STORM FORGED

DEATH BEFORE DRAGONS
BOOK SIX

LINDSAY  R

STORM
FORGED

CHAPTER 1

"I believe this one summons a djinn."

"Did your books tell you that, or are you guessing because it's shaped like an Arabic genie lamp?" I picked up the bronze charm, one of a dozen that I'd taken from bracelets around my previous employer's wrists.

His wrists, as well as the rest of his body, had been charred and smoking at the time. I was a little conflicted about claiming the charms, since I'd been on the payroll as his bodyguard when he'd died, but as an assassin who regularly battled magical bad guys, I needed all of the advantages I could get.

"Arabic genie?" Freysha's elegant elven eyebrows rose. "I am familiar with the cultures of the denizens of the Cosmic Realms—" she waved at books stacked on the kitchen table around us, most of the tomes written in goblin, elven, or dwarvish, "—but I am only now learning about the cultures of this planet. Earth is considered one of the wild worlds and, until recently, was of little interest to anyone in the rest of the realms."

"So I've heard." I set the trinket down with the rest of the eclectic collection. "I appreciate you helping me research all of these, but my priority is to figure out which one let Weber resist the compulsions of dragons. I not only need that one badly for my own charm necklace, but I might even push Sindari—" I tapped the feline figurine at the center of my leather thong, "—off to the side to give it a more prominent position."

I heard that, sounded Sindari's voice in my mind.

I thought you were outside getting your ears rubbed.

I looked through the open back door to the back yard of the rickety old Victorian house I'd recently moved into with Freysha and my other new roommate Dimitri. Zoltan, the vampire alchemist, was also technically a roommate, but he lived in the basement, didn't come out during the daylight hours—and only rarely during nighttime hours—and didn't pay rent, so I was more inclined to think of him as a feature of the house.

It took me a moment to spot Sindari, since more than the usual number of people were in the back yard.

Dimitri was hosting a barbecue get-together. He stood in front of his newly purchased gas grill, tending to hot dogs and hamburgers, while Corporal Clarke and a couple of guys Dimitri knew from the Seattle club scene chatted amiably and played a game involving tossing hoops onto the pointed ears of a gargoyle. Dimitri had constructed the gargoyle out of recycled bicycle parts and plumbing fixtures, and it was supposed to zap anyone who climbed over the back fence and into our yard. It didn't react to the hoops assailing it.

Nin, whom Dimitri had lured over to his shindig by promising they would discuss plans for the coffee shop we all owned together, kept trying to turn the conversation to profit-and-loss statements and the need to closely monitor inventory. Sindari, my huge silver tiger from the distant realm of Del'noth sat beside her, his tail swishing on the patio pavers.

I was allowing Nin and Dimitri to stroke my head in a respectful manner, but then one of his dubious acquaintances came over and rubbed the fur on my back the wrong way. It was all I could do to refrain from biting his hand off.

That wasn't Corporal Clarke, was it?

No. He knows he's not permitted to pet me. I roared at him.

I hope that wasn't the roar that makes your enemies wet themselves, because we just got the back yard looking respectable. Pee stains on the patio aren't cool.

"It hasn't been a simple matter to determine which charm does that." Freysha moved the genie lamp aside and picked up three other trinkets from the collection. Unlike the elegant bronze, silver, gold, and ivory charms, these were a mishmash of tiny pieces of warped metal and rocks that looked to have been smashed together into lopsided balls by pliers and then glued into place with resin or pitch. They were as attractive as gum stuck to the bottom of one's shoe. "It may be one of these."

"Don't even suggest that. There's no way I'm moving Sindari's charm aside to put one of those around my neck."

"I know what the elven ones do without even researching them." Freysha pointed to two silver charms she'd already set aside. "I'm familiar with the magic of my people. And I believe those two dwarven trinkets are designed to help you become a better crafter."

"Guess I'll give those to Dimitri and Nin. I already make wicked friendship bracelets out of thread. No need for magical enhancement."

Freysha's eyebrows drifted north again, and I reminded myself that she hadn't been on Earth for long and didn't have a frame of reference for my jokes. I should save my sarcasm for those who could appreciate it. Though I wasn't entirely positive anyone appreciated it. Zav only liked it when I turned my sharp tongue on his enemies.

"I will keep studying these," Freysha said.

"Thanks. I really do appreciate your help. And your help with the magic lessons too."

I waved toward the sunroom—Dimitri insisted on calling it a conservatory, but that was a lofty name for a drafty greenhouse full of cracked glass—where we'd been having our morning practice sessions. Each lesson started with me sticking my fingers into dirt and helping Freysha pot plants, but as surprising as it seemed, I was learning how to use the magic that had been flowing through my veins unbeknownst to me my whole life. I couldn't do anything cool yet, like levitate or hurl fireballs, but I was getting better at speaking telepathically to others and keeping intruders out of my mind.

If I could learn to magically make my lungs work better, that would be fantastic. As I'd feared when we signed the lease papers, the old house had a mold smell in a couple of the bathrooms, including the one next to my bedroom, and I'd woken up from nightmares more than once and the need to reach for my inhaler. Maybe I should confess my problem to Freysha—I hated admitting my health weaknesses to anyone and hadn't even told Zav—to see if she had any ideas for fixing them. But as far as I could tell, she wasn't a healer. Her specialty was forest magic, whatever that was.

Freysha lifted her head and looked toward the living room, or maybe beyond. Her eyes were distant and unfocused. "Your mate comes."

"Zav?" I hadn't seen him for a few days and wasn't sure if he had gone back to his world or had been chasing a criminal on a distant part of Earth. "Maybe he'll know which charm can keep dragons out of your head."

Freysha gripped her chin and picked up one of the junky resin balls. "If it is one of these, I will be surprised. They were made with goblin magic, and their shamans don't usually have the power to create anything strong enough to resist dragons."

"Trinkets pieced together from beer cans and paper clips aren't effective weapons against dragons? Who would have thought?"

Zav flew within range of my modest senses. He was alone this time, not with his sister, Zondia, and that was a relief. She still hated me and made snide comments if Zav and I kissed or looked at each other with ludicrous mushy eyes—that was her term for it.

"I do not know what those items are, but I assume you refer to the goblin knack for reusing and recycling the detritus of other races. They are quite resourceful." Freysha smiled fondly. "Few of the other lesser species give goblins much credit."

Zav landed on the lawn out front but did not take his human form and come into the house. That disappointed me, because it probably meant he wasn't staying. Now that I was learning to protect myself better from the powerful magical beings who liked to use me against him, I thought he might want to take our relationship to the next level. Maybe not during Dimitri's barbecue... but my evenings were open this week.

Are your lessons progressing? Zav asked telepathically.

Yeah. If you come in, I'll show you how I can punt Freysha out of my mind while rubbing my fingers in the dirt under a fern. I hoped to quickly get past the stage where I needed the *peace of the soil,* as Freysha called it, as a focal point.

I would like to come see this— it didn't sound like Zav found dirt rubbing odd, —*but I must return to my world to assist my mother for a time.*

Is something wrong?

Zav hesitated. He hadn't filled me in on all of the details of the dragon political situation, but I'd gotten the gist that, though his family was in power and had been for some time, they were losing their hold, and the Silverclaw Clan—and who knew how many others—wanted to take over. *My uncle Ston'tareknor has gone missing. It is possible he's dead.*

Due to foul play from dragons?

That is a possibility, but he was sick before he disappeared. This has happened before with other dragons in our family.

Sick? My lungs tightened in sympathy, and I walked outside, both to see him and for fresh air. *I wouldn't have guessed dragons could get sick.*

It is rare. When it comes to the few viruses that have the potential to affect us, our scientists have mostly found ways to combat them with magic, but a dragon still occasionally falls ill and flies to the stars.

Flies to the stars? Is that a saying? I found Zav still in his dragon form, taking up the entire lawn with his tail spilling down to the road. People were pushing strollers along the sidewalks and riding bicycles down the street toward Green Lake, but none of them noticed him, either because they lacked magical blood or because he was using his power to keep them from seeing him. Thanks to a road construction crew working with a jackhammer down on Green Lake Way, he probably could have roared, and it too would have gone unnoticed.

Zav lowered his head to the level of the covered front porch and gazed at me with his violet eyes. Usually, when he was in his dragon form, it was hard to read emotion on his face, but his gaze seemed uncharacteristically glum today. *A saying, and also reality. When a dragon believes he is dying, he will often disappear—fly off somewhere never to be seen again—to die in solitude rather than showing others his weaknesses.*

I almost said that was nuts, but then I remembered my ongoing reluctance to let anyone but my doctor and my therapist know that I'd been having health problems this last year. In my business, the last thing I wanted was for anyone to know I had an Achilles heel they could take advantage of.

That's what you think happened to your uncle? He was sick for a while, and now he's disappeared?

Yes. He is—was—one of my mother's most staunch supporters as well as her brother. She will miss him and also miss that he stood beside her in the Ruling Council.

Do any of those Silverclaw Clan dragons get sick and disappear? Maybe this was a dragon thing that had been going on for millennia, but I was immediately suspicious that his enemies had something to do with it.

Occasionally.

Oh. Recently?

They lost a female a couple of centuries ago.

I said recently.

Zav's head tilted slightly. *That is not recent?*

Not by human standards, no.

A familiar SUV pulled up to the front of the house, the driver parallel parking in a tight spot without trouble. Colonel Willard got out, wearing jeans and a T-shirt instead of her army uniform. She raised a hand toward me as she walked around and pulled two potted plants out of the passenger side of the SUV.

I waved back, though I worried those were housewarming gifts and we were getting *more* things for Freysha to grow. "I guess Dimitri invited everyone to his barbecue."

Barbecue? Zav had been spreading his wings and crouching to spring into the air, but he paused. *I smell meat.*

"I'm not sure hot dogs count as real meat, but the burgers looked okay. You're welcome to stay and eat before you go." I smiled slightly, imagining Dimitri's horror-stricken expression as Zav strolled back and vacuumed up everything on the grill.

You would feed me? His gaze locked on to me again.

I doubted he was thinking randy thoughts while in his dragon form, but we both knew where feeding him in his human form could lead. "Sure. Unless you think it's too dangerous. Then I could have Sindari feed you."

Imagining the big tiger swatting burgers off the grill and into Zav's open mouth also amused.

Funny. Continue your magic lessons, and then I will return and let you feed me.

"Let me. You honor me so." Maybe I should have stuck to telepathy instead of speaking out loud, because Willard was giving me a weird look as she came up the walkway. She glanced at the yard a few times, since I was looking in that direction, but she didn't see Zav.

"Who are you talking to, Thorvald?"

"Zav. He's hidden on the lawn."

Willard looked toward the rhododendrons under the windows.

"Yeah, behind one of those."

I must go. I will return later for meat.

I wanted to give him a hug, since he sounded glum, but that would have been hard to manage while he was in his dragon form. And Willard would think I was crazy for embracing something she couldn't see. All I did was think, *I hope your uncle is all right and that you find him.*

Yes. Dragons didn't seem to have the concept of thanking people in their culture.

As Zav sprang into the air, the wind from his wings buffeted Willard and me. She blinked and looked in the right direction as he flew off.

"I'd wondered," she said, "how all those firefighters putting out the flames at Weber's house failed to see the dragon tussle you reported going on concurrently."

"Magic."

"It's disconcerting to know they can be that close without being detectable."

"You still want me to marry him?"

"Of course." Willard smirked. "Who else would have you?"

"Thanks so much."

She climbed the stairs and put the two pots in my hands. "Your housewarming presents."

"You sure these are for me and not Freysha?"

"They're herbs. Rosemary and mint. They're anti-inflammatory. Good for someone like you. Put them on the kitchen windowsill."

"Someone like me, huh?" I hadn't told her about the mold, but she knew about the inhaler and my wayward lungs. The military knew everything.

"I thought about getting something with even greater benefits, like a maritime pine tree—the bark is fabulous—but they grow a hundred feet tall and prefer a Mediterranean climate. It seemed ambitious for your windowsill."

"How do you know such things?" And who ate *pine bark*? I imagined Willard out in the woods licking a tree.

"I read books. You should try it."

"*I* read books."

"*Harry Potter* and *The Hobbit* don't count."

"Bite your tongue, herb woman." I eyed the plants. "The leaves on this one have been chewed on."

"I bought them last night. That was long enough for Maggie to sample them."

"Does cat saliva inhibit growth?"

"You'll have to ask your elf."

"You can ask her yourself. Dimitri's having a barbecue. Do you want to join us?" I pointed at the door, inviting her in, despite her disrespect for quality literature.

Before she answered, Thad parked across the street in his BMW, bringing Amber for her sword-fighting lesson. I'd offered to drive up to Yost Park in Edmonds, the spot we'd met the last few times, but I'd also mentioned that I had a private yard now that we could use.

"I did want to talk to you about something," Willard said.

"You'll *have* to stay then." Guessing what it might be about, I added, "I'm researching the charms I got from Weber. Have your people gone over all those artifacts that you looted from his estate?"

"We didn't loot them. We confiscated them for study until such time as it can be determined if they were legally obtained."

"How does one determine the legality of artifacts taken from another planet?"

"It's not easy. It could take decades."

"Do we get to use them in the meantime?" I thought of the magical weapons that had been in the stash.

"No."

"You're a buzzkill, Willard."

Amber and Thad were walking up, so Willard dropped the subject.

"This place is *old*." Amber peered up at the house—including the turret I'd claimed for my bedroom—and wrinkled her nose.

"It's a classic," I said.

"A '69 Mustang is a classic. This is just *old*."

"Uh huh. Head out back. I've got the practice swords waiting. You can grab a hot dog before we start if you want."

Amber walked inside obediently, but the words, "It smells like old people and mold in here," floated back.

"Your daughter is exactly what I expected," Willard said dryly, reminding me that they hadn't met before. Technically, they still hadn't met since Amber hadn't hung around for introductions.

Thad stopped at the bottom of the stairs and lifted an apologetic hand. "She tends to be blunt."

"That's what I meant," Willard said.

"When do you want me to pick her up, Val? An hour?"

"That's fine, or you can stay and join the barbecue group, if you want." I questioned the words as soon as they came out. If *the girlfriend* who hated me found out that Thad had hung out at my house for an hour, she might lop off a few of his favorite appendages. "There's a bunch of people. And a tiger."

Maybe that would make it all right. I would be busy with Amber, not chatting with him.

"Uh, all right." Thad's face creased with uncertainty—maybe he was also thinking of ramifications with the girlfriend—but he shrugged and managed a smile. "I wouldn't mind seeing how the lessons are going. There have been fewer bruises than I expected thus far."

"I'm an expert, not a brute."

Willard snorted.

I glared at her but waved for them to go through the house to the back yard. Another magical being registered on my senses, and I paused before following them. It wasn't a dragon, but it did feel like someone with full magical blood, someone coming up the street in this direction.

What if an orc or a shifter had already found out about my change of address and planned a drive-by shooting?

But the aura didn't belong to any of the more belligerent species in the magical community, those who usually targeted me. I hadn't met many full-blooded gnomes, but the aura reminded me of Nin, with her one-quarter gnomish blood.

The owner came into view, darting from recycling bin to mailbox to garbage can, a hood covering his face and a cloak flapping around his ankles. It might have been a her. It was impossible to tell, but the being was short—only about three and a half feet tall—which would be the right height for a gnome. The skin of the hands gripping the cloak was leathery brown.

The figure kept stumbling, as if injured, and glancing back. I stretched out my senses, trying to detect other magical beings who might be chasing him.

At first, it looked like he would run past the house and have nothing to do with us, but the figure halted with a lurch and looked over at me. The sun was behind him, and with his hood pulled up, I still couldn't see his features, but he teetered as he stood, and I had the impression of someone in pain.

"You need help?" I called.

He glanced back the way he'd come, looked at me again, and then ran toward the side of the house and the gate into the back yard.

"I guess that's a yes."

CHAPTER 2

After making sure I still didn't sense any trouble coming—at least not *magical* trouble—I jogged through the house to warn everybody about the intruder before he made it into the back yard. But the little gnome was fast. By the time I exited the kitchen, I found him in the middle of the patio—sprawled on his face and completely covered by his hood and cloak.

Nin, Thad, Amber, Willard, Freysha, Dimitri, and his guests were all gaping down at the unmoving figure. Even Sindari gazed at him in puzzlement.

Willard looked at me. "Did you *shoot* someone?"

"Did you poke someone with a sword?" Amber sounded more curious than alarmed.

What did it say about me that my friends assumed that if there was a body, I was responsible?

"You would have heard it if I had." I wasn't even wearing my weapons. "He came in off the street. I think it's a he."

"Yes." Freysha crept forward warily and crouched beside him. "He is a gnome. An older gnome."

"He ran back here and collapsed." Dimitri glanced toward the wooden gate leading into the yard. Left open, it thumped in the breeze.

"I told you that you were burning the hot dogs," Corporal Clarke told him.

Dimitri frowned and waved his barbecue tongs. "What does that have to do with anything?"

"Isn't it obvious? When he ran back here, he was overcome by the smoke and passed out."

"Ha ha."

"Freysha, can you see if he's, uh, alive?" I waved to the gnome. He *had* to be alive, right? "I'm guessing he overexerted himself and passed out. I'm going to get my weapons in case there's trouble." I glanced at Willard. "Someone was chasing him. At least he *thought* someone was."

"My gun is in the car." Willard raised her eyebrows. "I didn't think I'd need it to bring you herbs."

"Might want to get it."

I ran into the living room and grabbed my sword scabbard and pistol holster, the weapons they held recently cleaned and ready for action. As I turned to go back out, I sensed the enemies I'd expected since I saw the gnome. Two orcs.

At least orcs were something I could handle, assuming there weren't a lot more of them and they weren't like those crazy tattooed orcs—Way Rovers—that Sindari and I had battled outside of Weber's house.

I considered going out front to face them, but I wanted to know more about the gnome, such as if he was still alive. It wouldn't be worth getting in a fight to defend a dead guy. Also, if I stuck my cloaking charm in his hand, was it possible the orcs would lose his trail and continue past the house?

When I got back outside, Freysha was rolling the gnome onto his back. For the first time, his hood fell away, revealing his wizened face and a bald pate save for wispy white hair around his ears. His face was scratched and bloody, as if he'd fallen several times on the sidewalk, and his eyes were closed.

Nin gasped, her blue pigtails bobbing as she drew back.

"What is it?" I hadn't gotten a chance to talk to her yet today—the profit-and-loss statements discussion hadn't driven me outside with an intense urgency to participate.

She stared down at the gnome, her hand to her mouth. I didn't know if she'd gasped because of his injuries or for another reason, but she was riveted.

"Nin?" I moved to her side and rested a hand on her shoulder, even as I used my senses to monitor the orcs. There were four within my range now, damn it. At least they were advancing slowly, as if sniffing a trail.

"This is my grandfather," she whispered.

My ears were more sensitive than average, and I heard her clearly, but that didn't keep me from issuing a startled, "What?"

"My grandfather."

"The grandfather you last saw in Thailand twenty years ago?" I'd heard the story before, of how he'd taught her to build and enchant weapons before he mysteriously disappeared, leaving Nin, her mother, her grandmother, and all her siblings to take care of themselves.

She nodded. "He has barely aged. But he is hurt." She stumbled forward and dropped to her knees opposite Freysha. "What is wrong with him? He ran in here. Why did he pass out?"

Not having an answer to that, I removed my charm thong and unthreaded the cloaking charm. Even though the thought of putting it in the hand of a stranger and potentially losing it unnerved me, I crouched and wrapped the gnome's calloused fingers around it. Fortunately, they were still warm and pliable enough to move.

"I'm not sure it'll activate without him willing it to," I admitted.

"I'll see if I can get it to work." Freysha nodded, understanding my intent.

"My sword-fighting lessons aren't usually this weird," Amber whispered to Thad.

They stood several steps back from the gathering, his hand protectively on her shoulder.

"I thought you said they were always weird," he murmured back.

"No, I said *Val* was always weird."

"Oh, right."

I was about to shoot him a dirty look for his lack of defense, but the side gate banged. Cursing, I jumped to my feet, expecting an enemy even though the orcs were still a block away. The orcs I could *sense*. There could be others with camouflaging magic of their own.

But it was Willard, back with a gun that had a magical signature. It was one Nin had made.

Willard pulled up short and stared at the gnome. "Where'd he go?"

"Camouflaged." I was relieved Freysha had used her magic to get the cloaking charm to work for him. I was still close enough that I could see through it, regardless, but Willard had stopped several feet away. "There are four orcs coming this way," I added.

"We should go out front to confront them." Willard looked at my unarmed group of houseguests, including Thad and Amber. "Clarke, did you bring a weapon?"

"Just my guns, ma'am." He was in a T-shirt, and his biceps popped when he flexed them.

Judging by the eye roll and mutter of, "Lord save us," Willard wasn't impressed. She pointed at the group and raised her voice. "Everyone, stay back here." She jerked her hand for me to follow her to the front yard.

I held up a hand to Thad and Amber, wanting to emphasize that they should stay. Sindari had been sitting and eyeing the gnome, but he joined me now.

I had feared there would be no battle to engage in today.

I was hoping there wouldn't be, especially since my daughter is here.

You do not wish her to witness your martial prowess and the way we eviscerate our enemies?

Not when there's a chance she could be hurt. And I prefer shooting enemies to eviscerating them.

That is not the way of fang and claw.

Just don't get blood all over your fur. That'll seriously cut down on the number of people willing to pet you.

Perhaps that would be an ideal way to keep away those with presumptuous hands.

Dimitri isn't going to pet a bloody tiger either.

Hm.

"I'm hoping they'll think they lost him now that he's cloaked," I whispered.

As I trailed Willard toward the gate, the gnome disappeared from my sight and my other senses. Seeing my charm work on someone else was odd.

"We'll hide and only attack if they turn this way," Willard said. "And then only if they refuse to go away. We don't have any way to know why they're following him or what the gnome did."

After we exited through the gate, I shut it firmly behind us. "True, but I think we can assume it's a good idea to protect Nin's grandfather."

We crouched behind some of the bushes in front of the house. It was a tight fit and the foliage wasn't as dense as I'd hoped. Now I wished Dimitri hadn't trimmed them when we'd moved in.

"The grandfather she hasn't seen for twenty years?" Willard asked. "What if he's a mafia leader who's been stealing babies from orcs for decades?"

"A gnome mafia leader? They're tinkerers."

Sindari lowered into a crouch beside me. Since his magic would camouflage him, he didn't try to fit behind the bushes.

"I'm just pointing out that we don't know his story and shouldn't open fire wantonly," Willard said. "You still sense four?"

"Yeah."

"How far?"

I lowered my voice even more. "Only a couple of houses down and still coming this way."

We fell silent to wait, but I winced when I heard voices from the back yard. Dimitri's buddies.

"Do you always let the women go out and do the fighting, bro?" one asked.

"Whenever I can, yeah." Dimitri didn't sound that worried about slights to his masculinity.

"I offered my guns, but they didn't want them," Clarke said.

"I hear you have that problem a lot with women."

"Can you shut them up?" Willard muttered.

"Not without shouting loudly enough for the orcs to hear," I whispered.

"I thought you were learning telepathy."

"Oh. Right."

I was used to only being able to talk to Sindari and Zav—and dragons who butted into my thoughts without permission. As the orcs crept into view, two on the sidewalk and two in the street, I envisioned Freysha's face and focused on her aura as I asked her to quiet everyone up.

The seven-foot-tall, broad-shouldered orcs wore cloaks with raised hoods—as far as I could tell, magical beings all shopped out of the same Fashions of Tolkien mail-order catalog—but the tips of their tusked snouts were visible. Unease crept into my gut as I sensed magical charms—or weapons—under their cloaks. Two of the orcs carried crossbows, and I thought I glimpsed the hilt of a sword sheathed at another's waist.

The orcs on the sidewalk spoke to each other in their native language, and I slowly lifted a hand to tap my translation charm.

"...don't sense him anymore."

"He's here. I *smell* him."

"We're screwed if we don't find him and bring him back."

"Shh. I sense elf."

I grimaced, not sure if that meant me or Freysha—maybe both.

Two orc snouts swiveled in my direction. That answered that question.

I unfastened Fezzik from its holster, the weight of the submachine pistol comforting in my hand. Chopper was a more powerful weapon when it came to battling the magical, but I had to get close to use the sword. When I was outnumbered, I preferred to get a few free shots in from a distance.

As I was about to stand—there was little point in continuing to hide in the bushes when they were staring right at me—Willard gripped my forearm.

"Don't start a fight if you don't have to." She'd seen me draw my gun.

"I'm not planning to." I walked out with Fezzik in hand. "This is how I negotiate."

"I guess that means I better be ready to cover you."

"Guess so."

All four orcs had gathered on the sidewalk to look at me. If they knew Willard was there, they ignored her.

One orc's nostrils flared, testing the air. "Another elf is behind the house."

"Deal with this one first," one of his buddies said. "She is armed."

"I'm armed because this is my house, and you're creeping up on it like a neighborhood gang. What do you want?"

"What is she saying?"

"I don't know. It's the vermin language of this crotch of a world."

Uh oh. These guys weren't locals. Most of the orcs who'd taken refuge on Earth, those I typically dealt with, spoke enough English to get by.

Sindari, are these more of those Way Rovers?

I fear they may be. Two of them carry magical weapons.

Can you communicate with them?

I may be able to do so, but that would give away my presence at your side.

Your presence may keep them from attacking. Despite my gun, they didn't look that worried. Two had crept off the sidewalk and onto the lawn, nostrils still sniffing.

Sindari roared, the tremendous noise rolling throughout the neighborhood. Distant walkers whirled to look back and then sprinted away.

I was imagining you communicating with them telepathically.

I am doing that now. I like to start a conversation with the power of thunder at the beginning of a summer storm.

Half our houseguests probably flung themselves into the bushes.

Do you wish me to tell them you're the Ruin Bringer? Sindari asked.

The orcs were frowning around the yard now, looking vaguely in the direction the roar had come from.

I doubt that means anything to them if they're not from around here.

Don't be too sure. The Dragon Justice Court knows all about you.

Don't remind me.

And they told the elves.

All four orcs roared—their roars weren't as impressive as Sindari's, but they conveyed suitable ferocity—and I expected them to rush at me. But they drew their weapons and paused as if waiting for something. Uh oh. What now?

An orc with a crossbow lifted his gaze toward the roof of the house. At first, I thought he was trying to trick me into glancing away so he could shoot me when I wasn't looking. Then a surge of magical power came from the rooftop. I'd felt something similar before when a portal had opened.

A new enemy comes, Sindari warned me.

Fantastic.

He was crouched, ready to spring at the orcs, but he whirled to face me. No, not me. Whatever was coming out of that portal on the roof.

Before I could figure out what new enemy was emerging, and if I needed to worry about everyone in the back yard, the orcs charged at me.

One flicked his wrist, chucking something that had been hidden in his hand. I dove sideways and into a roll as a throwing star whizzed past and slammed into the siding of the house above Willard's head. I opened fire before I finished my roll. Willard leaned out from behind the bush and shot at the orcs charging me.

My bullets slammed into the chest of the lead orc, but dull tinks instead of fleshy thuds told me he was wearing armor. As he sprang for me, I fired at his unprotected face, then rolled out of the way again. My bullet slammed into his eye, and he tripped and tumbled to the grass.

Willard's bullets slammed into the neck of one of the other orcs, and he roared and fired a crossbow at her. I had enough time to rise into a crouch and shoot at the other two, but the air buzzed with magic as an invisible barrier appeared to protect them. My bullets hit it and bounced away. One ricocheted back and came within inches of striking me. It clanged into a drainpipe near the porch.

Sindari had rushed to the other side of the yard and sprang to meet a shadow coming down from the roof. Not a shadow. A four-legged, scaly creature with a wolf's face and fangs. It was as large as Sindari, and when it crashed into him, they tumbled across the yard in a tangle of flying fur and snapping jaws. They crashed into the bushes along the property line as they bit and clawed at each other, growls and yips sending chills down my spine.

The two uninjured orcs drew swords and rushed toward me. I gave up on firing and pulled out Chopper. When the orcs tried to flank me and come in from both sides, I sprang away and skittered backward up the stairs to the high ground of the porch.

A gasp of pain came from my left. Willard? She was still trading fire with the other orc, but I worried that first crossbow bolt had hit her.

With my allies busy, I would have to take care of both orcs in front of me. I was prepared, blade ready and the railing of the porch steps providing some cover for my flanks, but then a tickle of power touched my mind. A magical compulsion urged me to drop my weapons and bare my neck to my enemies' blades.

"That's not going to happen," I growled as I deflected a barrage of sword blows from the closest orc.

The second orc stood slightly back, his eyes intent as he stared at me. He had to be the magic user.

Even as I relied on years of battle training to parry and block the closer orc, I focused my mind on the insidious mental attack. As Freysha had instructed, I imagined ferns growing up to wrap around my mind and protect me from compulsions.

The magic-flinging orc scowled and produced another throwing star. Knowing I couldn't deflect that and parry a sword at once, I switched from defensive to offensive against the one I faced. I flowed halfway down the stairs, trying to place myself so that he was in the way of the one with the throwing star.

My opponent was momentarily surprised by my speed and aggression, and I spotted an opening as our blades crossed over his head. I twisted and slammed a side kick into his groin.

The other orc chose that second to spin his throwing star at my face. I ducked as I retracted my kick, my other foot precariously close to the edge of the step. The throwing star almost took off my braid on its way to embed itself in the door.

Gunfire from the side almost made me jump. It was Willard. Her orc was rolling on the lawn, grabbing his arm, and she was firing at the magic user. He'd been busy attacking me and didn't have his defenses up. Bullets slammed into the side of his torso and one skimmed the top of his head—he ducked in time or it would have burrowed through his ear.

I leaped down the stairs to press the sword fighter while his buddy was distracted.

A canine squeal of pain came from the bushes. Sindari had come out on top, his teeth sinking into the neck of the scaled wolf.

The orcs exchanged glances, then sprinted toward the side of the house. Even the injured one leaped up and raced after them.

Terrified that they would run into the back yard and get hostages, I yanked out Fezzik again and fired after them. But they didn't run into the side yard. They climbed up the trim at the corner of the house, somehow finding handholds to support their massive bodies, and made it to the rooftop even with Willard and me firing at them.

Their magical defenses were back up and our bullets bounced off. They disappeared onto the rooftop where I could sense the portal still open.

I ran out onto the lawn, hoping to get another chance at them, but as the silver portal floating behind my turret came into view, two of the orcs dove through it. One paused and glowered back down at me.

"You harbor a fugitive," he snarled in his own language, my charm still translating, "and we will be back with powerful allies to collect him. Then you will die horribly, mongrel bitch."

I fired at his forehead. Alas, the bullet bounced off. He gave me what was likely the orc equivalent of the middle finger and walked backward into the portal. He and it disappeared, leaving one orc dead in the yard and the beast pinned under Sindari.

I'd thought it defeated, but with a great thrashing, it tore away from Sindari and rolled onto the lawn. Half of its throat had been ripped open, but it wasn't dead yet.

Willard and I opened fire, careful not to aim close to Sindari. Fortunately, the creature, despite having a strong magical aura, didn't have any shields. Our bullets pierced its scaly hide and sank deep. It howled with pain.

Sindari pounced, rolled it onto its back, and raked his claws into its belly, tearing out entrails. The creature twitched in its death throes, and I lowered my weapons, looking toward the roof where the portal had been.

The orc's threat rang in my mind, and I feared it was an honest one and that he would be back. With reinforcements.

CHAPTER 3

In the aftermath of the fight, I wanted to rush back to check on Amber and Thad and everyone else—and see if Freysha had gotten the gnome to wake up—but what was I supposed to do with the bodies? The orc had died off to the side and behind a bush, but the scaly wolf creature lay in the middle of the front lawn. Any dog walker or couple with a stroller who passed by would see the eviscerated—thank you, Sindari—corpse and blood spattering the walkway leading up to my porch.

"Is it dead?" Willard stepped up beside me, gore and grime on her T-shirt ensuring it would need the attention of a triple-powered, late-night-infomercial stain remover.

"Yeah. You've got a van or something that picks up the bodies of magical creatures, don't you?"

"You know I do." Willard pulled out her phone. "You've left enough of them behind for me to have picked up."

"Usually, I leave them behind on someone *else's* lawn."

"I'm aware. Don't think I've forgotten the dragon you left in the Sammamish River. We had to get a helicopter to airlift the corpse out."

While Willard called her contact, I kept watch, my sword still drawn. For the moment, the neighborhood was quiet, though from the lawn, I could see down the street and across to Green Lake where a vigorous soccer game was going on while people jogged on the paved path that followed the shoreline. I was surprised the fight hadn't drawn attention, but the road construction had probably drowned out the gunshots.

"Which van?" Willard had already given the person my address. "The big one, I guess." She paused for a response. "I don't know how much the beast corpse weighs. Or what it is even." She looked at me.

I'd never seen one before and couldn't guess what species it was, so I offered, "It's kind of like the scaly Klingon lizard-dogs."

Willard frowned at me. "The what?"

"Klingon dog?" a male voice asked from her phone. "Original movies or *Next Generation*?"

"Original movies," I said, "and bigger. This thing is probably four hundred pounds. Almost as big as Sindari but not nearly as regal."

Certainly not. Sindari was in the process of washing blood off his foot and did not look up.

"Got it," the man said. "Thanks, Val."

Willard hung up. "You're more of a geek than I realized."

"Someone with a Garfield mug collection doesn't have room to talk." Trusting the van would show up soon, I pulled tarps out from under the porch and covered up the bodies, then jogged toward the back yard to check on everyone.

"Two mugs isn't a collection," Willard said, striding after me.

"It is if you add in all the Flintstones and Smurfs mugs on the shelf with them." My heart lurched when I found the back yard deserted except for Clarke and the other two guys. What were their names? Jeremy and Juan. "Where's my kid? And the gnome? And everyone else?"

"They took the gnome inside to put him on a bed," Clarke said.

"*Whose* bed?" I assumed Dimitri's, since his room was on the ground floor, but when I ran through the kitchen—Thad and Amber were standing around the table, thankfully unharmed—and peeked inside, there were too many boxes of reclaimed junk for his projects for anyone to lie down. "How could anyone who was living in a van a week ago have accumulated so much?"

Willard was following me, but she didn't offer an opinion. Using my sense for the magical instead of common sense, I realized the gnome was on the second floor. So was Freysha. Why did it seem like they were in *my* room?

"This place is big," Willard said as we tramped up one of the two staircases in the house and past a library, a study, and two bedrooms before reaching the turret. "But badly in need of work. What are those stains on the carpet?"

"Someone probably killed a Klingon dog."

Afternoon sunlight streamed through the tall windows in the rounded walls of my bedroom. My theoretical bedroom since the mold on this floor had been bothering me and I'd been sleeping downstairs on the couch when nobody was looking. I was even less inclined to sleep in here now that there was an injured gnome lying on the pillows and comforter. The king-size, four-poster canopy bed was huge, which brought attention to how small he was.

Nin stood at the foot of the bed, nibbling on her knuckle. Freysha sat on the edge and held the gnome's hand, though he was as unconscious as he had been before.

"You have a giant poster bed?" Willard sounded amused. "That's new, isn't it? It's bigger than your entire previous apartment."

"It came with the house. I doubt the previous renters could get it out."

Freysha gazed across at me. "I don't think his injuries alone would explain why he's unconscious. He does have a lot of wounds, new and old, but I also sense..." She groped at the air with her long delicate fingers. "I believe there is something unusual in his body, something *unnatural*."

"Uh." I glanced at Willard, thinking of the *something unnatural* in her body that had nearly killed her a few months back.

Judging by her grimace, it came to mind for her as well.

But I'd sensed the magic that had been affecting her. Even when I stepped closer to the bed and examined the gnome with my senses, I couldn't sense anything similar from him.

"You're sure?" I asked.

"I do not sense magic but something foreign. Something that does not belong."

"Like a poison?"

"That is... possible." The wrinkle to Freysha's upper lip suggested skepticism, but maybe she didn't have a better word for it. "Unfortunately, I am not a healer. If we could take him to my world, I could easily find someone who could examine him. It is also possible one of your Earth doctors would be sufficient."

"Earth doctors don't believe gnomes exist," I said.

"That may make treatment problematic."

"Is it possible to travel to your world, Freysha?" Nin asked.

"Certainly, but I am not skilled in travel magic." Freysha spread a hand. "Lord Zavryd could do it easily. I sensed him here earlier. Would he help?"

"Probably, but he went home. He's got some trouble of his own with his family."

"Anything we need to worry about?" Willard eyed me. She hadn't been happy when I'd passed along Zav's warning that Earth had come more fully on the Dragon Ruling Council's radar of late and that it was possible some officious dragons would come to see our world leaders.

"I don't think so. Not this time. A relative of his has gone missing."

"There is nothing that can be done to help here?" Nin gripped one of the bed posts. "I have not seen my grandfather for twenty years. When he disappeared, we all thought he was dead, that some angry client had killed him or he had been a hapless victim to violence. He was not the kind of man to leave his family, especially after my deadbeat father walked out on my mother and all of us." Nin shook her head. "I do not know where he has been or how he found me here at your house, but we must help him."

It hadn't occurred to me that the gnome had been specifically seeking out Nin, but I realized he must have been. Chance wouldn't have brought him to my doorstep—or my back patio, rather.

"Maybe Zoltan can do something once he wakes up." I squinted at the afternoon sun, realizing it would still be several hours before our basement roommate stirred.

"He has medical training?" Freysha asked.

"Just the alchemy, as far as I know, but he researches a lot of stuff. Maybe he's got a potion that would work."

"I believe he would need a diagnosis to prescribe a formula. A healer would be ideal. Is there anyone here who treats those in the magical community?" Freysha frowned thoughtfully at the window. "I suppose I could ask Gondo if he knows of any goblin shamans. They mostly heal their own kind, but…"

Willard sighed dramatically—which was startling because drama wasn't her thing. "I have someone I can ask to come take a look."

She dug out her phone, her mouth twisting in displeasure.

"An ally or an enemy?" I asked.

"Both."

"Really? Do I need to stand on my lawn with my gun again when he or she arrives?"

"It's a he, and he's some kind of cat shifter with the arrogance of a dragon, even though he's lived on Earth his whole life, as far as I know, and has no right to be as cocky as he is."

"I'm not sure if that answered my gun question."

"He's not an enemy, just vexing." Whoever he was, Willard had his number programmed into her phone. "He probably won't even come. He's extremely sought after, or so he tells me. Whenever he comes to the office, he reminds me how much more he makes in private practice than by helping the government."

"Such vitriol. This sounds more like an ex-boyfriend than an army contractor."

"I'd gnaw my foot off before dating him."

Her vehement denial made me want to probe further, but Nin was watching with pinched lips, and I reminded myself that she *knew* the stranger passed out on my bed.

"What's his specialty?" I asked as Willard's call dropped to voice mail.

She hung up and tried again. "Reconstructive surgery."

"You're calling a plastic surgeon to come help a mysteriously injured gnome?"

"That's his current practice and how he makes his money, but he was in the army and can do just about anything. He started out operating as a GP specializing in magical beings, but the goblins, trolls, and orcs all wanted to pay him in chickens and daggers and stolen loot from muggings. He switched tracks, and now he fixes people's faces if they get burned or mangled in a car accident. He also helps non-humans blend in if they want. He turned a teenage orc girl into someone who could fit into your daughter's school and get hit on by football players."

"You're sure that was a service?"

"Apparently."

"Colonel Willard," a smooth male voice answered—it was quiet enough in the bedroom that I had no trouble hearing it, "you've called three times and refuse to leave a voice mail. You must be breathless with need for me."

"Yeah, my female bits are aching." Willard ignored my eyebrows flying up. "Also, I have an unconscious gnome that's been poisoned and attacked by orcs. Can you come take a look?"

"It's Saturday."

"So you're not busy? Good."

He snorted. "Never too busy for you, Colonel. You're at the office?"

"No." Willard shared my address for the second time in ten minutes.

I doubted my new home was going to remain a mystery to the magical community for long. I hoped this shifter could be trusted. He sounded smarmy.

When she hung up, I asked, "Am I supposed to find some chickens to pay him?"

"No." Her mouth twisted in distaste again. "He insists on cash and charges even more exorbitant fees than you do for his consulting time."

"I didn't know charging more was an option."

"Don't get any ideas. It's not."

"But this doctor gets away with it?"

"He has multiple advanced degrees."

"So, if I start taking correspondence courses, I can raise my rates?"

"No." Willard glared at me and strode out.

I didn't know if she was truly irked with me or just annoyed that she'd had to ask this guy she didn't like for a favor, but she didn't look back as she stomped down the stairs.

"I will pay for the doctor," Nin said gravely when we were alone with the unconscious gnome.

"You don't have to do that. As you could tell, Willard is delighted to work with him, and her office will be happy to foot the bill."

Nin looked dubiously toward the open door. "I do not believe you are good at reading people."

"Why do you think I became an assassin instead of going into the hospitality business?"

In her sweet precise English, Nin asked, "You like to blow shit up?"

"Well, that too, but mostly I suck at dealing with people. It's why Dimitri hasn't asked me to take a shift at the coffee shop." I smiled at her.

Nin managed a fleeting smile, but her focus returned to the gnome.

"For so many years, I have believed he was dead. That is what my mother and grandmother believed and told us children. I loved him very much as a little girl and was so pleased to learn the interesting skills he taught me. I also wanted to tinker and build things, not play with dolls. I only reluctantly learned to cook because my mother insisted that we girls learn skills to properly please a man."

"And cooking works? I suppose that's true. Zav is into it when I feed him." I was trying to lighten her mood, but she didn't crack another smile. Maybe I needed to let her talk about it, not make jokes. Nin was right. I *was* bad at people. "What's his name?"

"Ti."

"Ti? That's it? He can't possibly have a name that I can pronounce."

"It is possible he has a longer name and that it is short for something in gnomish, but I do not know what it is. I was only ten when he disappeared. He told me a little of his home world and how he had been looking for interesting crafting components on the wild worlds when he met my grandmother and fell in love with her and her country, but I do not remember that many of the stories. It has been many years now."

"Yeah."

A soft knock on the doorframe made me turn. Thad stood there.

"Oh, I'm sorry." I'd forgotten about Amber and our sword lesson, not that there hadn't been a good excuse to.

"I need to get back to my office for a meeting," he said.

"On Saturday?"

"Don't you work on Saturdays?"

"Yeah, but I'm weird."

"As Amber reminds me." He smiled, but as with Nin, it was a fleeting gesture. "I'm going to take Amber home. Don't take this the wrong way, but I don't think sword lessons at your house are a good idea."

I grimaced, but how could I object after he'd been here to witness a gunfight in the front yard? The orc's parting words rang in my mind again.

"An hour ago, I would have said you were wrong, but I'm forced to agree. If everything works out okay here—" I waved to the gnome—to Ti, "—maybe we can try again tomorrow afternoon, back up at the park in Edmonds."

"How about one evening this week?" Thad asked. "Tomorrow, we're back-to-school shopping. That usually takes eight or nine hours."

"So few."

"Yes. She offered to let me stay home if I just gave her a credit card." His mouth twisted wryly.

"Teenagers are extremely thoughtful."

"I thought I better go along and pretend I have some say in placing spending limits and yeaing and naying purchases."

"She tried to get me to buy her a Prada purse. Apparently, that brand is superior for clubbing enemies."

"I have no doubt. How about Wednesday evening?"

"That should work." I was relieved he wouldn't put an end to the sword-fighting lessons permanently after witnessing a deadly battle at my house. They were my only chance to see Amber regularly.

"Are you all right?" Thad asked softly, touching Nin's arm.

They must have had time to introduce themselves to each other and exchange a few words while Willard and I had been fighting.

"Yes." Nin smiled at him. "Thank you for offering to stand in front of me if the enemies made it into the back yard."

"You looked small and fragile. That was before you pulled out a miniature magical gun."

"It was only a pistol ring. Val did not inform me that I needed to come well-armed to her barbecue."

"I'm getting the feeling anyone who visits her should be well-armed."

"You guys are hilarious," I said.

"This does seem to be true," Nin said, ignoring me. "Next time I come to Val's home for a barbecue, I will bring semi-automatic weapons."

"I'll bring spoiled potato salad," Thad said.

Nin's brow creased in confusion.

"So the bad guys eat it and get food poisoning," he explained, then shrugged. "I'm not much of a combatant."

"Oh, I see."

I rubbed my head. Thad hadn't gotten any smoother with women over the years. It was a wonder that he'd managed to snag a girlfriend, though from what I'd seen of Shauna, it might have been better if he *hadn't* snagged her.

It had grown quiet outside after our battle, and my keen ears picked up the rumble of a vehicle pulling up in front of the house. Expecting Willard's monster-disposal van, I went to the window in case they couldn't figure out that the bodies were under the tarps. But it wasn't a van. A gleaming fire-engine red SUV pulled into a spot that had opened up between Willard's Honda and my Jeep. It had a similarly boxy frame to my Jeep, but the Mercedes emblem on the grill promised the similarities ended there.

"Is that Banderas?" Willard walked back into the room to join me at the window.

"Not unless the government is paying a lot more for corpse-pick-up vehicles than I thought."

Willard curled her lip when she saw the SUV. "That's our doctor. In his outrageously priced box on wheels."

"I didn't know Mercedes makes SUVS," I admitted.

Thad walked over. "Oh, that's the AMG G 63. They're posh."

"It looks like a red toaster oven," Willard said.

"The seats are heated and have a massage function," Thad said.

"If the front window flipped down, you could slide a Hot Pocket right in."

"Colonel Willard is impressed by ostentatious displays of wealth," I informed Thad.

"I see that." He didn't look offended, maybe because his BMW was only half the price of that thing.

"I'll go get him," Willard growled and stomped out again.

"I think they may have dated," I whispered to Thad.

"And it didn't end well?"

"I don't know, but I hope to tease her mercilessly about it."

CHAPTER 4

Dr. Daku Walker wore an impeccable navy-blue suit, blue tie, and dress shoes, despite the warmth of the late-August afternoon. He was a handsome man in his forties with skin dark enough that he ought to meet Willard's previously expressed tastes, though maybe the thick mane of red-blond hair threw her off. I assumed that was natural—a byproduct of his lion-shifter heritage—and didn't represent a dye job, though his trimmed nails and perfect cuticles suggested a passion for salons, so it was hard to tell.

When Willard had said he'd been in the army, I'd assumed the US Army, but he spoke with an Australian accent, so maybe that was wrong. While examining the still unconscious Ti, Walker mixed terms like "Buckley's chance" and "a few stubbies short of a six-pack" with "liver sinusoidal endothelial cells" and "tissue macrophages," none of which I found comprehensible, though the latter was part of an explanation about Ti's liver and detoxification pathways being overwhelmed.

"How can you tell that without a blood test?" Willard asked.

"I'm gifted."

"Please."

"And have highly refined magical senses to go with my medical knowledge. I can see with my mind's eye what mundane humans would need a microscope to glimpse. But I don't know *what* is overwhelming his liver, nor can I tell if his unconscious state is due to hepatic encephalopathy—a buildup of toxins in the brain—or is magically induced."

"When I examined him with my senses," Freysha said, "I thought I detected a hint of something foreign in his bloodstream."

Walker's brow creased. "Did you?"

"Are her magical senses more highly refined than yours?" Willard asked.

"It is possible. Elves are sensitive and sophisticated magic users."

"And here I thought he'd deny anyone could be more refined than he," Willard told me.

"With your permission, ma'am—" Walker raised his eyebrows toward Nin, "—I'll take some blood samples and have my lab run them on Monday."

"Of course," Nin said.

"Not until Monday?" Willard frowned.

Walker glanced at a gold-and-crystal watch on his wrist. "They're already closed for the day today, and another lab won't do. My people can check for evidence of magical tampering as well as mundane problems." He smiled at her, flashing white teeth. It was only in my imagination that his fangs were more pronounced than a normal human's would be.

"Your laboratory in the plastic-surgery clinic where you work?" Willard asked.

"It's restorative surgery, and we have several kinds of practices in the building, including a lab with a half-gnome analyst who is precisely the right person to run this."

Willard's lips thinned, but she didn't object further.

"Now, if you'll allow me to work—" Walker patted the medical kit he'd brought along, "—I'll suture his wounds and set up an IV to hydrate him and give him some nutrients that may help his liver."

"You can do that in someone's house?" I asked.

"I can. As you pointed out, a gnome arriving in a hospital would flummox the staff. And I find it unlikely he has a health insurance card." Walker opened his kit. "If I'm not able to rouse him, I may have to insert a catheter as well."

"Uh." I raised a finger. "Could we take him to a guest bedroom before messing with his bladder?"

"Who's going to monitor that stuff?" Willard asked. "Thorvald's about as likely a nurse as a sasquatch."

"Hey, I completed the combat-lifesaver course in the army."

"Were catheters covered?"

"Not… explicitly."

"Have no fear, Colonel," Walker said. "I can send someone over to help with nurse duties this weekend, and I'm capable of turning this into a first-rate care facility."

"I'll show you to the bedroom you can use for that." I pointed out a guest room, then went outside to get some fresh air.

Dimitri's barbecue guests had left, only a sad platter of charred hot dogs and cold burgers evidence of his attempt at an afternoon shindig. He'd switched to poking into the various raised planters around the back yard, digging out weeds and putting in fresh bark. I remembered he'd worked for a landscaper back in Oregon, something that had paid the bills better than his yard-art-creation hobby.

"How are Nin and her grandfather?" Dimitri asked when he saw me.

"She's worried. I hope they get Ti to wake up, because I'm sure she has questions for him. *I* have questions for him. Like how did he know to find her at our new house? And did he know he was leading a passel of trouble to us?"

Dimitri's phone rang. "It's the shop. I hope Tam doesn't need me to come in. This is the only day I've taken off all week."

I spotted Freysha walking out to the conservatory and left him to talk to his barista.

"Hey," I said, joining her inside. "I kept an orc from compelling me to bare my neck to his sword. The lessons are paying off."

"That's excellent." Freysha didn't head to her growing plant collection, as I'd expected. Instead, she pulled out the box of LEGOs that Willard had given her and started setting up piles on the brick floor.

"New project?"

"Gondo and Tari are coming over for a block-construction contest. Also, to look over my homework for my engineering class."

"Are you sure you want input from goblins? They'll probably suggest you add more repurposed auto parts and road signs to whatever it is you're designing for your homework."

"A sewage-treatment plant."

"Carburetors add flair to those, I hear."

"Val?" came Nin's voice from the kitchen. "Freysha?"

"Out here," I called.

"The doctor found something in my grandfather's pants." Nin ran out with a folded paper clenched in her hand, her expression extremely earnest, so I resisted the urge to make jokes about what men—and presumably male gnomes—kept in their pants. "But he cannot read it."

Nin stopped in front of us and unfolded the paper. No, that looked like *parchment*. She held it up toward us, and I gaped at a portrait drawn in black ink.

"Is that a picture of me?"

"It looks very much like you." Nin pointed to two columns of symbols below the portrait along with another small drawing. It was of a sword that looked a lot like Chopper.

"That's the most predominant of the three dwarven languages." Freysha held out her hand for the parchment.

"Dwarven?" I asked. "Not gnomish?"

How many races were mixed up with Nin's grandfather?

"Dwarven, yes."

"Can you read it?" I scratched my head.

Did this mean Nin's grandfather had come looking for *me*? Not Nin?

"Yes, I believe so." Freysha laid the parchment on one of the potting benches and scrutinized it.

Behind her, Nin paced.

"Val," Freysha said, "have you ever met a dwarf named Belohk?"

"Uh, yes. A few months ago. He was chained up and being forced to make magical ammunition for some shifters up in Bothell."

"He signed this." Freysha pointed to four symbols at the bottom of the parchment. "He may have written the whole page."

"And the page says what?"

"It speaks of a mighty half-elven warrior who fearlessly battles dragons and carries what he believes is one of the original Dragon Blades from more than ten thousand years ago." Freysha glanced over my shoulder, though I'd removed Chopper's scabbard after the battle. She realized that and turned her gaze toward the open kitchen door. Her eyes grew unfocused, as if she was using her senses to study the sword for the first time. "I do not know enough about dwarven workmanship to know if that's true. It is a powerful sword and certainly made with superb workmanship."

"So I've heard. But why was this guy writing about me? This isn't a bounty poster or something like that, is it?" I'd thought I'd parted on good terms with old Belohk.

Freysha ran her hand along the ragged top edge of the parchment. "I believe this was torn from a workbook. It looks much more like a diary entry or a letter than a mass-produced document. There is no mention of a reward or bounty."

Dimitri walked in, sticking his phone in his pocket. "I need to go to the shop. Trolls got in a fight and broke more of Zoltan's tinctures. I'm going to have to build some kind of troll-proof display case. I'm envisioning poured cement and transparent aluminum."

I lifted a hand to acknowledge the *Star Trek* reference but was too distracted by this new development to look away from the parchment.

Dimitri followed our gazes to it. "Everything okay here?"

"Dwarves in other realms are writing about me in their diaries," I said.

"Did that answer my question?"

"I don't know. Freysha, what else does it say?"

"It reemphasizes that you've got one of the ancient Dragon Blades and that you're a great warrior who has slain dragons with it."

"That isn't something I want getting out. So far, every dragon I've met has taken exception to that, and it's only the fact that Zav claimed me and told his people he'll be responsible for my further actions that I haven't been shackled by the Dragon Justice Court for years of punishment and rehabilitation."

"I was going to ask if you wanted to help me clean up the shop while I build the display cases," Dimitri said, "but I see you have problems of your own to deal with."

"No kidding. I'll help you with the display cases later if you help me tear out the walls in the bathrooms upstairs, dry out the framing, and repair the leaks."

Dimitri looked puzzled. "I said I would. I didn't realize it was that urgent of a project."

Only if I wanted to be able to sleep in my bedroom without crazy nightmares and my inhaler clenched in my hand. I didn't say that out loud. I hadn't told Dimitri about my weak lungs or susceptibility to mold, and I was hesitant to bring it up now. Or ever. Even if these people were my friends, I didn't want to admit to my weaknesses. Wasn't that why I was seeing a therapist? I'd complain to her at my next appointment.

"Freysha," I said, "any idea how Nin's grandfather—her *gnomish* grandfather—got ahold of a dwarf's diary entry?"

"No. The only person who knows is unconscious in your house." Freysha looked contemplatively at me.

"I do not understand," Nin said. "Why would my grandfather be interested in Val? Does he want her sword? He is not a warrior, and he knows how to craft magical weapons of his own."

"Maybe he wants *Val*," Dimitri said.

"I'm kind of tall for him, don't you think?" I smiled, but nobody else did.

Freysha folded the parchment back up and returned it to Nin. "I believe the only way to get answers is to figure out how to wake him up so you can ask."

"Or wait for some more orcs to come attack me and ask *them*." That wasn't the option I would prefer.

"Let's hope the doctor figures out how to heal and rouse him," Freysha said.

After Dimitri left, I guided Nin out of the conservatory. She drew the parchment out to look at it again.

"Are you okay?" I asked. "I'm sure the doctor will figure something out. If not today, then when his lab analyzes the blood sample."

"Yes. I will be fine. I am just..." Nin lowered the parchment. "Is it wrong of me to have hurt feelings because my grandfather came to Seattle to see *you* instead of me?" She waved her hand in front of her heart. "I feel upset. It is childish and not important right now, but... it is my feeling."

"It's not wrong to have feelings, but maybe we should get his story before we judge him."

"I do not wish to judge him. I am merely admitting to feeling hurt."

"Let's get his story before you feel hurt." I patted her on the shoulder.

"I wish he were awake now. I so badly want to talk to him."

I wished I could help her more.

Willard walked out of the house and joined us on the patio. "Walker has done everything he can for now and said he'd drop the blood off at his lab and send a nurse to help. I'm heading home."

"Wait." I lifted a hand, realizing we had access to another lab that might be as viable as Walker's. And that could run the sample *tonight*.

"Can he get another vial of blood before he goes? For our vampire in the basement?"

"I don't think Nin wants Zoltan to drink her grandfather's blood."

Horror flashed in Nin's eyes.

I shook my head. "Zoltan has a bunch of alchemy equipment he brought when he moved in. I bet he can analyze blood and find magical substances too."

"Ah. I'll catch Walker before he goes and ask." Willard jogged back inside.

I called Zoltan on my phone. The sun was a few hours from setting, so I didn't know if he would be awake. Dimitri's first home-improvement project had been, per Zoltan's request, completely blocking in the basement windows so his lair was pitch dark around the clock. Providing nobody was rude and opened the door.

Dear robber, a text came in. *Why are you calling me during the middle of my night?*

Though a phone conversation would have been quicker, I texted back, *I have some blood for you.*

He replied before I could send a second message more fully explaining.

You're offering some of your fine half-elven blood that is enhanced by the magical mark of a dragon? I accept. I will even allow you to enter my abode during the day so that I might enjoy this feast.

Gross. I need you to analyze some gnome blood for a magical poison or spell or something that we believe is afflicting him.

I would prefer your blood. It would not be beneficial to my health to consume tainted blood.

Nin will be relieved to know you're not going to lick the vial. This gnome is her grandfather, and he's very sick. We need your help.

I will be glad to help. At my usual hourly consulting fee.

"Zav is right. Earthlings are overly concerned with money." *Fine,* I texted him back.

"America is a capitalist society," Nin informed me. "But the opportunities are many. Soon, I will have enough money to buy a house and bring my family to this country."

"You think so, but that's only because you haven't yet seen what Zoltan charges for his help."

CHAPTER 5

I had an appointment with my therapist the first thing in the morning, so I left the house before any news came up from the basement about Zoltan's blood analysis. A part of me had wanted to reschedule on Mary, since Nin's grandfather was still passed out in the guest bedroom, and now a nurse I didn't know was wandering around the house, but I'd already rescheduled on her three times this month. She'd gone out of her way to come in and meet with me on a Sunday, so I couldn't cancel again.

Nin was at the house. She would keep an eye on things. The evening before, she'd only left long enough to go home and pack an overnight bag. This was the longest she'd been away from her business since I'd known her—she usually thought nothing about working seven days a week and being there from opening to closing—but this was an extenuating circumstance.

The scent of brewing coffee filled the air as I walked into the marble-floored waiting area.

"Good morning, Val." Mary lifted an empty mug from the beverage station. "Coffee?"

"No, thanks." Coffee always smelled better than it tasted, so I was happy to give the burbling pot a wide berth and head straight to her office.

Since Mary was the only therapist working this morning, I didn't have to pass any weirdos waiting for appointments. An inordinate number of clients at the clinic liked to pace and mutter to themselves, occasionally while straightening magazines or chanting rap lyrics. Mary kept promising me that plenty of normal people came in to see therapists, but she lumped me into that category too, so I knew not to believe her.

I sat in my usual chair, the back to the wall and arranged so I could see her desk, the window, and the door. As I preferred it.

Coffee in hand, Mary came in and sat down. "How's your weekend going so far?"

"A portal opened on my roof, I battled a bunch of orcs, my tiger eviscerated a monster creature on the lawn, and I found out I'm now infamous in other realms."

"If someone else said that to me, I'd think it was an odd joke."

"But it's me, so you know it's only odd."

"Yes. Do you want to talk about it?" Mary set down her coffee and pulled a pad of paper into her lap.

"I don't know. I'm still processing the situation."

Technically, *Zoltan* was processing the situation—while tallying up hours to bill me.

"Aside from portals and battles, how have your relaxation exercises been going?"

"Not well."

She didn't frown at me, but I felt like she was oozing disappointment. It wasn't that I didn't *want* to try to relax and lower my stress levels and hopefully find a way to get off the damn asthma medication I now took morning and night. It was that my life wasn't cooperating. And the new house…

"I'm not sure I should have moved," I admitted.

"Oh? When you described moving into a house with other people, I thought it sounded very promising. You need company, people who care about you and who you can talk with when you need to. I'm here for you, of course, but it's important to have a supportive community around you."

"Did I mention that one of my new roommates was a vampire?"

Her brow furrowed. "No."

"Ah. Actually, I'm not having problems with my, uh, community. It's that the house is old and musty, and it's been bothering my lungs." And my sleep. I'd had hours of nightmares the previous night and woken up sweating and disorientated several times. I doubted I had managed to string together two hours of solid sleep.

"Did you speak with your doctor?"

"Yeah, he said not to live in a moldy house."

Mary gazed blandly at me.

"I bought drywall and a sledgehammer and crowbar. I'm going to start watching HGTV and figure out how to fix it all. In my copious free time."

"Perhaps your roommates could help."

"They will. Or at least one of them will. Dimitri already agreed. From what I've observed, Zoltan isn't into physical labor. He can hurl cybernetically enhanced bears across a laboratory if he's threatened, but if you ask him to help move furniture, he's always in the middle of an experiment and can't leave it."

"Perhaps you can focus on the more helpful roommates."

"Oh, I do."

"Have you seen Amber lately?"

"I have. I'm giving her sword-fighting lessons."

Mary's eyebrows rose.

"Is that not a typical mother-daughter bonding thing? We also shopped, but that was extremely expensive, and now I'm stuck with dresses I don't need."

Mary took a few notes. I wondered if she'd liked it more when I hadn't opened up to her about my life.

"Are you still seeing Mr. Zavryd?" She insisted on calling him by name, not *the dragon*. Or *your incredibly bizarre boyfriend who claimed you as a mate but hasn't actually had sex with you*. I appreciated that.

"Yes."

"You said he has magical powers?"

"Incredible magical powers."

"Perhaps he could assist you with your mold problem."

"I don't think dragons mind mold. They sleep in caves. Occasionally on the roof." Admittedly, Zav hadn't tried that since I moved into the Victorian house. There were a lot of slanted and pointy bits up there.

"But *you* mind it. Have you told him?"

"We don't discuss my vulnerabilities."

"No? Who do you discuss them with?"

"You."

"I appreciate that you trust me."

"It's more that I'm pretty sure you'd get your license revoked if you gossiped about me to my enemies."

"Do you believe Mr. Zavryd would do that?"

"No." I leaned back in the chair. What was she angling for? "But he's a super powerful dragon, and he thinks I'm a mighty warrior who vexes his enemies."

"Aren't you?"

"I'm excellent at vexing. As for the rest, I have my moments. But look, I'm already this half-human mongrel, as he called me so often early on. It took me a while to climb up to a respectable status in his eyes. I don't want to admit that I have this... what's becoming this chronic weakness." I grimaced, hating to admit that it might be chronic. That seemed to imply forever. That I wouldn't find a solution. So far, I hadn't wanted to accept that, but at the same time, I hadn't managed to do many of the things that could help my body relax and maybe stop being so reactive to everything.

I dropped my face in my hand.

"If you were one of my less bristly clients, I would ask if you wanted a hug," Mary said, "but I'm a little afraid you would punch me."

"Only if you didn't warn me first." I lowered my hand. "I'm just having a moment. Is that what it's called?"

"We can call it whatever you wish. I will say that I haven't seen any relationships succeed where either partner withheld crucial personal information from the other."

"Are you sure? Because I'm positive I've heard stories of guys with three wives in different states who didn't know the others existed."

"I wouldn't call any of those successful relationships."

"You've got high standards." My phone buzzed, and I pulled it out.

A text from Zoltan read: *It is well past the hour that I go to sleep, but I believe I've found what is ailing your gnome. A bacterial infection that may have been created in a laboratory employing both science and magic. I have isolated the bacteria in a Petri dish and found a couple of chemicals that can kill them, but they are extremely toxic to gnomes, humans, and similar beings. I have researched natural substances that are less deadly and could hypothetically do the job, and I've selected a recipe for a promising formula. However, I may need you to acquire the core ingredient. Do return before I slip into the cozy confines of my coffin for a well-deserved sleep, or you'll have to wait until tonight to speak with me.*

I thought about pointing out that I knew where his coffin was and that I could knock on it anytime, but it sounded like he had a solid lead, so I refrained from snark and texted: *Thank you. I'll head back to the house soon. Tell Nin.*

"I have to go." I put my phone away. "My friend's grandfather is in trouble, and I need to help her."

Mary had used my distraction to fill in several lines on her notepad. "Of course. Will you do me a favor?"

"Pay my bill?"

She smiled. "You always do that. In cash."

"You say that like it's unorthodox and weird."

"We usually bill people's insurance, but we're happy to take payment however is convenient. A favor?"

"What?" I couldn't keep the wariness out of my voice.

Mary wasn't going to ask me to go to that float-tank place again, was she? I'd looked into it. Some people might find floating in a dark coffin of warm water appealing—Zoltan, perhaps—but there was no way I was getting naked in some commercial establishment and climbing into an enclosed box with my weapons on the outside.

"If you trust him and feel comfortable enough to do so, please consider telling Mr. Zavryd about your health problems and discussing your fears with him. Your relationship will be stronger if it's based on honesty and disclosure."

My shoulders slumped. It wasn't that she was wrong; it was just that we hadn't even had sex yet and I didn't know for sure that we would have a lasting relationship. Peeling back all my armor and sharing my fears, insecurities, and weaknesses with him would make me feel so vulnerable. I *hated* being vulnerable.

"I'll think about it," I said, more because Mary wanted to hear it than because I thought I would do it.

"Good. I hope you're able to help your friend."

"Me too."

CHAPTER 6

Maybe it was because Mary had brought him up, but as I drove back to the house, I found myself missing Zav.

He'd only been gone a day, but he'd been scarce the previous week too. My understanding was that the ordeal with the stolen egg had riled up the entire dragon populace. I had no idea how many clans they had or how many dragons were in each one, but at least three clans were far too aware of Earth now for my liking. And Zav seemed to be in the middle of all their politics. It couldn't be a healthy place. I wished we could take a vacation somewhere and hang out and have fun, me being snarky, him being pompous, and our enemies having no idea where we were or how to find and pester us.

"Wishful thinking."

There wasn't any street parking, so I drove up on the curb at the corner and onto the lawn. The perks of having a Jeep. If the landlord objected, he could put in a driveway.

My senses told me Ti was still inside and that Nin was in the basement. Dimitri had gone to the shop that morning, and Freysha had gone to Willard's office to help out with a weekend organization project, and a twinge of unease filled me at finding out Nin was alone in the basement with Zoltan. Even if he was a putative ally, he *was* a vampire. If he was hungry after a long night of research, would he be tempted to sample the blood of the nearest human?

With that thought in mind, I was running flat out by the time I leaped down the stairs to the basement and flung the door open.

A male scream echoed from what had once been Jimmy's blacksmith shop and was now Zoltan's laboratory. Belatedly, as daylight streamed inside with me, I realized the reason why.

"The door!" Zoltan cried. "Shut out that light."

I was already closing it. Since Dimitri had covered all the windows, doing so plunged the basement into darkness, save for a soft red glow coming from the laboratory.

"That was unacceptable," Zoltan groaned.

"Sorry. I was worried you were down here gnawing on Nin's veins." As soon as I made sure the door was too well latched to blow open, I hurried around the corner to check the status of those veins.

Nin was sitting on the magical anvil—apparently, that was an immovable piece of equipment that Jimmy hadn't been able to take— with her neck unmolested.

"*Gnawing?*" Zoltan crept warily into view, glancing toward the door before pinning me with a glare. "Really, dear robber. How little you think of me. Even when I drink the blood of my neighbors, my touch is so light that they don't rouse from their sleep."

My fingers strayed to my own neck, though I hadn't noticed any puncture wounds there since moving in. I also slept so poorly that I doubted a dust mote could sneak up on me, much less a vampire.

"I have been studying your blood sample," Zoltan said tartly. "All night. For many hours. I'll have an invoice delivered directly to your bedroom."

"The kitchen table is fine. You said you found the problem? Some weird bacteria?"

"A bacterial infection, yes. The bacteria are like nothing I've seen before, but that isn't surprising if the gnome came from another world and was presumably infected there. I wish I had a DNA sequencer. That would help me determine which world it originated on and whether it's something natural or, as I suspect, was made by scientists."

"Which races have scientists advanced enough to make bacteria? Can *we* even do that?" Maybe I was arrogant in believing Earth was more technologically advanced than the worlds in the Cosmic Realms, but I'd been to Elf Land, and they wore buckskins and lived in trees.

"Certainly, we can. As can scientists of many other races, most using magic the way we yield gene-editing tools. Dragons could have done it, gnomes themselves could have done it, and so could elves, dark elves, and even top-of-the-line goblin and troll shamans."

"I *hope* dark elves weren't involved. I don't want to see them again this year. Or ever."

"My guess from my analysis would be sunlight elves or dragons."

I curled a lip. I didn't want dragons to be involved either. But why would an elf poison a gnome with some bacterial infection? Why would *anyone*?

"He's not awake yet to explain how he got this infection, is he?" I looked at Nin.

She shook her head. "I wish he were. I want to know what happened, and also where he has been these last twenty years. My grandmother still lives, and I know she would dearly wish to speak with him, to know why he left all those years ago. I have not called home to tell my family about this yet. Not until I know... that he will survive."

"If he doesn't receive a formula that will eradicate the infection," Zoltan said, "he won't."

Nin slumped. I frowned at Zoltan.

"But as I told you, dear robber, I believe I've found a formula that will work without harming the host. The gnome, in this case." Zoltan walked to the counter, grabbed an open book that was older than the house, and brought it over to show me. It wasn't in English. He pointed at what looked like a list of items. "I have this, this, this, and this. *This* is not inexpensive, so your bill will rise, dear robber."

"*I* will pay for the ingredients." Nin pressed her hand to her chest.

"Very good. But there is one that cannot be purchased and is not a native plant on Earth." Zoltan turned the page to a drawing of a stalk of small bell-shaped flowers.

"It looks like foxglove," I said.

"Similar, but the flowers are teal, and the stigma protrudes. See?"

"I guess." It was hard to envision the color from a black-ink drawing.

"It's native to the troll home world and is called *guk-laruk*."

"Sexy. If plants here had that name, they would fly off the shelves at the home and garden center." I propped a fist on my hip. "Does this mean we have to find someone who can make a portal and visit the troll home world?"

"That would be the easiest way to acquire the plant," Zoltan said, "as it grows rampant in the wetlands there."

"Since the only person I know who makes portals isn't on Earth, it's not easy."

"Elves are known to cultivate it on their worlds. Since elves and trolls have warred often throughout the millennia, elves started growing some of the plants in wetlands near their cities. They are used in several formulas that can protect against common troll poisons."

"We'd still need a portal to get there." Unless Freysha had been lying to me and could make one, we were out of luck until Zav came back. I wondered how Freysha planned to get home. Maybe our father made portals and planned to pick her up eventually.

"True. Will your dragon return soon to bask in your wit?"

"I'm sure he wants to, but I don't know."

"I ask because…" Zoltan glanced at Nin. "I would guess that even with your marsupial shifter's intervention, the gnome only has a few days left to live if he doesn't receive an effective antibacterial."

Nin closed her eyes and leaned against a wall for support.

"Dr. Walker? He's a lion, not a marsupial." Not that I cared about that. I was worried about Nin. I hated seeing her distressed, and it was a cruel twist of fate that would bring her living grandfather to her side only to die before they had a chance to speak.

"He is a marsupial-lion shifter. The Thylacoleonidae are believed to have gone extinct during the Pleistocene era, so I don't know his story, but I imagine it's fascinating."

I barely heard him. I was trying to think of a way to open a portal to one of these worlds with the plant.

Was it possible one of the artifacts Willard's people had recovered from Weber's house could create portals? As far as I knew, Weber had been gathering security artifacts, not means of transportation. I might have better luck asking Gondo if his people could make a portal generator out of dented traffic signs.

"Oh, wait." I snapped my fingers as an idea came to me. "You say elves cultivate these plants? Is it possible they would have brought them to Earth to grow when they created their sanctuaries here?" I remembered the different climate inside the elven sanctuary I'd visited in Idaho. It had been similar to the Pacific Northwest, which was full of wetlands.

Wetlands that might support this plant?

"I have not been to an elven sanctuary," Zoltan said. "It is possible. *Guk-laruk* is a perennial, so if some were planted decades ago, it might still grow wild."

"Maybe it's time to visit the goblins that settled into the sanctuary near Granite Falls." It might be a waste of time, but unless Zav returned soon and could give me a ride to another world, I didn't know what else to try.

"Would Freysha know if the elves who visited Earth had planted such things?" Nin asked.

"Maybe. I'll call." I dialed Willard's office number.

When someone picked up, something that sounded like a staple gun firing over and over greeted me along with a perky, "Captain Willard's office. This is her assistant speaking. How may I be of service?"

The thwacks of the stapler continued.

"It's Val, Gondo. Is Willard there?"

"Let me see if she's available to speak with you." *Thwack, thwack, thwack.*

"That's not your typical hold music," I muttered.

Nin lifted her eyebrows.

"She's finishing up her current call," Gondo informed me, the stapler finally winding down, "and she will talk with you shortly."

"Great. What was that noise?"

"One of the junior officers who's been assigned to teach a class to the police department on ogres, trolls, and orcs brought in a ridiculous amount of duplicated papers that he wanted stapled together into booklets. Naturally, a goblin as important as myself can't manually staple together two hundred booklets, so I automated the process."

"Uh huh. What exactly did you do to Willard's stapler?"

"It now staples across the desk and returns to its original position in time to receive a new stack of papers, much like the carriage return on the typewriter I found in the basement. Point of interest, I *used* the carriage return of the typewriter I found. I also created a paper sorting and gathering machine."

"What parts went into that?"

"A fan motor, the gas cylinder from a broken office chair, and items called Tic Tacs."

"*Tic Tacs?* What role did they play?"

"Goblin fuel. Crafting is hard work."

"I've heard that. Gondo, have you been out to the elven sanctuary that your people took over?"

"Only once, but yes. It's not nearly as interesting as living in the city. There is no way to brew high-quality coffee in the woods."

"Tragic."

"Indeed. Woodland goblins don't seem to mind, but I'm a city goblin now."

"Are there a lot of plants there? Flowers?" I described the picture to him, though it occurred to me that even if the plant did grow out there, it might be past the flowering season now.

"I don't know," Gondo said. "Maybe? I can't *make* anything out of flowers, so I don't look at them much."

"What part of the plant do you need, Zoltan?" I whispered.

"The root."

"Okay. Write me up a detailed description to go with a copy of that drawing, please."

"I'll take it now," came Willard's voice in the distance. "And don't start up that stapler gizmo again while I'm talking."

"Yes, ma'am."

"We won't get results back from Walker's lab until tomorrow," Willard told me without preamble.

"I know, but I have results back from my basement lab. It's possible your doctor will find something else, but Zoltan is convinced it's a bacterial infection, probably from another world. There's a plant that he believes can be used in a formula to eradicate it in Ti's system without hurting him. He's got a name here. Uh." I squinted at Zoltan's open book, and he was polite enough to hold it up to the infrared light and point out the word for me to read, but not without eye rolling for my execrable memory. "*Guk-laruk.*"

"Hang on. I'll write that down."

"Here. In case you need to write it down correctly." I took a photo of the page and sent it to her cell phone. "It's a troll word."

"Thanks. Why didn't you call me on my cell to start with?"

"Because I enjoy being patched through by your assistant. Also, I'm looking for Freysha, not you. I thought she might be hanging out with Gondo."

"She was in there earlier, but the noise of the staple-whatever hurt her ears."

"You're fortunate you can close your door on that."

"It's not *that* soundproof of a door," Willard grumbled. "Hang on."

She put me on hold, hopefully to find Freysha. I kept hoping that Zav would fly into my range, so we could more easily find this plant, but I had no such luck.

Freysha came on the line. "I am familiar with *guk-laruk,* Val. I have even grown it before."

"I don't suppose you brought any seeds with you to Earth?"

"No. I am not certain if it is capable of growing here."

"I'm going out to the elven-turned-goblin sanctuary to check. Do you want to come with me?"

If she knew the plant by sight, that would be far better than taking a list of attributes and a black-and-white sketch.

After a pause, Freysha said, "The colonel agrees that I can go. She insists we take Gondo."

"To serve as a diplomat and ensure his people will let us in?"

"Because his staple machine is giving her a headache."

"I'll pick you guys up in twenty minutes."

"I will go with you," Nin said as I hung up. "If the goblins require that we trade for the plant, I will offer them my goods."

"I think if you offered them aluminum cans and shoes full of holes, they would be delighted."

"I will offer whatever it takes."

Nin started for the door, but I held up a hand. "You don't need to come. This could take all day. You should stay and watch your grandfather and be around in case you're needed at your food truck—or the coffee shop. If the plant exists in the sanctuary, I'll get it for you."

"You do not believe I could be useful?"

"I'm more worried about leaving your grandfather here alone. I can leave him my camouflage charm again and activate it before I go, but it needs to be reactivated regularly. If those orcs show up and can sense him... I need you to call me, and I'll do my best to get back in time to help." I rubbed the back of my neck as I debated how likely it was that the orcs would return with their promised reinforcements while I was away. "I think I'll leave Sindari with you too. To help fight if necessary."

I didn't like the idea of going into the woods without my tiger ally or my cloaking charm, but hopefully, there wouldn't be trouble in the sanctuary.

"Oh, yes. I understand. I should have realized that he could still be in danger. I will stay here with Sindari. He is a good companion."

"Yes, he is."

"I am *also* here," Zoltan pointed out. "She will not be alone."

"Ti is in a sunlight-filled, south-facing guest bedroom. I doubt you're going to want to hang out there."

"It does sound dreadful. If you go to our shop, have Dimitri fetch some of the Mechanics' Muse lotion for you. If you need to trade with the goblins, you will find they are very fond of it. It makes them joyous."

"Wouldn't a thermos of coffee do the same thing?"

"Possibly."

Once Nin and I left the basement—giving Zoltan time to hide himself in a closet or coffin or whatever light-proof structure he'd built—I summoned Sindari.

I need you to stay with Nin and help her if any enemies show up, I told him.

He gazed at me with his green eyes. *You are not going off into battle without me, are you?*

No, I'm going to look for a plant.

That sounds boring.

Exactly. That's why you're staying here. I hoped that another battle wouldn't come to the house and that Sindari would also find it boring here. Maybe he and Nin could watch sports on TV together. Or the robins at the new birdfeeder Dimitri had put in. *Also, I haven't removed the pine-tree scented air freshener from the Jeep yet, and I know how you feel about that.*

It's odious.

I patted Sindari on the back, then unthreaded his charm from my thong. "He's agreed to stay with you, Nin." I placed the charm in her palm, trusting she knew its value and would keep it safe. "He's pleased."

"Oh? I'm not very interesting."

"Yes, but you don't smell like a fake pine tree."

Nin gave me an odd look as I left the house. What was new?

CHAPTER 7

Despite it being a weekend, traffic was a snarl, and it took more than an hour to stop by the shop to grab a bribe for the goblins, pick up Freysha and Gondo for the trip, and get onto I-5 heading north out of Seattle. It would be another hour to get out past Granite Falls and to the spot where I'd dropped those goblins off in the U-Haul truck earlier that summer.

I was glad I didn't have another gig at the moment. Willard hadn't given me anyone to hunt down, and I wasn't serving as anyone's bodyguard this week. The only time concern was that Sindari could only stay in this realm for about six hours—maybe longer if he was just lounging on the patio in the sun. Once his time was up, Nin would be alone, save for a vampire who couldn't come up into the daylight-riddled house to help, even if he wanted to. Maybe I should have asked Willard to send someone over to keep an eye on the place. I would if this started looking like it would take all day.

"What's in that thermos?" Gondo asked from the back seat, his nostrils twitching.

Freysha was riding shotgun. She regarded his sniffing nose curiously.

"About thirty espresso shots being kept warm by stainless steel vacuum insulation." Since all I wanted to do was wander around and look for a plant—and I'd helped these goblins before—I didn't expect to have to deliver a big bribe, but a gift of caffeine might make them more amenable to offering assistance.

"Is it the French Sumatra from Lighthouse Roasters?" Gondo gripped the backs of our seats as he focused on the thermos. "That's my *favorite*."

"I didn't ask."

"You didn't? I can sample it and let you know if it has the dark caramelized flavor and deep complexity of the French."

"That's not necessary." As I turned off the interstate and headed east, the traffic opened up. Good. I didn't know how long I could keep Gondo's lips out of the coffee thermos.

"Will you give it to Work Leader Nogna?" he asked. "Her palate is primitive. The nuances of good espresso will be lost on her."

"I'm sure she'll like it."

Gondo humphed and started exploring the tools in the back of the Jeep. What were the odds that I could get there before he built something out of my jack and tire iron?

Freysha watched out the window as I drove past Lake Stevens. Even though we'd been roommates for the last couple of weeks, we hadn't discussed many topics beyond looted charms and my training. I didn't know much about her, other than that she was my half-sister and that my father had sent her to spy on me and see what kind of person I was.

I wondered if the mission bothered Freysha. Eireth had admitted she'd been preparing to study engineering on the goblin home world, not on Earth. Her plans had been derailed when he'd learned of my existence and decided to send her here. She was perky and friendly, but did she resent this at all? Resent *me*?

"What do you think of Earth so far?" I wasn't good at small talk and wondered if she would find my questions awkward.

"It's an interesting place. It's so very busy, though, with so many people."

"You might like today's trip then. The old sanctuary is between hiking trails, so I doubt we'll run into anyone until we find the goblins."

"It will be good to walk in the woods and listen to nature. Your neighbor has a very obnoxious machine that he uses frequently in the mornings."

"The guy with the leaf blower? Yeah, I agree. Especially since all he does is blow the leaves into the street and toward our house."

"Would you ever consider leaving Earth?"

"To go where? I wasn't welcome when I visited your world."

"No?" Freysha lifted her eyebrows.

"The greeter elves were snooty and said I couldn't stay in your tree city. Later, a randy dragon sang to me in the woods, but that wasn't enough to make me want to stay."

"I am surprised."

"Then you've clearly never been sung to by a dragon."

"Not about that. I am surprised you were turned away. You are Father's—the king's—child, even if you are only half elven. You should have some rights among our people."

"The welcoming committee wasn't informed. It's not a big deal. What are you going to do with the engineering knowledge you gain here?" We passed through Granite Falls and headed into the Mt. Baker-Snoqualmie National Forest, the openness of the agricultural areas we'd driven by giving way to towering moss-draped evergreens.

"I wish to repair and improve some of our older cities that are tethered together with magic instead of engineering. The magic fades over time and must be continually renewed by the builders. When I was younger, I saw a boy fall through a railing and to the ground below before anyone with magic enough could stop him. He died."

I was about to answer when I sensed Zav. We were almost to the place where I planned to park and hike into the woods. *Now* he showed up.

As I pulled over to the side of the road, he came down fast and right in front of us, wings tucked so he could fit between the trees. The landing was abrupt enough that I worried he was in trouble. Or *I* was.

Problem, Zav?

His eyes flared violet as he looked at us through the windshield, his magical power radiating from his big dragon form. *A problem. Yes.*

He shifted into his human form—he wore his robe with his usual slippers today, no new experiments with footwear—and strode toward us as I opened the door. A skinny green arm reached up between the seats. I grabbed the coffee thermos before Gondo could snatch it. He would implode if he drank all those espresso shots by himself.

"I will speak with you alone." Zav stood in the road beside my door.

He radiated irritation, though I doubted it had anything to do with me. I hadn't seen enough of him lately to irk him, so I assumed his meeting with his family had not gone well.

"I need a favor, so I'm not going to point out that you're supposed to say please after a statement like that."

"What favor?"

A car drove around the bend, heading straight toward him. I closed the door and waved for him to get off the road. He ignored the gesture and glared balefully at the oncoming car. There weren't any other cars in sight, so the driver moved into the other lane, but he honked self-righteously at Zav.

A wind blew up out of nowhere, whipping my braid around to slap me in the face as it blew against the side of the honking car. Tires squealed as it was forced off the road.

"Zav." I lunged out and grabbed his arm.

The wind subsided, and the driver managed to maneuver back onto the pavement, but not before he lost his driver-side mirror on a mossy tree trunk. It crunched loudly and fell to the earth. The driver sped away without stopping to retrieve it.

Zav glowered at me. "The vermin on this planet are *not* properly respectful of dragons."

"This is true, but dragons probably shouldn't stand in the middle of the road." I smiled and patted him on the chest.

My smile did nothing to alleviate his peevish mood. Aware that Freysha and Gondo had gotten out of the Jeep and were now standing and watching us from the other side, I held a finger up to Zav, and trotted the thermos over to them.

"Would you mind going ahead to the sanctuary and telling them about the plant we need? Zav wants to talk. I'll catch up as soon as we're done."

"We can handle this." Freysha nodded.

Gondo reached for the thermos. I held it above his head as I handed it to Freysha.

"As a thank-you for helping us, please offer that to all of the goblins who are interested. If there's any left over, Gondo can have it."

"You're giving *all* of the French Sumatra to wild goblins that drink out of streams?" Gondo moaned. "They won't properly appreciate it."

"I will, Val." Freysha accepted the thermos and headed into the woods in the right direction, despite having never been here before.

"Val." Zav spoke the syllable in a clipped you-will-attend-to-me-now manner that had my hackles up, but if the sanctuary was a dead end, I would need him to take me to another world for that plant, so I decided to hold my tongue and be conciliatory.

"What's wrong?" I returned to his side as another car came.

He glowered in that direction, as if he couldn't believe the rudeness of humans who presumed to use the road he'd chosen to land on.

"Let's go talk in those trees over there, eh?" I pointed.

"Yes." He clasped my hand and strode across the road at a brisk pace.

The car whizzed past behind us as he led me down a slope toward a creek trickling past in the distance. Before we were out of sight of the road, he halted and gazed down at me with a heated expression, his eyes still glowing.

When we stood close together, I was always conscious of the power of his aura and the way it crackled in the air around me, flowing over my skin and making me intensely aware of him. Even when he was annoyed, it had a magnetic quality that made me want to get closer to him. I found my hand straying up to rest on his chest again.

"What's wrong?" I repeated softly.

I thought he would explain why he was so angry, but he stepped close and wrapped his arms around me and kissed me.

You are my mate, he growled into my mind, as if I'd been questioning it. Or as if someone *else* had been questioning it? *I've claimed you because you are a superior warrior who stands at my side and vexes my enemies.* His hand slid down to grab my butt and pull me closer, our bodies molding together as he kissed me with intense longing that left me breathless and grabbing him back. *Also, when I am in this form, I am extremely attracted to you. Even when I did not know that I liked your sharp tongue, I wanted to do this with you. And more.*

I didn't know what to say, and I was so distracted by this unexpected ardor that I wasn't sure I could have formed words regardless. Zav lifted me from the ground, and I wrapped my arms around his shoulders and my legs around his waist, intensely aware of every inch of his hard body under his robe. I found my back against a tree, pinned even as I gripped him with no intention of letting go.

This wasn't how or where I'd imagined we would have sex for the first time, but like him, I'd wanted it long before I decided I'd liked him. As tendrils of magic flowed from his fingers, igniting pleasure in me like human hands never had before, I groaned against his mouth.

I want you too. My fingers twined in his short hair, and I kissed him as passionately as he kissed me, his body an exciting contrast to the gnarled trunk of the tree at my back. He shoved my jacket off my shoulders, and it tumbled to the ground. I was seconds away from yanking off the rest of my clothes—and yanking that robe off him—when he pulled back from the kiss and looked toward the forest canopy. He didn't release me, but the magic teasing my body disappeared.

"Zav!" I panted, my arms tightening around him. "You can't start this and then stop."

"I don't want to stop."

"Then *don't.*"

He still wasn't looking at me, so I kissed his neck, nipping at the strong tendons, trying to draw him back to me. I didn't sense anything out there—he couldn't be distracted by some squirrel running overhead or a bird flying past, could he?

His gaze returned to mine, his eyes full of the desire I felt. "I ache to be with you."

He pressed his hand against the tree behind my head, his tendons taut. His whole body was taut and hard.

"I can feel that. Why—" Then I sensed what he must have sensed. Another dragon.

This time, my groan had nothing to do with desire as I dropped my face into his shoulder. "What now?"

His hand shifted from the trunk to the back of my neck and he massaged my muscles, tingles of magic flowing from his fingers.

"Zav," I protested. That was going to make it harder to collect myself, if that was what I had to do. I assumed so. Even though I didn't recognize the aura of this new dragon, I assumed he was coming toward us for some unfriendly reason.

"Perhaps…" He rubbed his cheek against the side of my face and nuzzled my ear. "Perhaps if she came upon us in coitus, she would leave in a huff and never speak with me again."

I lifted my head. "*She?*"

So far, the only female dragons I'd met had been his sister, who hated me, and his mother, who also hated me.

"The queen is attempting to arrange a political pairing for me," Zav said as the female dragon flew closer. "She wishes me to dissolve my *Tlavar'vareous* with you and mate with an appropriate female dragon."

I unlocked my legs from around Zav and let my boots settle to the ground. My knees felt weak, so it was a good thing the tree was behind me for support. Not that Zav had released me. He was still holding me, his eyes narrowed as he contemplated the idea of being caught in coitus when his visitor showed up.

"We're not having sex in front of another dragon. I don't want to be incinerated by some jealous lover."

"She is not a lover. This is all political. I'm not sure it's even that. My sister reported back to the queen—our mother—that you were integral in retrieving the Starsinger egg and keeping our clans from going to war. I thought the queen would be pleased to know I had chosen a superior female, but I've since learned that she was angry. She wants me to mate with one of our kind and have hatchlings who will grow and add numbers to our clan."

"And I'm from the wrong side of the tracks."

His brow furrowed. He was still rubbing my neck, and it felt insanely good, but I made myself clasp his hand and push his fingers away.

"You figure it out with her. I'll stay out of it." Actually, I planned to run to the Jeep and grab my weapons. Just in case. I assumed Zav could and would protect me, but... better to be holding a dragon-slaying sword than not when an angry female showed up.

Her powerful aura blazed above the trees overhead, and I remembered Zav's warnings that female dragons were the most powerful and that males acted to serve them.

The canopy opened up as if it had been unzipped by a giant, and sunlight streamed down to the forest floor. Worried we were still compromisingly close, I pushed Zav farther away. He let himself be pushed, but there was a stubborn set to his jaw, and he eyed my mouth, as if he still thought his idea was a good one.

His idea seemed like a great way for me to land on the radar of another dragon who might show up to kill me when he wasn't around.

A great red dragon descended, trees and branches leaning away from her to make room for her to land. She radiated such power and magic that my senses ached from being in proximity to her.

Zav sighed and turned to face her.

"I'll wait at the Jeep while you guys figure it out." I grabbed my jacket and started to jog away from them, hoping to escape the female's notice entirely, but I hadn't gone more than five feet when the power of a vice wrapped around me, keeping me from moving.

Hell.

CHAPTER 8

As I stood frozen with one foot in the air, crushing power making it difficult to breathe and impossible to even move my head, I wished I hadn't told Freysha and Gondo to leave. Not that they could have driven off an irritated female dragon, but maybe they could have brought me my weapons. Or Freysha could have given me a crash course in how to escape magic binding me.

"Release her!" Zav boomed out loud, as well as telepathically.

It is true! the red dragon's feminine voice boomed even more loudly in my mind, causing an instant headache. *You have a female here on this vermin-infested planet!*

More power wrapped around me, and I winced, imagining myself being squeezed to death. But this was Zav's power. He peeled the other dragon's bindings away from me.

You dare pit yourself against me! You dare test your mettle against a superior female dragon?

Apparently, Zav dared, for I was able to get my legs working. I scrambled up toward the road, afraid that if I looked back, a tree trunk or some other piece of the forest would slam into me from behind and kill me instantly.

I will not allow you to harm my mate.

The queen said you wished me *to be your mate. That you were available for a mating as soon as our families ironed out a treaty.*

A treaty. How romantic.

I rushed across the road and grabbed my gun holster and sword scabbard from the back seat and strapped everything on.

The queen knew I was mated already. She should not have told you that.

I knew you were up to something when you fled from the Eyries of Evenlor so quickly. I knew I would find your secrets if I followed you to this prison planet.

And so you have. But Val was never a secret, not to my family, and not to the queen. She should have told you that I have a mate.

You name her! Some mongrel who stinks of this filthy vermin world? A loud sniffing noise reached my ears. *And you stink of her. I sensed you entwined, planning to rut against a tree like an animal. You are not worthy to be my mate, Zavryd'nokquetal Stormforge.*

I stood beside the Jeep, feeling better with my weapons on, but not sure what to do. If she was angry enough to lash out at Zav, I should stay and help him. But maybe it would be better—easier for him to deal with her—if I wasn't anywhere around. I wondered what the odds were that the elven sanctuary with its magical border would keep the female from finding me.

That is correct, Zav replied calmly. *You may leave and tell the queen that you are not interested in her proposal.*

You dare reject me! For a mongrel slut! Magic crackled in the air as the female hurled power.

Even though I'd run far enough that I could barely see them through the trees, I knew with all the certainty in my being that she'd lashed out at Zav.

Anger infused me, and I yanked out Fezzik and rushed toward them. How dare some self-righteous female dragon, who probably didn't even know Zav, assume that he would hook up with her?

Power whirled about like a cyclone. It uprooted a tree, flung it in the air, and slammed it down not ten feet in front of me. The unbroken branches stretched upward, blocking my view of the dragons.

Had she done that intentionally? To keep me from running down and helping him?

Fear replaced my anger as I imagined her utterly destroying him. Again, I thought of how he'd said that females were the strongest. Were they above the dragon laws and willing to kill those who spited them?

More magical power swept through the area, ripping more trees from their roots. They slammed down hard enough to shake the earth. The wind whipping about was a hundred times stronger than what I'd felt when Zav nudged that car off the road.

It wasn't directed at me—the snarls and thumps and snapping of jaws coming from the other side of the tree promised the dragons were focused on each other—but it impeded me all the same. I felt like I was in a wind tunnel as I leaned into the gale, determined to claw my way over the trunk blocking me. Even though Chopper was the only weapon I had that could harm a dragon, I would fire at her with Fezzik. That would distract her, and maybe Zav could take advantage of that.

The tree was so ancient and massive, and the tumultuous wind such an obstacle, that it took me far longer to climb to the top of the trunk than it should have. Zav had changed back into his native form. Clumps of dirt and broken branches flew as the dragons thrashed about on the ground, throwing magic as they bit and clawed at each other.

Gripping a thick branch for support, lest the wind tear me back down from my perch, I leveled Fezzik at the red dragon. Only to realize that Zav had gained the upper hand. The female lay on her back, taloned feet up and trying to push him away, but he stood unmovable as a mountain atop her, fangs bared as he stared down into her eyes.

An irreverent comment—was this still a fight or foreplay?—leaped to my tongue, but I quashed it. I hadn't expected Zav to win, but now that he had the upper hand, maybe I should disappear.

The female dragon looked over at me, and I tensed, finger tightening around the trigger. Zav also looked over at me.

If they were still speaking telepathically, they were excluding me from it. I hoped the female didn't feel that she had to kill me now that I'd seen her lose face—or at least lose the fight. It wasn't as if losing to Zav was uncommon.

Release me! the female commanded, turning her eyes back toward Zav, and I had no trouble hearing that.

Agree not to touch my mate, and I will let you up, Zav replied, his gaze also shifting back toward his opponent.

You presume to pin a superior female.

I will protect my mate.

You cannot have spawn with a mongrel two-legs. That you rut with her at all is an embarrassment to your family!

Is that what the queen said? Zav's anger and irritation leaked into his tone.

She didn't have to say it. It is obvious to all. That is why she sought me out to claim you as a mate.

Zav stepped off her, but he kept his gaze on her. Expecting shady business, I also kept Fezzik trained on her.

You dare to strike a female. She growled as she spoke to him, staring straight into his eyes. With amazing litheness for such a large creature, she flipped herself onto her feet. Her tail swished, rattling the undergrowth, reminding me of a cat about to pounce on a mouse.

Why did I get the weird feeling that she'd liked fighting with Zav?

I protect what's mine, he said.

Was that me? I thought about protesting being anyone's property, but again, I didn't want to draw attention to myself. Even if Zav could handle her in a fair fight, that didn't mean she couldn't come to Earth sometime when he wasn't here and flatten me.

She gazed at me again, a dismissive gaze, and flicked her tongue at me. *What a strange, pathetic creature you have claimed.*

She is a brave warrior.

If the wind blew, she would fall off that tree.

If you attacked her, Zav said, *she would drive her sword into your heart, as she has my other enemies.*

But I do not wish to be your enemy, Zavryd'nokquetal. I am here to offer to let you hold my tail and to unite our clans so that we will both be more powerful. Together, we will maintain control of the ruling council for all eternity.

I am not interested. I have a mate. As the queen should have told you.

For the first time, a twinge of uncertainty ran through me. Even if this dragon seemed like as much of an arrogant shit as every other dragon, maybe an alliance between clans was something Zav should consider. He'd admitted his people weren't as powerful as they'd once been and that others were plotting against them. If he married—or mated to—this female, could he change the fate of his family?

The dragon political scene made my head hurt, and I was glad when the female sniffed disdainfully and sprang into the air. Once again, the trees parted so she could fly up between their branches.

You will see the error of your ways and come to me, Zavryd'nokquetal, her parting words entered my mind as well as his. *And you will realize that I am what your clan needs. It does not need some short-lived verminous mongrel who isn't of our species. The embarrassment for one of your stature! You will see.*

Fortunately, she was flying away as she dissed me. Unfortunately, she didn't simply make a portal and disappear off to some other world. Did that mean she planned to stick around on Earth? To what end? Wooing Zav?

I curled my lip. If he ever did decide that he should make a sacrifice for his family and mate for an alliance, I hoped for his sake that he could find a dragon with a halfway pleasant demeanor.

But I would prefer he stay here with me, hanging out on the couch, watching movies, and gnawing on piles of takeout barbecue ribs. I snorted at myself. I was starting to sound like an old lady. Maybe after we watched movies and ate, we could rub liniment into each other's joints and get out the cribbage board.

Zav shifted into his human form. I returned Fezzik to its holster as he climbed toward me, hopping up onto the massive trunk, aided by a magical burst of wind. It ruffled the hem of his robe and put some of his leg hair briefly on display.

"Did the patch you shaved ever grow back?" I waved toward his leg.

He gazed at me. "I was about to express my appreciation that you stayed nearby and were willing to endanger yourself to fight a female dragon if I needed assistance."

"I'm sorry. Did my leg hair interest derail you?"

"Yes."

"You know I'm not very good at wrangling my tongue to stick to proper topics."

"I know this. I was hoping you would vex her." Zav arched his eyebrows as if to ask why I hadn't flung insults about the size of her butt and called her a grotsky little byotch.

"She seemed dangerous. I didn't want her to come back when you're not around and pulp me."

"Ah. You've grown wiser when it comes to dealing with dragons."

"Yes, I can be taught." I jerked my thumb toward the sky. "Any chance she's leaving Earth forever?"

"She has not left yet. I do not know what she plans next." Zav sighed and gazed sadly at me.

His earlier anger had bled out of him—his aggression worn off by the battle, perhaps. I didn't like that he seemed resigned.

"To woo you, it sounded like." I raised my eyebrows.

It wasn't so much that I wanted an explanation—I'd gotten the gist—but I wanted to know if he found the idea completely deplorable and wasn't remotely interested... or if I should brace myself for him ultimately giving in because it would be best for his family. He'd told me before that he supported his mother. Would he walk away from his lowly half-elf to do what she wished?

"I was hoping she would find the queen's suggestion unpalatable," Zav said.

"But she doesn't."

"It seems not."

"She only finds *me* unpalatable?"

"Because you are an obstacle and not a dragon."

"Grievous flaws I've tried often to remedy but alas failed."

His eyebrows twitched. "You still are not properly respectful of dragons."

"I know." I lifted a hand and rested it on his cheek, not sure what I should say but needing to say something that wasn't sarcastic or a joke. But I wasn't sure what. Mary could have suggested something appropriate, but Zav would think it weird if I texted her for a suggestion. She would want me to be honest instead of nonchalant, to let him know I cared. Why was that so hard?

His gaze turned toward my hand and then my eyes.

"I know you came up with this whole mating scheme to save my butt, but I do like you Zav, and I would miss you if you left to marry a dragon." There. Honesty. If he proceeded to tell me he had to leave me, I'd fire rounds into the nearest tree in a huff, but at least I wouldn't have driven him away with flippancy.

"A dragon does not leave his mate for another. The queen knows this. She is being..." A muscle in his jaw flexed. Like he wanted to deliver an appropriate insult, but he also didn't want to be disrespectful to his mother. "*Overbearing.*" He clasped my hand.

I squeezed his. "Mothers are difficult."

"Yes."

"Are you going to tell me if you got that patch of hair to grow back?" Normally, I would have assumed it had, but he'd told me his hair and beard always remained the same.

"Perhaps later when we are truly alone, I will let you check."

I offered a flirtatious smile, but that *when we are truly alone* put me on edge. The female dragon had flown out of my range, but I had a feeling his words meant she was still within Zav's. What did she plan to do? Spy on him from a mountaintop? Fly down and throw a few trees at me if I kissed him?

"I'll look forward to that." I pointed past the road toward the forest Freysha and Gondo had disappeared into. "Do you want to help me find a plant?"

I expected him to ask why, but, still clasping my hand, he said, "Yes."

We clambered down from the log and headed after the others.

CHAPTER 9

"You seek another plant for the princess to grow in your house?" Zav asked as we maneuvered our way up a fern-crowded slope toward the sanctuary.

I couldn't sense its boundaries, as the old elven magic had been designed to keep outsiders from finding their home, but I'd been there before and remembered the way. Mostly. A couple of times, Zav steered me in one direction when my feet tried to take me in another.

"No. This is an ingredient Zoltan needs to make a healing formula. Nin's gnomish grandfather showed up, chased by orcs from another world, but he's unconscious and dying from an infection so we can't ask him what happened."

Now that Zav was back, I was tempted to ask him to open a portal to the elven world and help me find the plant there, but as long as we were this close to the sanctuary, I figured we should look here first. Freysha might have already found it.

"I am frequently capable of healing unconscious and dying beings."

I glanced at him, though he was looking toward the sky to the south instead of at me. Why did I have a feeling that dragon was still lurking nearby? If I kissed Zav, would she swoop in to object? We were still holding hands—Zav seemed reluctant to let me go, even when we maneuvered around bushes, trees, ancient stumps, and over logs. A few times, he incinerated stumps so our route would be easier.

"I would appreciate it if you'd be willing to try healing him." I squeezed his hand. "But we might as well look for the plant since we're already here."

If Zav could flick a finger and heal the gnome, that would be fantastic, but I didn't want to come back out here again if it turned out he couldn't.

My phone buzzed. Willard.

The reception was weak, but I answered and hoped for the best.

"Dr. Walker got one of his people to come into the lab and run the test this morning," Willard said, the words broken up but not so much that I couldn't piece them together. "He also found evidence of some weird bacteria cavorting through his bloodstream."

"Thanks for verifying that."

"Walker was irked when he found out we already knew. I think he pulled in favors to get someone in there on a Sunday, because he wanted to show off that he could get results faster than your vampire."

"Is it my bad connection, or do you sound tickled that he was irked?"

"I'm not that immature, Thorvald."

"I've seen your cartoon mug collection; I don't believe you."

"This is why I don't invite subordinates to my apartment."

"Except to help you move in. Please let Walker know that he was useful. I doubt Zoltan would have been able to set up an IV or a catheter." Not if it involved leaving his dark basement anyway.

"No? Vampires should know how to puncture people."

"With teeth, not needles."

"Are you out at that sanctuary now?" Willard asked. "Your reception is horrible."

"Walking to it now, yes. I left Sindari back at the house in case the orcs show up again."

"Let's hope they don't. I received reports of suspicious activity in a neighborhood in Green Lake."

I grimaced. "They popped out of their portal somewhere else?"

"No. The suspicious activity is centered around your house. Your neighbors noticed the glowing portal on your roof yesterday and reported noises from a fight."

"I'll try not to invite any more bad guys to the house for a brawl."

"Good. It would be awkward to send you to investigate yourself. Keep me posted on the gnome."

As I ended the call, Zav guided me around a clump of bushes, incinerating a branch that would have been in my way.

"If you ever retire from working for your family," I told him, "you could make a decent hiking guide."

"*Decent?*" His brows lifted. "Dragons are superior, not decent. In all things."

"*All* things?"

"Yes."

"So, if I asked you to knit an afghan for my couch, it would be a superior afghan?"

"Certainly."

"Do you know what an afghan is?"

Zav squinted suspiciously at me. "Your dictionary says a native or inhabitant of the region of Afghanistan, or a person of Afghan descent."

"There should also be a definition that includes a blanket. Though I'm intrigued that you think you can knit a person."

"I am a dragon. I am gifted."

And so humble. "I guess that's why the ladies love you."

I meant it as a joke, but he frowned and glanced skyward again.

"*Some* ladies, as you call them, only seek me out for political reasons. Lesser species may flock to a dragon simply because of his power and magnetism, but other dragons are not impressed by such things. They mate for personal and clan gain."

"Always? Don't your people have a concept of love?"

"We are not as driven by emotion as the lesser species. Occasionally, two dragons will find harmony together for apolitical reasons of camaraderie and resource gathering."

"Romantic."

"We have songs about this."

"I wonder if that's what that Starsinger dragon was crooning to me."

That earned me another squint. "If he was, I shall tear off his tail in a duel."

A tingle of magic washed over me, distracting me from whatever appropriately snarky response that deserved. We'd reached the barrier hiding the sanctuary, and the world around me wavered as we passed through.

Inside, the types of trees, and the temperature and humidity of the air, weren't as drastically different from their surroundings as they had been in drier Idaho, but a soft mist curled through the undergrowth, and the sun filtering down through the canopy was muted.

The last time I'd been here, it had been wild and overgrown, the paths obscured by foliage. That had been less than two months ago, but the sanctuary was starkly different now. The landscape hadn't changed a lot, but the paths had been cleared, and buildings of three and four stories rose from the earth. They appeared structurally sound, as if professional home builders had created them, but they were made from recycled junk instead of lumber or brick or anything else humans used to build dwellings. A few *No Trespassing* and *Private Property* signs that had been liberated from their original locations were incorporated in the sides. Some of the other components were more difficult to identify, but I spotted mattress coils, a swimming pool diving board, and a china hutch in the walls of the closest building.

"They've redecorated," I observed.

Zav sniffed. "Goblins are *not* superior."

"What? You don't like the style? Don't dragons sleep in caves?"

"Caves are natural and sublime."

"And dank and mildewy and littered with bat guano."

"It is a simple matter to incinerate guano."

I was about to ask if it was a simple matter to incinerate mold and mildew when dozens of goblins flowed out of the buildings toward us. They weren't armed, and I recognized a few faces, but by habit, my hand strayed toward Fezzik before I caught myself.

Freysha was in the back of the group, covered with grease stains that hadn't been there before. What had she been doing? Working on a car? I'd expected her to go straight into the woods to search for the plants.

Work Leader Nogna was in the middle of the crowd and waved forward two goblins carrying silver trays covered with matching cloches. What junkyard had they visited to find those? Or was a distraught butler somewhere even now searching for them?

"The Ruin Bringer is here!" one goblin hollered back into the village with more enthusiasm than had ever accompanied my sobriquet.

Several of the goblins sketched wrenches in the air with their forefingers—a traditional goblin greeting—and others simply gathered and came forward. The group looked like it would swarm around us—

Zav also tensed, probably more because he didn't want grubby green hands touching him than he worried about them being a threat—but the goblins stopped several feet away and fanned out in a semi-circle around us.

"Her mate is also here," one whispered, looking at Zav with wide eyes.

"We knew they would come," Nogna said. "Bring forth the water box."

Whispers went through the crowd, and a few goblins in the back darted off into a structure akin to a pole barn.

"Uhm, what's going on?" I met Freysha's gaze, figuring she would be more likely than the goblins to give me a straight answer.

Gondo was in the group, but he was busy passing around the thermos—how had he gotten ahold of it?—with his buddies.

"They are pleased that you've returned and wish to help," Freysha said over the excited murmurs of the crowd.

"The only help I need is to find the roots of some of those plants."

"I told them about that." The corners of her eyes crinkled with amusement. "They think you need more."

The barn doors were pushed open and squeaking noises came from inside.

Goblins are ridiculously theatrical, Zav told me telepathically.

Do you know what's coming? I knew he could read their minds, but I didn't know if he would bother.

Yes. He lifted his gaze heavenward. This time, it seemed like more of an eye roll than a check for the female dragon.

The squeaking grew more pronounced as a circular wooden tank was wheeled out on a large, flat cart with wobbly wheels. Water sloshed over the sides, but it took me a moment to realize this was a hot tub. One of the *original* hot tubs. A cedar-sided circle, it looked like the bottom half of a whiskey barrel, though it was large enough for a couple of people to sit in. Or several goblins. Or... a half-elf and a dragon?

I smirked at Zav. "It seems they remember the first time they met us."

The crowd spread, opening a path between us and the tub on the cart. In case we wanted to hop in?

"The water is not hot," he informed me.

"We can build a fire underneath," one of the goblins said. "The cart is metal. It will heat up quickly and warm the water."

"We appreciate that you were thinking of us and had this prepared..."

And they truly *would* have had to have it prepared, wouldn't they? It wasn't as if they could have made the tub and filled it in the twenty minutes they had known I was on the way. "But we came because we're looking for a plant."

"Yes, yes. The elf informed us. Rowul." Nogna clapped her hands, her bicycle-chain bracelets rattling. "Show them."

One of the goblins holding a silver tray knelt and lifted it toward me. Was I supposed to remove the cloche?

Freysha smiled and nodded from the back. A little wary, I stepped forward and took off the lid. Stringy roots of a plant lay on the tray, the stems and a few leaves attached, along with one jumble of bell-shaped flowers. They were wilted and past their prime, but this was unmistakably a match for the plant in Zoltan's book.

"Huh." I took it and stuck it in a collection bag I'd brought for the purpose. "Thank you."

The other goblin with a tray knelt beside the first and lifted his in a similar fashion. Another plant?

I lifted the cloche, but this tray held a baked good, not a plant. Vaguely Bundt-cake shaped, it was brown with a darker brown frosting. It appeared very homemade. Did these guys have ovens?

"For you to take with you on your journey," Nogna said. "Gondo informed us that humans love coffee, so we concocted a recipe and invented an original and delicious cake. We call it *coffee cake*." She spread her arms to the sky in triumph.

I decided not to mention that humans had invented coffee cake a long time ago. This looked a little different from the crumble-coated versions I was familiar with.

"You may share it with your mate," she added.

"Thank you. Zav loves sweets." I didn't have to look back to know he was glaring at me. *I'll buy you some ribs later,* I told him silently.

Unfortunately, Velilah'nav will swoop down and object if I let you feed me.

Was that her name? I hadn't expected anything pronounceable, and I was right. Though the implication that she might be spying on us indefinitely bothered me, I ignored that for now and kept my response light. *Then I'll drive through the fast-food place and get you some chicken strips. You can feed yourself.*

This is acceptable.

"Take the cake, please, Ruin Bringer," the goblin holding the tray said. "We are thankful that you found this home for us and kept our people from being destroyed. We will have offerings for you each time you visit us."

"Thank you," I made myself say, though I was a little concerned. Who knew what kinds of offerings goblin ingenuity could come up with?

As I attempted to pick up the crumbling coffee cake with its sticky frosting, I grew even less certain that this was a boon. I hadn't brought a bag capable of containing this. At least it smelled good wafting up to my nostrils. It was an interesting mix of earthy and sweet with the coffee undertones staying subtle, and when I licked my finger, a hint of salt and maple syrup teased my taste buds.

A whir and clacking noises echoed from under the cart. A goblin had laid tinder and kindling and was spinning a contraption for making sparks.

"We don't have time to use the hot tub right now." I held up a hand. "I appreciate the gifts—especially the plant. Maybe next time, I'll bring a swimming suit."

"Swimming suit?" Nogna asked.

"For getting in the hot tub."

"You weren't in a swimming suit last time." Gondo smirked. "You and the dragon were in the water box naked and *klukklik*." In case I'd missed the meaning of the word, he pumped his hips in a self-explanatory rhythm.

Heat flushed my cheeks as the goblins tittered. I had to get out of here.

"Freysha, are you ready to go? It's a long ride back to the house, and Zoltan needs this plant."

A few giggles went through the crowd as more goblins whispered, "*Klukklik, klukklik.*"

Zav's eyes narrowed further, and it looked like he was contemplating incinerating a few of them.

"It is important to get the plant back, but as I was searching for it, I found something that might interest you." Freysha pointed off into the woods behind the village. It must not have been something that could be tossed on a tray under a cloche. "I can lead you to it."

"Now?" I asked dubiously.

"Perhaps Lord Zavryd would consider flying the plant back to Zoltan so that he can start? I can show you what I found. Your mother came here before, did she not? With our father?"

The questions piqued my curiosity, but with all the goblins listening, I kept myself to a terse nod. And looked at Zav. He hadn't mentioned if he had criminals to hunt down—or a female dragon to talk to—but I didn't know if he would be willing to run errands.

Surprisingly, he was staring contemplatively at the hot tub.

Will you take the plant back to the house? I asked. *Nin is there. You can give it to her if Zoltan is hiding in the basement. And can you look at the gnome? If you can cure him without the need for alchemical formulas, that would be excellent.*

Zav accepted the plant bag. *You do not know this gnome, but you would be pleased if I healed him.*

I wasn't sure if it was a question or a statement.

Yes. His name is Ti. He's Nin's grandfather.

You will be so pleased that you will acquire a water box for your house? He gazed at me with his eyes half-slitted. His version of bedroom eyes. *A proper one that is warm and does not require goblins lighting fires under it.*

You want me to get a hot tub? Did you actually like sitting in that one? Even though the jets scrubbed out your lower, uhm, orifice?

I liked kissing you in it.

Oh. My cheeks heated again, for a different reason this time, and I flashed back to Zav pressing me up against that tree and where that might have gone if we hadn't been interrupted. *I liked it too.*

I know. Once I convince Velilah'nav that I will not mate with her, we will mate. Finally.

I should have told him that he couldn't unilaterally decide that for the two of us, but it wasn't as if I didn't feel the same way. *I'm ready.*

I know, he repeated and gave me a smug smile. Was that a nod to how horny I'd been against the tree? *Your training is progressing well. I am pleased.*

If we hadn't had an audience, I would have kissed him for acknowledging that.

"See how they look at each other," a nearby goblin whispered. "They will mate soon."

"In our water box!"

"One of our kind has never mated with a dragon before. The Ruin Bringer is so brave."

I cleared my throat and looked away from Zav. Nope. Kissing was not going to happen right now.

"I will go to your house." Zav stepped back after shooting a dirty glare at the chatty goblins.

"Good. Thank you. Here, take this too." I put the messy cake in his hands, pieces crumbling and falling to the ground.

He curled his lip as the sweet scent wafted up to his nostrils. "How am I supposed to fly with this?"

"I don't know. How were you going to fly with a plant in a bag?"

"By storing it in an extra-dimensional nook."

"Put the cake in the nook too."

"It will make a mess."

I scratched my head. "I don't think magic works quite how I imagined."

"You still have much to learn."

"This I know."

Though grimacing, he walked out of the village and changed into his dragon form as soon as he had room. The cake and the bag disappeared into his nook. Magic flowed from him, and the trees and the canopy parted so he could spring up and fly away.

Freysha nodded to me from behind the crowd of still-tittering goblins. Time to see what she'd found about my mother and father.

CHAPTER 10

"Please have your weapons ready," Freysha said as we walked side by side away from the goblin village and deeper into the sanctuary.

"They're always ready, but why?"

I eyed the wilderness around us, vines as well as moss hanging from the evergreens and deciduous trees, several of the species not native to Washington—and possibly not to Earth. We had left the last of the goblin paths and were picking our way through dense undergrowth. Without Zav there to incinerate bushes and stumps, the going was slower.

"There is a creature back here."

"It's not a Klingon monster dog, is it?"

"A what?"

"Remind me to schedule a *Star Trek* marathon so I can get you caught up on Earth culture. The geeky part of it anyway." I waved toward the woods—so far, I hadn't sensed anything magical, except for the auras of Freysha and the goblins. "This creature isn't like the one that came through the portal on top of the house and attacked us, is it?"

"It is not the same. It is from my home world, from the wild marshes that are full of very dangerous predators. A *trogwarth*. They are not dissimilar to your large felines and not usually long-lived, but this one has either been here for more than forty years, since our people left Earth, or it is the offspring of others that were here with them. I cannot sense others in the area, so it may be the last of its kind."

"Meaning endangered species activists would kick our ass if we killed it."

"It is not endangered on my world. They are smart, deadly predators."

As the wind rustled the branches and leaves rattled on the bushes, the sanctuary felt a lot less inviting. The undergrowth rose above our heads in places, making it difficult to see far and leaving plenty of room for creatures to get close. Now and then, I heard small animals skittering through the leaf litter. I *hoped* they were small animals. The mist had grown thicker, adding to the poor visibility.

"Why would your people have brought them here?" I rested my hand on the butt of my pistol as we walked.

"They are excellent guardians. They cannot be won over by mundane means, but someone with good animal magic can ask such creatures to protect their borders or specific individuals, and they will do so. Earlier, the *trogvarth* saw me in the distance as I was searching for the plant but did not rush to kill me. I hope it can smell my blood and recognize me as an elf and will not consider me an enemy. Your blood may not be elven enough for it to treat you the same way."

"Even elven predators snub mongrels. Wonderful."

She gazed at me. "I am sorry. It wasn't my intent to snub you. I simply want you to be prepared."

"Don't worry about it. What exactly did you find back here that you want me to see?"

"I believe it was our father's home when he was visiting this world. Some magic protects it and a few others, and they are in good repair. I thought there might be some remnants left behind that would…" Freysha spread her palm toward the sky. "Explain more."

"What is it you want explained?" I'd assumed she had all the answers when it came to King Eireth and that I was the only clueless one around.

"More about what he did here and about your mother."

"My mother? Why would she matter to you?" I hadn't yet introduced the two of them—Mom had gone back to Oregon after her search-and-rescue conference, so she hadn't seen the new house or met my new roommate.

"I am curious. My—our—father and *my* mother—" Freysha touched her chest, "—have always seemed more like polite acquaintances than husband and wife. They fulfill all their societal and political obligations together, but they rarely spend time with each other outside of that. It has often made me sad. I like both of them and wish they seemed to like each other more. They've both said their marriage was arranged for the good of their families and our people, and I understand that. It happens frequently among the royalty and our leaders—much as with the dragon clans—but I've often wondered why they didn't fall in love. Neither of them are unpleasant people."

Maybe my father still loved my mother. Was that possible after all this time? If he'd cared that much, why had he left her in the first place? Because of the pending arranged marriage? Was such an arrangement for political purposes truly more important than love?

I tripped over a root as it occurred to me how similar this sounded to Zav's situation. Dragons might not have the concept of love, but he liked me and was *pleased* by me. At least some of the time. It sounded like he wanted to keep me as his mate, but what if in the end, he realized he needed to go back to his people and do what his mother wished? He'd emphasized often that he was loyal to her and the rest of his clan, even if they seemed to be fighting a losing battle. What if it turned out that the only way for their clan to become strong enough to fight off their enemies was for him to mate with this female dragon and gain the allegiance of her family?

A depressing thought.

"I do not know if I will find any answers here, but I am curious and thought you might be too." Freysha shrugged.

I didn't know if I wanted to find something that would explain why Eireth had decided being a king and marrying a queen was more important than my mother, but I kept following Freysha. We'd come out onto a white pebble path that radiated a faint magical signature, probably designed to keep trees and bushes from encroaching on it. Even though it had to be more than forty years old, the pebbles looked like they could have been laid yesterday.

A granite bench rose up to one side, all gentle curving edges as if it had been coaxed out of a slab of stone instead of carved from it. A muddy paw print on the ground behind it reminded me about Freysha's creature. The print was as large as the ones Sindari left on the ground. Maybe larger.

Faint snuffling came from the brush ahead and to the right, and

Freysha paused. I pulled out Fezzik. It sounded like it was twenty or thirty feet back from the path, but a large feline could cover that ground quickly.

We stood still, listening and waiting. Freysha didn't have any weapons, other than whatever she could do with her magic.

It is backing away, she spoke telepathically, the first time I could remember her doing so. *I do not know if it has decided we are permitted to come here or if it's waiting for a more opportune moment to attack.*

Maybe it sensed my weapons and got scared.

It is possible.

The mist thickened more as we followed the path deeper into the sanctuary, and I almost missed the first of the elven dwellings. If not for the faint magic emanating from them, I never would have seen them.

Wooden platforms had been built high off the ground and around the tree trunks in a style similar to what I'd seen on their home world. The dwellings, however, were external structures here, mounted atop those platforms. Maybe on Earth, the trees didn't grow wide enough to live inside of them.

Freysha walked to the base of one of the trees. I could make out the seams of a trapdoor in the platform above, but there wasn't a ladder or any obvious way to go up. She rested her hand on the trunk, and I sensed a tingle of magic as she did something.

The rough bark re-formed in spots, bulging outward to create bumps. Or handholds? It wasn't exactly a ladder, but I could climb up them easily enough.

"Val?" Gondo's voice drifted down the path from the direction we'd come. "Are you back here? Where'd you go?"

Freysha paused with her hand still on the tree. "I didn't think to tell him what we were doing. I thought he was too busy socializing with his kin to notice us leave."

"We're checking out old elf houses," I called. "You better go back. There's a—"

Foliage rattled and thrashed off to the side of the path. The creature.

At first, I thought it would attack me while I was distracted, but in the dense undergrowth, the noise of its passage marked its path. It was rushing toward Gondo.

Cursing, I yanked out Chopper and sprinted back down the path. If

I could *see* the creature, I would have opted for Fezzik, but all I would be doing was shooting blindly into the bushes.

"Run back!" I yelled, afraid I wouldn't reach Gondo in time.

Even having to bound through the dense growth, the creature was fast. I spotted Gondo on the path ahead, his hands raised as he stared in horror toward the thrashing bushes. He gripped a wrench in one hand—as if that would do anything against some giant feline predator.

I was less than ten feet from Gondo when I first saw it, a huge gray lion-like creature with shaggy fur. It bounded over the bushes, long fangs revealed by its open maw. Its yellow eyes were focused on Gondo instead of me.

I reached Gondo in time to dive into him, bowling him to the pebble path as the pouncing creature flew through the air where his head had been. Claws raked as it went by, and I felt the wind of a near miss on the back of my neck.

Before it landed in the brush on the far side of the path, I leaped up, standing over Gondo and brandishing my sword. The creature whirled and snarled at me. I bared my teeth back at it.

Freysha ran down the path toward us, but I didn't take my focus from the shaggy feline. Its gaze shifted from my face to my bared sword—the mist didn't quite mute Chopper's blue glow—and back to my face. Its large nostrils twitched—they were on the sides of its snout, more like a horse than a lion.

The creature started toward us, but rustling sounded under its feet. It tried to jerk its foreleg up. But it couldn't. Something had grabbed its foot.

I stared in puzzlement, imagining bear traps. Would an elven sanctuary have such things?

The creature's shoulders flexed as it tried to back up. Then it snarled and lowered its head to bite at its feet—or whatever had its feet trapped.

"I made vines," Freysha explained, stopping beside me.

Gondo was on his back where I'd knocked him, but he scrambled to his feet and glowered at the creature, waving his wrench menacingly.

Freysha spoke sternly in elven to our trapped foe. I reached up to activate my translation charm. The creature lifted its head and glared at her. Defiantly? It was hard to tell.

"Attack no goblins," she said, my charm translating this time. "We are the descendants of the elves you served. We will do no harm to this place." She waved her hand.

The vines disappeared back into the ground, leaving the creature free. I crouched, not trusting that it understood her or agreed with her even if it did.

It snuffled again, looking back and forth between us. It ignored Gondo completely, which emboldened him to wave his wrench again and curse at it in his native tongue.

"Don't goad it," I muttered. "You don't want it to go after your people when we're gone."

"They have set traps around their village and can defend themselves. Though it would have been nice if they'd told me *why* they'd set the traps—and to be careful leaving the area." Gondo shook his head. "They were distracted by the show they thought they were going to get."

"What show?" I asked as the creature backed slowly away.

"You having sex with the dragon in the water box."

If an enemy hadn't been less than ten feet from us, I might have dropped my sword. "*That* was what they thought would happen?"

"Yes."

"Why would they want to watch that?"

"Who wouldn't?" Gondo flashed a grin, said, "*Klukklik*," and copied the hip-thrusting motion he'd made earlier.

"You guys need to get cable out here."

The creature kept slinking away, finally disappearing into the brush. Its departure was a lot quieter than its approach had been.

"I think it may recognize you as well as me," Freysha said, "as descendants of the elves who lived here. And it's decided it's all right for us to visit."

"And Gondo?" I eyed him.

"He had better stick close to us. In addition to being set by our people to guard this area, *trogwarths* in the wild like to eat goblins."

"That's disgusting," Gondo said.

"Let's hurry up and find out what it's been guarding." I waved for Freysha to lead the way back to the tree and for Gondo to follow. "I need to get back and make sure my gnomish houseguest is going to live."

CHAPTER 11

Freysha climbed up the tree to the trapdoor in the platform first, and as I started after her, Gondo announced, "I shall stand guard from down here."

He was eyeing the small handholds Freysha had magically coaxed out of the trunk. For goblin arms, they were far apart.

"The creature might come back for you," I pointed out.

"I shall stand guard from two feet behind you," he corrected.

"Wise."

Despite his eyeing of the handholds, Gondo scrambled up behind us easily enough. As Freysha headed for the first of two dwellings built on the platform, which extended around four trees, I sensed an aura I'd been hoping wouldn't return.

Freysha must have sensed it too, because she looked back at me with a frown. "There is a female dragon nearby. I am not familiar with her."

"I wish I weren't."

Freysha arched her eyebrows. "I sensed her earlier, but she flew in the other direction, so I focused on finding the plant."

"She flew toward Zav and me," I said dryly. "She wants to date him."

"Date him?"

Gondo had reached the platform, and he stuck his head through the trapdoor, looking below for the creature rather than a dragon, and kicked it shut. Then he set his wrench down on it. But only for a moment. He must have considered that too lightweight an object, for he pulled over a broken branch and centered it on the trapdoor. "Can those creatures jump this high?"

"I don't believe so," Freysha said, "but they can climb."

Gondo groaned and went to retrieve more broken limbs that had fallen onto the platform over the years.

"Maybe dragons don't date," I continued my conversation with Freysha. "I gather they get to claiming each other as mates quickly."

I watched the sky, though we weren't high enough that much of it was visible through the branches, and briefed Freysha on the female-dragon situation. What advice she could give me, I didn't know, but elves knew a lot more about dragons than I did.

"Do you think she plans to kill you?" Gondo asked, dragging over another branch. He was building something to barricade the trapdoor. It looked like the wilderness version of The Club.

"She didn't mention it," I said.

"She's circling the area," Freysha said.

My very own dragon stalker. "I sent Zav back to help Nin's grandfather. I was hoping she would leave Earth—or at least stalk him instead of me."

"She may struggle to figure out exactly where you are, but I am not certain of that. Dragons can more easily see through the magic of the elven sanctuaries than other species, and this barrier has not been renewed for a long time."

"Let's look inside for whatever and get out of here." I still didn't know what Freysha thought was back here that would interest us after all this time.

"Of course. You look in that dwelling, and I'll check this one." Freysha glanced toward Gondo, but he was busy with his project.

I had a feeling we wouldn't be able to leave that way when he was done.

When I walked into the two-room structure, a twinge of déjà vu or some other weird feeling I couldn't pin down came over me. I hadn't been there before and hadn't ever been inside an elven house, but something felt familiar among the alienness of the elf-designed furnishings.

After all these years, dust cloaked the chairs and table, but they were similar to the granite bench we'd passed, all made from single logs and appearing worn by wind or water—or magic—instead of carved by tools. A bookcase on the far wall had a similar construction. The lack of books on the shelves disappointed me, though I wouldn't have been able to read them even if they'd been there. My mother had studied the language enough to read it; she would have loved a new elven book. Maybe I could find something here that I could give her.

Though the bookcase had been cleaned out, the place wasn't entirely devoid of decor. Something that looked like a crystal ball registered faintly to my senses as magical. Dimitri's psychic neighbor would probably love it.

I drifted to what might be considered a desk, though it was round, and where I would expect drawers, there were cubbies covered by what looked like living lily pads. Thinking they were like cabinet drawers, I tried to grab the edge and open one. It twitched at my touch and furled to the far side.

A few ordinary-looking if aged envelopes lay inside atop what might have been a journal. It had a green plant-like cover with a silver ribbon holding it shut. Even though I knew I wouldn't be able to read anything, I pulled out the contents of the cubby.

I started to open the journal, but the writing addressing one of the envelopes to Eireth caught my eye. My stomach did a weird flip-flop. That writing not only used English letters but was familiar.

All of the envelopes were addressed to him and all written by the same person. Even though they had all been opened long ago, my fingers had an uncharacteristic tremble as I pulled out one of the letters inside. It was normal Earth stationery, but the color—a pale blue—had faded with time. The writing was in pen and still legible. Even before I glanced at the signature at the bottom, I knew my mom had written it.

What did it mean that these letters had been left behind when all the books had been taken? Had my father known he couldn't take them home where his elven kin might see them? Or had he known it was over between him and my mother, so he had simply shoved them in a desk and left them behind?

It had little to do with me, but the idea made me hurt on my mom's behalf. He'd been the love of her life. To waste that on someone who hadn't returned her feelings or had dismissed her as some inconsequential fling…

I stared at the page without reading it, not sure I wanted to read it.

This had been a private letter from my mother to Eireth.

Warily, I skimmed the first paragraph. It wasn't gooey, and there weren't any love poems or sonnets or whatever it was infatuated people had written to each other back in the seventies. It said she wasn't sure his people would find her letter and give it to him, but she'd enjoyed meeting him in the woods and fishing in the creek and playing the elven gambling game he'd taught her.

"Huh." I imagined Mom and Eireth playing Tic-tac-toe in the dirt beside some waterway.

As I skimmed more letters, they became more friendly, and she referenced things that he'd said or that he'd written in letters to her, so it grew clear they hadn't been one-way communications. Not that I'd expected that. I'd come from somewhere, so things had escalated at some point. But of course, there weren't any letters here from Eireth. If they still existed, they were in a desk drawer in Mom's cabin somewhere. Even if they hadn't been a state away, I doubted she would have shown them to me. She was an even more private person than I was, and she would give me the frostiest glare imaginable if she knew I was reading her old love letters.

Feeling guilty, I put them back in the cubby, but my guilt didn't keep me from checking the journal. It was in a different hand, the penmanship elegant and fluid—and in the elven language. My translation charm allowed me to understand the spoken language, but as I'd learned on previous occasions, it didn't help when it came to reading.

I sensed Freysha heading toward me. My first instinct was to shove the journal back into the cubby and shut the leaf-door before she caught me snooping. But we'd *come* here to snoop. It had been her idea. And she knew how to read this language.

The idea of asking her to read my father's diary, if that was what this was, weirded me out though. He was her father too, but if he'd been writing about my mother instead of hers, Freysha wouldn't want to read that. But it was possible he'd been writing about fishing and trapping here on Earth or taking weather readings for scientific studies. Maybe this had nothing to do with Mom or she was only mentioned sporadically.

I was still looking indecisively down at the journal when Freysha walked in.

"You found something?" she asked.

"Some letters in English. A journal that's not." I lifted it with feigned indifference. "Want to see if he wrote it?"

"Our father?"

After so many years without a father, it was odd to think of myself as having one at all, much less sharing him with someone else, but I managed to say, "Yeah."

As Freysha came forward and took it from me, thumps and clangs came from outside.

"Is that trouble?" I asked as she opened it to read. "Or is Gondo further battening down the hatches?"

"The latter. So far. I shouldn't have told him that *trogwarths* can climb."

"I shouldn't have told him where we were going. Wait, I didn't."

Freysha flipped the page. Since she was engrossed in reading, I didn't speak again. I resisted the urge to pace, though I did walk over to check on Gondo. That trapdoor was doubly secure now.

"This is getting… intimate," Freysha said after a time. Her cheeks had grown pink.

"You don't have to read it. I just wondered what it said."

"Some of it talks about the reason his group came here—they were studying the plants here and on other wild worlds to see if any had medicinal or magical promise that could be useful for our people—but then it goes into detail on a local woman he met. Sigrid."

"My mother."

"Yes."

Freysha sounded like she'd already known. Eireth must have told her something about my origins when he'd sent her to spy on me.

She bit her lip, read a few more pages, and then closed it.

"You don't have to read it," I repeated. "I'm sure it's weird when it's not about your mother. I mean, that would probably be weird to read about too. If elves are like humans—or at least Americans—they get uncomfortable thinking about their parents having sex."

"It's not that. Well, it is a little that. But it's strange because he cared about her so much, and as I was telling you, I've never seen evidence that my parents feel that way about each other."

"But have you read any journals or letters they wrote to each other before you were born? Maybe they fell in love back then. You're older now, and they're older, so maybe they're just not as passionate about things as they used to be."

"I *have* read some of their correspondence from before I was born." Freysha twitched a shoulder. "I'm a curious person."

"Obviously. You led me here." I smiled, hoping she would too.

But she looked forlornly down at the journal. Now I wished I'd put it away and said I'd found nothing.

"It makes me sad that they married only for political reasons and didn't care for each other," Freysha admitted softly. "And that my parents don't truly love each other. You probably don't feel fortunate, since he left, but…"

"No, I don't. I always thought he was a jerk for doing that, even though I never knew him."

"His parents and our people pressured him. He must have felt honor-bound to do the right thing. He may have also realized that since humans are not long-lived, it would have been difficult for them to have a relationship. For him to watch her grow old when he barely aged, for him to lose her."

"If that's a reason not to have a relationship with someone, then I guess I shouldn't be hanging out with Zav."

Freysha lifted her eyes. "That is not what I meant to imply."

"I know, but it's been on my mind." I walked toward the empty bookcase, though there was nothing to look at.

"Maybe they made a mistake. Maybe *he* made a mistake." Freysha put the journal away. "I think that if you're lucky enough to fall in love with someone, you should take a chance and pursue it and not worry about the rest of the Cosmic Realms. Though I wouldn't exist if Father hadn't gone back to do what he believed was his duty, so perhaps I shouldn't vote for that." Freysha smiled, but it was a sad, miserable smile.

"It's good to exist."

"Yes. But there is a part of me that wonders what it would be like to have come from people who genuinely loved each other, rather than out of some political arrangement."

"You can't change how other people feel about each other, and you'd be a different person if you'd come from different parents. Do you want to change who you are? You seem pretty rocking."

"Rocking?"

"Smart and badass."

She mouthed, "Badass?" but she must have gotten the gist, because she smiled. "Thank you. You are also rocking."

I snorted, but she seemed genuine. Maybe I needed to learn how to accept a compliment. Since I'd started meeting dragons and full-blooded elves, I'd begun thinking of myself as the mongrel most of them called me at one point or another. A half-breed. They had all made it out to be a bad deal, as if I was a deformed mutant that had crawled out from underneath a rock.

Before I'd met them, I'd appreciated my elven blood. In my line of work, having extra agility and better healing had helped me survive many deadly missions. It was sad that the perceptions of others could change one's perceptions of oneself.

Freysha gazed around the room. "I was curious, and now I have satisfied some of that curiosity. I want to peek into one of the other dwellings, and then we can go."

After she left the room, I grabbed the journal and stuck it in my waistband. Mom might be interested in reading it, and I doubted anyone from Elf Land was coming back for it.

I walked out, ready to head home, only to find an unfamiliar elf standing on the deck. An unfamiliar elf with blazing red hair and the powerful aura of a dragon.

Damn it. How had she gotten down here without me sensing her?

CHAPTER 12

I n her elven form, Velilah had silver eyes, a beautiful face, and pointed ears, but she oozed dragon arrogance as she looked me slowly up and down with a sneer on her pouty lips.

I did not fully examine you before. She spoke telepathically even though she had a human—or elven—tongue now.

"I imagine it's hard to examine things when you're being squished by another dragon."

Her eyes flared with silver light, and I reminded myself that irritating a dragon was not a good idea. She wouldn't be like Zav and tolerate my lip.

You are not as eager to please as the females of most lesser species who seek to seduce dragons. The way her head tilted was more reptilian than elven or human. Maybe she didn't spend a lot of time shape-shifting into *lesser species. Or are you different with him?*

"With Zav? No, I'm flippant to him too. He says I'm not properly respectful of dragons, but he likes it when I vex his enemies."

Her eyes closed to slits. *He told you to vex me?*

"No, I think we were both hoping you and I would never meet."

I wished to see what mongrel trash he was letting hold his tail. Judging by that disdainful expression, Velilah couldn't see my sex appeal.

"Here I am." I spread my arms. "I look better when I haven't been rolling around in the mud fighting elven guard creatures. You should see me in the green dress with the leg slit."

If you wish to survive to see the next moon, you will tell Lord Zavryd'nokquetal to go back to his own kind, that you have no wish to be his mate. And I suggest you use his proper name when you address him.

"I can't pronounce it. Mongrels are inferior."

Obviously.

"If you want him, you'll have to win him yourself. I'm not telling him anything."

"Val?" came Freysha's soft whisper from the side. She'd come out of another dwelling and stood in the doorway. "What are you doing?"

"Vexing a dragon."

"That's unwise."

"I know."

Power flowed from Velilah and gripped me. I drew Chopper and willed the blade and my own power to keep her from holding me immobile—or squishing me like a grape—again.

You will tell him you no longer wish to be his mate, Velilah spoke into my mind, magical compulsion urging me to obey, to drop to my knees in front of her and do whatever her lofty greatness asked.

My legs threatened to buckle as my muscles turned as limp as cooked pasta.

Though her power was as great as, or maybe *greater* than, that of any of the male dragons I'd faced, I hurried to bring Freysha's exercises to bear. I formed the fern fronds in my thoughts, willing them to wrap around my mind and block her while protecting me from the compulsion. Would such puny mongrel magic work against her? I had to believe it would. It had worked to push away Xilneth's compulsion.

If you get involved with dragons, you will die, she told me. *Send him away, and dragons will not have a reason to come to this world any longer.*

After the egg theft, I doubted that was true, but it was hard not to believe her, to think that never seeing Zav again would be a good thing…

Growling deep in my throat, I redoubled my efforts to form the protective magic in my mind. I wished I'd grabbed a handful of dirt before coming up here. Either it would have helped me focus, or I could have thrown it in her eyes.

Tell him to leave you, she tried again, *that you no longer want to be his mate. It would be better for him and for you if he left. You know this to be true.*

Damn her for playing to my own doubts.

Another's power joined mine, reinforcing my barriers, and the power of the compulsion lessened. Freysha was lending her magic to mine.

If you don't tell him to dissolve your bond, Velilah said, *you will die. Painfully.*

More than a compulsion wrapped around me now. The same power that held me in place started squeezing. A magical vise wrapped around my heart, and painful pressure built in my chest.

"You would kill someone of another species?" Freysha asked angrily. "That is not the way of the Dragon Justice Court."

Stay out of this, elfling. This is not your affair.

As they spoke, I managed to use the mental tricks Freysha had taught me to lessen the pain in my chest. Maybe it was just that Velilah was distracted, but I also managed to inch my foot forward. Toward the dragon. I still gripped Chopper, my hand tight around the blade. Taking a swing at her would get me in trouble, I had no doubt, but I wanted her to know I could protect myself and to leave me the hell alone.

More of Freysha's power flowed into me, and I strode forward at full speed.

"Leave me alone, and leave Earth," I said. "If you want Zav, you'll have to convince him yourself. I'm not telling him to take a hike."

Before I was close enough to truly threaten her with my sword, Velilah flung up a hand and a tsunami of power struck me. As I flew backward and smashed against the wall of the nearest dwelling, I saw Freysha fly backward too. Since she was in the doorway, she tumbled inside, all the way to the far wall and struck it. A gasp of pain escaped her lips.

I scrambled to my feet, Chopper still in hand.

Velilah sprang off the deck and shifted in the air to her dragon form. She flapped her great wings and opened her maw, showing sword-like fangs that could chomp me in half.

But they didn't come in to bite me. Smoke roiled out of her throat and nostrils.

"Dragon attack!" I shouted for Gondo's sake, wherever he was. "Get out of here!"

I didn't heed my own advice. I ran into the dwelling Freysha was in, afraid she was too injured to escape on her own.

Velilah spewed fire, the flames bursting through the doorway after me. My fire-resisting charm activated and kept me from being charred to ash instantly, but the extreme heat still struck with an inferno's intensity. The wooden walls of the dwelling burst into flame, and the light turned reddish orange all around me.

Where had Freysha gone? If she didn't have a similar charm, she wouldn't survive this.

Velilah paused to draw in a breath of air before spewing a second gout of flame at the dwelling. I spotted a weird green lump of giant leaves hunkered in the far corner.

Outside, the platform burst into flame. Snaps and cracks hammered my ears as the air threatened to broil me alive. Worse, smoke filled the dwelling, tendrils curling down my throat and assailing my sensitive lungs. I broke into coughs as I ran to the leaf pile. Hot air scorched my windpipe and nostrils, and tears ran down my face.

"Freysha!" I grabbed the foliage—it was surprisingly damp, as soaked as seaweed freshly plucked from the ocean. "We have to get out of here."

The lump of leaves parted, and Freysha reached up toward me. I tried to pull her out, intending to leap down from the platform and sprint somewhere safe—wherever that would be—but she grabbed *me*.

She pulled me down beside her inside the cocoon of wet leaves. That cocoon expanded, making room for two, and then sealed over us.

In the dark, tight space, claustrophobic fear gripped me. I barely resisted the urge to cut open the leaves and run out. It was wet inside and surprisingly cool. I could imagine us being steamed like wontons, but that wasn't happening. At least so far.

I gripped Freysha's arm in case my fire charm could spread its influence to her and hoped Gondo was all right wherever he was. Inside the cocoon, the snaps and cracks were muted, but I still heard them. The tree was burning all around us.

"This is against the rules put forth by the Dragon Justice Court," Freysha said, surprisingly tart and irritated. "As soon as I get home, I intend to report her through the proper ambassadorial channels."

"I was thinking of—" coughs broke through my words, and tears ran down my hot cheeks, "—sticking my sword in her."

"Unfortunately, that would also be against the rules. But she deserves it." Freysha paused. "She's flying away." She lowered her voice, sadness creeping into her tone. "The trees are burning. It's difficult to put out dragon fire. This whole village might be destroyed."

"We—" The platform shuddered underneath us, then collapsed, and I didn't get to finish the thought.

We plunged twenty feet through heat and smoke and flames to the ground below. I managed to twist in the air, land on my feet, and turn it into a roll. Freysha did something similar, and we rolled into each other. Painfully. At least I didn't hear any bones crunch.

The flames were mostly up in the trees, but fallen branches burned and sputtered on the ground. We sprinted for the pebble path as I continued to cough, my lungs trying to turn themselves inside out and escape my tortured body. I flashed back to the miasma of hot gaseous air in Mt. Rainier's volcanic ice caves, but as we ran into clear air, the imagery faded.

Freysha slowed and turned around. I ran farther before realizing she was doing more than glancing back. I stopped to wait, though all I wanted was to get in the Jeep and drive back to my hopefully enemy-free home. I couldn't sense Velilah and hoped she'd flown off, but I wasn't sure. I hadn't sensed her approach up on the platform either.

"I'll just be a moment," Freysha called.

She lifted her hands with fingers splayed as she faced the fire. It burned heartily in dozens of trees. I hoped the goblin village was far enough away that it wouldn't be in danger, but I couldn't be certain. This late in the summer, the foliage was dry by Pacific Northwest standards.

I couldn't see what Freysha was doing, but magic flowed from her fingers. A long moment passed before I noticed anything, but gradually the flames burned less fiercely. Water dripped from the needles and leaves on the branches, and the scent of damp foliage mingled with that of burning wood.

Gondo crept out of the bushes to the side of the path, bits of ash and charred twigs in his shock of white hair. "A dragon tried to incinerate me."

"If it helps, she was trying to incinerate me, and you just happened to be nearby."

"That doesn't help. Goblins aren't fire-proof. I've been attacked by a crazy elven creature today and now a dragon. I do not believe my association with you is good for my health."

"Probably not. You should stick with Willard. She mostly stays in the office, and it's almost never visited by dragons."

"A good idea. I will still come to your shop for coffee."

"Dimitri would be crushed if you didn't."

"I know. Goblins are his best customers. We don't destroy anything. And we improved the toilet-paper dispenser in the bathroom."

"Was the carriage return of a typewriter involved?"

"No. Parts from an old Fourdrinier machine from a decommissioned paper mill. It's fabulous. The toilet-paper dispensing is fast and easy now."

I decided not to ask for more details. Or visit the bathroom at the coffee shop any time soon.

The branches continued to weep water, and the flames dwindled further. I kept an eye on the sky and my senses stretched out, but I didn't sense Velilah and eventually put away Chopper.

When Freysha lowered her hands, her shoulders slumped with exhaustion. Whatever she'd been doing, it hadn't been easy, but the last of the fire went out. The smoke hung in the air, and I was relieved when she joined me and we were able to continue away from the area. My eyes stopped watering, but I kept coughing, and my throat felt like someone had rubbed sandpaper up and down it a few hundred times.

"Thanks for the help." I patted her on the shoulder as we walked. "As Gondo has learned, being my acquaintance is dangerous. Being my sibling is probably even worse."

"You should do your best to avoid that dragon," Freysha said.

"Trust me. *I* didn't seek her out."

"I know. It is always problematic when we get involved in dragon politics. Our father has felt the pressure of their influence a number of times."

"Did one of them try to light him on fire too?"

"No, but they've used magic to try to manipulate him before. We need to figure out which one of those charms can protect you from that."

"I'm very amenable to that."

"I'll continue to research it." Freysha looked over at me. "Do you think—I haven't heard the whole story of how Lord Zavryd claimed you and if it was something you wished. Do you care for him? It might be better for your health if you did as the female dragon asked and let him go—or encouraged him to go."

Great. Another voice of reason.

"I care for him." I didn't respond to the rest. The idea of caving to some bitchy dragon's demands made me long to punch things, but I wanted to have a heart-to-heart talk with Zav to figure out how he felt before saying more.

"Oh," was all Freysha said.

"If you want to start sleeping at someone else's house, I'll understand."

"No. If you care for Lord Zavryd, and he cares for you, then you cannot give in to this dragon. Also, you are my sister. I will stay with you and assist you if more trouble comes."

This touched me—especially since she was only here on Earth because Eireth had asked or maybe ordered her to come. But it also worried me. What would I say to our father if she were killed because of me?

CHAPTER 13

As Gondo and Freysha and I were driving back into Seattle, my phone buzzed. Amber's number popped up.

I didn't want to miss her call—the last call I'd missed had been Dimitri wanting to tell me where his kidnappers had taken him—so I took an early freeway exit to pull over and talk.

"What's up, Amber?"

"They broke up!" she said with an excited squeal.

"Your dad and Shauna?" I assumed she wouldn't call me with news of some dating drama among her high school friends.

"Yeah. Nobody's getting a BMW from Dad now except for me."

"You're getting a BMW?"

"No, but if someone *was* going to get one, it would be me." Amber paused. "He got me a sic bag for school. Pink leopard print. With a phone charger."

"That's good." At least I was fairly certain *sic* was good.

"Anyway, I just called to let you know we can do the sword-fighting at our house now. I figured you didn't want her to bitch at you and that's why you suggested the park, but the teenage guys in the pool there ogle your ass. It's so gross."

"My daughter," I mouthed to Freysha, who was pretending not to pay attention but who no doubt heard everything with those elven ears. Her eyebrows had twitched at the last. Maybe she didn't talk to her mother that way. "I'm pretty sure you're the one they were ogling, kid. But if you want to practice in your yard now, that's fine."

"Good. No offense, Val, but I'm not going back to your house."

"You didn't like Dimitri's burgers?"

"I didn't like the orc bodies and dead alien dogs in the yard."

"Understandable." An uneasy thought jumped into my mind. "You haven't seen any dragons lately, have you?"

"No. Why? Are some coming?"

"I hope not."

Zondia had gotten all my records and researched me thoroughly to find out Amber existed. I hoped Velilah didn't care enough to bother with that. If she *did*, and if she tried to hurt Amber or make me choose between her and Zav...

"Are you all right?" Freysha whispered.

"I feel a headache coming on."

"Maybe you need espresso." In the back seat, Gondo sloshed the thermos around, but it sounded like very little liquid remained in the bottom.

"Who are you talking to?" Amber asked.

"An elf and a goblin." I thought about explaining that I had a half-sister and Amber had a half-aunt, but that seemed like a conversation for another time, such as when I wasn't pulled over on the side of the road with traffic whizzing past.

"Don't you know any normal people?"

"No."

"Maybe that explains you. Bye."

"That's your daughter, you said?" Freysha asked.

"She's a teenager."

That seemed a legitimate explanation, but Freysha's expression remained puzzled.

I drove us back onto the road and took the side streets to the house. As we drew nearer, I sensed Zav. He was the *only* dragon I sensed, but I glanced at Freysha for confirmation.

"The other one isn't lurking around somewhere, is she?"

"No."

"I hope she left Earth." The idea of Velilah flying around looking for friends or family of mine to torture had me clenching the wheel tightly and grinding my teeth by the time I parked in front of the house.

Nin's blue Volkswagen beetle was still here. This had to be the most time she'd spent away from her business all year. I hoped Zoltan or

Willard's doctor acquaintance would be able to bring her grandfather around. Or if Zav could wave a hand and cure him, that would also be wonderful.

"You guys head inside. I'll be there in a bit." I climbed out and waved them toward the front door.

My senses told me that everyone, including Ti, was down in the basement, so I headed around the house to go in that way.

"Does this mean we don't need to go back to work today?" Gondo asked Freysha.

"I am going to return to researching the charms so that Val will be better protected from dragons," Freysha said as they climbed the steps to the porch. "You can assist me."

"I don't know anything about charms."

"Some of them are goblin charms."

"I still don't know anything. I'm a builder, not a shaman."

The last thing I heard as they went inside was something about LEGOs.

Has everything been all right here while we've been gone, Sindari? I sensed him in the living room, standing guard from a reclining position on the couch. There would be silver fur to vacuum out of the cushions later.

It has been disappointingly peaceful, save for neighbors walking their domestic canines past. They sensed me from the sidewalk and insisted on barking.

I hope you ignored them like the mature regal tiger you are.

I roared at them. One wet himself.

So much for mature and regal. *We'll have you to blame if the grass in the front yard dies.*

He used the sidewalk, not the grass.

Gross.

I thought so.

I made a note to get a pressure washer for that sidewalk. Renting a house was turning out to be a lot more work than renting an apartment, and it hadn't even been broken into by my enemies yet.

Can you send yourself home for a while? I didn't think I could order him to do anything until I got the charm back from Nin. *I want to be able to call upon you if trouble more ferocious than barking dogs shows up.* I hoped it didn't. It had been a long day, and I was tired. I needed to figure out how to sleep better at night.

I will be ready, Sindari said before disappearing from my senses.

At the basement door, I made myself knock before entering.

Come in, Zav spoke into my mind. *The vampire has ensconced himself.*

I entered and closed the door quickly to minimize the pesky infestation of daylight. Inside, Zoltan's infrared lights were on, and I found Zav with Nin standing over Ti, who'd been laid out on a blanket on the floor. He was still unconscious.

"That's superior to the guest bedroom?" I asked.

"Zoltan is preparing the formula to administer." Nin gave Sindari's charm back to me, as if she'd been keeping it safe in her hand the whole time I'd been gone. Maybe she had.

"That was fast."

"He had everything ready except for the remaining ingredient."

Zoltan stepped into the room. "It's bad enough being awake in the middle of the day, but the constant threat of a light invasion is tedious. When I agreed to swap homes with Jimmy, I did not properly consider how inferior a basement is to a fully underground domicile."

"Maybe Dimitri can build something like an airlock at the door." I stood next to Zav and leaned against his shoulder.

He put his arm around me and turned his face down to my hair. Maybe he intended to smell my shampoo—or my naturally fantastic female pheromones—but he leaned back and frowned.

You smell like smoke. Were you in a fire?

Yeah. I hesitated to bring up Velilah, because he might overreact and leave in a huff to confront her. But it would be better that he deal with her, if he could, than for her to pop up and harass me every time Zav wasn't around. *Your would-be mate tried to burn down the tree Freysha and I were in.*

Zav tensed like a coiled spring and radiated anger. I could feel it in the energy of his aura, the energy that I usually found appealing but that now buzzed my senses like lightning about to strike.

We're fine. I glanced at him, catching an equally stormy expression on his face. *We got away without being hurt. Freysha plans to file a complaint with your legal system though. I hope Velilah gets a hefty fine.* I smiled to try to alleviate his anger, though my attempts at diffusing anger with humor hadn't been working well lately.

I told her to stay away from you. And to go back to her home world because I wasn't interested.

Yeah, but she got excited when you pinned her. I could tell. I wished that was also a joke.

Zav's frown only deepened.

"Airlock, ah." Zoltan was poking at his smart phone—looking up submarines. "Interesting. Dimitri could make me a *light* lock. That would be the appropriate term. I like that. All vampires should have light locks."

"Maybe Dimitri can perfect self-contained light-lock units and sell them out of the back of the shop. To the vampire clientele that we don't yet have." I waved toward my collection bag open on his counter. "Is that plant what you needed, Zoltan?"

"Indeed, yes." He put his phone away and returned to a burbling concoction on a burner. "I am preparing the formula now. Lord Zavryd—why is he brooding so ferociously, and am I in danger?—has helped stabilize the gnome, but we need the formula to kill the bacteria infecting his system."

"Zav is having family problems. He'll be okay." It felt a bit like hugging a starving lion, but I wrapped an arm around Zav's waist and patted him on the chest.

Do you want to talk about this? I asked silently. *Or anything else?*

I wish to find that female and bite her head off.

There's probably an even bigger fine for that.

He eyed me, then sighed and attempted to loosen his rigid stance. He was only partially successful. With my arm around him, it was hard to miss the tension in his body.

Let us go talk in private, yes.

"We're going upstairs," I told Zoltan and Nin. "Let me know if you need anything."

"For people to stop opening that door." Zoltan threw up his arms and stalked into the other corner of the basement.

"I'll text Dimitri about the light lock," I said as we headed out.

"Do so," Zoltan called from his dark nook.

I might have opted for talking in the back yard, but Gondo had found the LEGOs in the conservatory, so that wouldn't be private. We passed through the kitchen, where Freysha had returned to researching the charms, and headed for the stairs. My lungs had recovered from the smoke inhalation, but my airway still felt raw, and I grimaced at the omnipresent mold scent on the second floor.

"Can dragons incinerate mold?" I asked, pausing in front of the bathroom that I suspected was the main source of the problem.

"What?" Zav had been gripping his chin, lost in thought, and almost bumped into me.

"I think there are leaky pipes and mold under the floor or in the walls of this house, and I'd like to get rid of it."

He stared at me as if he couldn't figure out why I would be bringing this up when we had larger issues to worry about. A good question. Mary *had* wanted me to tell Zav about my health problems, but if I did, would he deem me an inferior mate? Not the brave warrior woman he thought he'd claimed?

"Never mind." I waved for him to follow me to the bedroom in the turret.

"Mold grows on things that can be incinerated," Zav said. "It would be difficult to destroy the fungi without its substrate."

"Meaning you could get rid of it, but only by incinerating the house?"

"Select walls perhaps." His eyes grew distant, as if he was using his magic or maybe his senses. "And floors. And part of the ceiling."

"Ugh."

"You do not like its scent? It reminds me of forest caves."

"Humans are sensitive to the spores. Some humans. Me." I shrugged, reluctant to go into detail about my increased nightmares and need for the inhalers. "Don't worry about it. Let's figure out the mate thing."

"I figured out my mate many moons ago." Zav still looked tense and broody, but he managed a smile for me.

"Many moons ago? When we first met, you wanted to kill me."

"Yes, but I changed my mind after we battled together." His smile grew a little more relaxed. "And after I saw you in the water box. When will you have one placed in the yard here?"

I imagined us making out in a hot tub while Gondo and Freysha puttered in the conservatory and discussed LEGO engineering. "After the mold problem is fixed."

And after I priced hot tubs. I doubted they were cheap. And what happened if we moved after our lease was up? They couldn't be easy to transport.

"Oh?" Zav appeared intrigued—and more interested in solving my mold problem. "Have the vampire's assistant bring replacement materials for that which must be destroyed, and I will use my magic to incinerate the problem areas."

The vampire's assistant? Was that Dimitri?

"Deal," I said without quibbling over Zav's inability to learn the names of my friends. We could work on that later. After the house was a healthy place for my lungs.

"Deal." Zav took my hands. "Val, I regret that the queen—that my *mother*—is causing this problem. I had thought when my sister reported back about how helpful you'd been in retrieving the stolen Starsinger egg, and averting an inter-clan battle, that the queen would realize your worth."

It was the closest I'd heard to an apology from him—dragons didn't ever say *please* or *thank you*. I didn't know what to say.

I rubbed the backs of his hands with my thumbs and gazed into his eyes. "Is it likely she would ever be happy with you having a non-dragon for a mate?"

"As the prime perch holder on the Ruling Council, she has always been forced to be politically minded, and I have not in the past told her that I would refuse a political mating, so perhaps that is part of the problem. In the past, I had not met a female who is willing to pick fights with foes who could crush her with a thought. All for me." His smile was a touch lopsided.

"I'm not sure if that was a compliment or if you're calling me a fool."

"It is natural that your adoration for me compels you to make foolish choices to ensure I am safe."

"You're full of yourself."

"All dragons know their worth." He lifted a hand to my face and traced my jaw with his thumb while lowering his eyelids to half-mast. "More half-elves should know theirs."

A tingle ran through me at that touch—and at the way he looked at me—and I grew aware of the nearby bed. I hadn't exactly proven that I could take care of myself against any magic user who wanted to compel me and use me against him, but I'd made progress. He'd seen that.

His hand shifted, his fingers tracing my neck down to my collarbone. He paused there, looking down at my chest.

"I wish to see you again without your clothes."

"Oh?" It was silly, but a titillating pulse of desire ran through me at his interest. "Did the goblin water box put thoughts in your mind?"

"I think often of you in the other water box. You were naked, and then you turned the light on so I could see you even better." His fingers drifted lower to trace the outline of my breast, and I suddenly wanted to see *him* without clothes too.

"I was trying to turn on the bubbles, not the light. To *hide* myself."

"You should not hide yourself from your mate." He seemed intrigued by fondling my breast, and the light exploratory touches felt way too good for me to protest.

I gripped his shoulders. "If I knew where the zipper or velcro or whatever holds your robe on was, I'd be removing it now."

"You wish to have sex with me," Zav stated, his gaze lifting to mine as he cupped me.

"Yeah."

"Good. I have wanted you for *many* moons." He pulled my shirt over my head, and before I could protest that he was still clothed, he tugged off the robe and let it pool on the floor.

I only had time to note that he still went without underwear before his mouth descended on mine. I kissed him back, running my hands over the powerful muscles of his chest. Our caresses in the hot tub had been so brief before we'd been interrupted. Finally, I could explore every inch of him with my hands as our mouths melded together, kisses heated and hungry.

How does this garment come off? He'd tugged one of my bra straps off my shoulder but seemed to realize that move alone wouldn't defeat it.

There are hooks in the back. My mouth was too busy to speak out loud. *Want me to do it?* Too bad that would mean taking my hands off him, but only for a moment...

I could incinerate it.

No, no, that's only for mold. I'll handle it. Maybe I would strip off the rest of my clothes at the same time, though I'd no sooner had the thought than Zav's hand drifted lower, to the button of my jeans. Maybe I'd let *him* strip me.

A hot spike of pleasure almost made me gasp as his hand brushed me through the denim.

"Val!" came Nin's call from the hallway. "Val, my grandfather is awake."

Only as she burst in on us, Zav as naked as a porn star and my bra straps drooping off my shoulders, did I realize we'd left the door open.

"That's good," I managed, pulling my bra strap back up and grabbing my shirt off the floor.

Zav squinted at Nin as if he had incineration in mind again. I patted his bare chest and stepped in front of him to hide his nudity—and the evidence that he'd been enjoying our kiss.

By now, Nin had realized her mistake and recovered from her initial gawking.

"Sorry." She lifted a hand and turned away. "I wanted to let you know. Also, he wants to see you when you are, uhm, not busy."

She fled down the hall.

"We will continue," Zav stated, turning me back to face him.

I was debating if I wanted to agree or not. That had been turning into something *extremely* promising, but I also longed to know why Ti had sought me out, and who was chasing him and why.

Before I finished the internal debate, Zav released me and scowled up at the ceiling. "Velilah'nav has returned to the area."

That made up my mind for me.

"Doesn't she have a job?" I tugged my shirt over my head.

"She is the first heir of the princess of Danlykosh Eyrie."

"I'm going to take that as a no. Maybe you can have a chat with her about leaving us alone, and I'll find out what our gnome guest wants."

Zav was still scowling when I left.

CHAPTER 14

As I entered the basement, I sensed Zav leave the house, off to tell Velilah to sit on her tail and rotate, I hoped. Night had fallen outside while Zav and I had been distracted, so I didn't have to worry about searing Zoltan's sensitive skin with daylight. Voices met me as I entered. Voices speaking not in gnomish but in Thai.

Nin's grandfather had been moved to a faded yellow chair, the one piece of furniture in the basement that wasn't laboratory equipment or a coffin, and Nin stood beside him, clasping his hand. He was still as wan and pale as Zoltan, but he managed to speak slowly, answering her questions. He had blue eyes that grew round when he saw me. He patted her hand and pointed.

"Yes," Nin said, switching to English. "This is my friend, Val."

He surprised me by also switching to English, though his accent made him harder to understand than Nin. "The Ruin Bringer who carries one of the fabled Dragon Blades."

"That's me. Apparently." I dragged up an old apple crate that had come with the house and sat on it facing him. "How's it going, Ti?"

He regarded me gravely and rubbed a shaky hand over his bald pate, then scraped his fingers through the wisps of white hair around his ears. "I feared I would not make it. I was so ill, and the orc mercenaries came after me."

"Yeah, we met them. They said they'd be back with reinforcements. Care to tell us why?"

"Very much so, yes." Ti looked at Nin, and she patted his hand. "I spoke to your mother and knew you lived in this city. I hoped to visit you if I survived this trip, but it is true that you are not the reason I risked everything to escape and return to this world."

"Escape?" I asked.

Nin didn't look surprised, so maybe she'd already gotten the story.

"Yes, Ruin Bringer."

"You can call me Val."

"That is very informal."

"I'm an informal kind of gal."

"You are said to be a great dragon slayer."

"I'm an informal kind of dragon slayer. And we better get something straight." I had no idea what rumors were flying about in the Cosmic Realms, but if the rest of the lesser species thought I could kill dragons, that was a problem. Especially if they were seeking me out because they wanted dragons killed. "I battled a dragon with the help of another dragon. Lord Zavryd-thingie."

Ti's white brows drew together.

Damn, if I was going to start thinking of him as my boyfriend and having sex with him—would we ever get a chance to do that?—I should learn to pronounce his name. Maybe I would have him write it down on a sticky note for me, spelling it out phonetically, so I could practice. Or at least pull it out of my pocket for introductions.

"Zav helped me. And by helped me, I mean he did all of the work. But he is a noble dragon and doesn't slay other dragons, so I was the one to jump on Dob's chest and plunge Chopper into his heart."

I was either shortening too many names or speaking too quickly, because Ti looked to Nin for a translation. She gave him a version in her native tongue, and I heard the name Dobsaurin.

"You can pronounce their names?" I whispered.

Granted, Dobsaurin was a lot easier than most of the dragon names, but they were all simpler when shortened.

Nin smiled crookedly. "My last name is Chattrakulrak. I can pronounce anything."

I snorted. "I'll bet."

She patted her grandfather's hand again and nodded for him to go on. She looked a lot more relaxed now that he was awake. I wondered what the total would be on Zoltan's invoice. He wasn't around, so I assumed he'd hopped into his coffin for a cat nap.

"You have killed a dragon." Ti nodded to himself, as if he needed to believe I was capable of that, though doubt lurked in his eyes now.

I hated to disappoint the guy, but if he'd come looking for a dragon slayer, he needed to hire Zav, not me. Zav was pretty badass. He'd even taken down the female after telling me that females among his kind were more powerful. Later, I would find him a T-shirt that said he was my *#1 Dragon*.

"Many years ago, I was kidnapped from this world because I was known to be a talented crafter among my people, and a gnomish crafter was what my captors believed they needed. You see, they'd had another gnomish crafter before me, one who made an impressive prison that funneled the power of the molten core of Nylunia—the gnomish home world—deep within the Crying Caverns. His wife was a gnomish scientist who crafted a special type of bacterium that invades the bodies of certain species and makes them very ill. They were a team working for my captors until the scientist died of old age and her husband took his life, grief-stricken by her loss and feeling great guilt over what they'd done."

I shifted on the hard crate, wishing I'd brought a cushion. And popcorn. This story was going to take a while. "Is this the same bacteria that infected you?"

"Yes. But I was originally told it was developed to affect wyverns, cockatrices, hydras, and dragons."

"Dragons?"

"Dragons. And the prison was designed to hold the dragons that were weakened by the bacteria and place them into a magical hibernation where they did not age and the infection did not advance. This way, they were held helpless but not killed, because it is a great crime for a dragon to kill another dragon, one punishable by death."

"So I've heard." I frowned, realizing the implication of his words. "Dragons were your captors and behind everything?"

"Yes. Once weakened by the bacteria, the dragons could be contained in this prison indefinitely. Some have been there for centuries."

"How *old* was that gnome couple when they died?"

"Five or six hundred years."

I looked at Nin. "I hope you're investing in the stock market. If you live even a quarter as long as a full-blooded gnome, compounding interest is going to be your friend. Big time."

"I am learning about investing and do have mutual funds and stocks in a self-managed SEP IRA." Nin smiled at me. "But you should be doing the same. A half-elf can live much longer than a quarter-gnome."

"You know a dragon tried to light me on fire today, right?"

"That happens most days, does it not? You are still alive."

"For the moment." I turned back to Ti. "Your captors snatched you to take over maintenance of their dragon prison? How many of these sickly dragons are there?"

"More than twenty. Dragons are not a fecund species, so that is a great many for them, especially since most of these are from one clan."

A hollow feeling of dread and certainty dropped into my gut. "What clan?"

"Stormforge."

"Zav's family." I rubbed my face, wishing he was still here. No, maybe this was for the best. When he heard about this, he might destroy the house in his fury. Unless he already knew. Did he? "Do they know?"

"It is unlikely. In the twenty years I was a captive in the Crying Caverns, only two dragons visited, aside from the ones that were brought in sick and placed in the life cells."

"Life cells?"

"That is the name for the enclosures that force the sick dragons into hibernation. Since they never wake, they cannot work on healing themselves or breaking out."

"For centuries."

Ti nodded. "That is what I've been told. None of the dragons that were imprisoned there when I arrived have ever been taken out."

If they were still alive, would it be possible to free them? Or, if taken out of the cells, would they die of the bacterial infection?

Maybe I was getting ahead of myself. "Are you sure they're alive and those aren't actually tombs?"

"I could still sense their auras when I walked past them, and I understand enough of the magic of the machinery to read their statuses. They are ill and unconscious but not dead. The life cells keep them alive."

"If these bacteria were designed for dragons and dragon-kin," Nin said, "why did it almost kill you?"

Ti grimaced. "My captors infected me with it as soon as they brought me to the caverns. I was not put in a life cell, because they needed me to work, to do the maintenance on the machines and place new dragon prisoners into cells as they were brought in. They used some magic to halt the spread of the infection in my body—that is what they told me. They said that as long as I remained in the Crying Caverns, I would live, but that if I left, I would die. I was never positive that was the truth, that gnomes could be killed by the bacteria, but I was always afraid it was so. Afraid enough that I stayed and did not try to escape back to Earth and my family." He gazed sadly at Nin and shook his head. "Even my wife whom I loved very much. And still love."

"She has missed you," Nin said. "She still loves you."

Ti's head drooped, and moisture glinted in his eyes.

I wanted the rest of the story, but I made myself wait while he took a moment. Questions built up in my mind, and as soon as he took a deep breath and looked back to me, I started in.

"Who are the two dragons that you've been working for? Who captured you and checked in on you?"

"Gythornishnar."

I hadn't heard that name before.

"And Shaygorthian," he added.

That name I knew. Dob's father. The dragon who'd tried to drag me back to the Dragon Justice Court for killing his son. One of many Silverclaw dragons who seemed to be plotting against Zav's family. No, not seemed to be. They *were*. If Ti could be trusted—and why wouldn't I trust Nin's grandfather?—this plot had been going on for *centuries*.

"Were any new dragons brought in recently, by chance?" I thought of Zav's story of his uncle gone missing. What had his name been? Ston-something.

"Yes. A male dragon. I used his arrival to enact my escape. Gythornishnar was busy forcing the sick dragon to one of the life cells. It was an opportunity I'd waited years for, though I might not have taken it, but I recognized the dragon. He was Ston'tareknor, the dragon who ruled over the gnomish home world. Who ruled *benevolently* over us.

"Our world was claimed long ago by the dragons, our ancient kings turned into governors, and there was great bitterness for a time as we were treated like slaves, but the Reform of 3835 came, and a treaty was signed with the Dragon Justice Court. We were still to have a dragon ruler, but he would allow us to govern ourselves and treat us fairly. He was a Stormforge dragon, the first of three that ruled our world over the last thousand years."

"And that went well?" I tried to imagine Zav as a ruler, but my wayward mind instead imagined him standing naked in front of me with his robe on the floor.

"Far better than it had been before. The second dragon was reputed to be reasonable, and Ston'tareknor followed in his footsteps. Of course, rule by dragons was not perfect, and not all gnomes stayed—I was exploring when I found Earth and Nin's grandmother. But we all knew there were worse dragons. And when Ston'tareknor disappeared, our people were told to expect a Silverclaw ruler to take his place. We'd heard all about how their rulers were treating those on other worlds they had gained control of." Ti shook his head slowly.

"How'd you find out about all this if you were stuck in those caverns?" I asked.

"My people were not unaware that I was imprisoned in the Crying Caverns. They would not dare defy dragons to try to break me out, but over the years, adventurers who came to hunt and explore on the continent where the caverns are located updated me." Ti touched his temple, which I gathered meant the messages had been delivered telepathically and from a distance. "But it was an old traveling dwarf friend who most recently came and updated me on current events important to our peoples. He also told me of a half-elf who had a Dragon Blade and wasn't afraid to slay dragons… I impulsively decided that it was worth dying if I could make it here in time and find a way to talk you into helping our people. I hoped my captors had been lying all those years and that the bacteria would not affect gnomes."

Ti leaned his head back in the chair and wiped his arm over his brow, as if he could wipe away his weariness. "I did not realize how quickly I would succumb and how hard it would be to find you. This world is so much larger than I remembered. I had to gather information and travel across the ocean to reach you."

"What is it you want me to do?"

120

I would give this information to Zav—if anyone could do anything, it was he—but I already worried about the consequences. He would want to free his people, and that could end up starting the war the two clans had been flirting with. It could draw in all the other dragon clans, who would be forced to pick sides, and the conflict could take down lots of innocent people living on the worlds across the realms. Would Earth be safe? I doubted it. Would Zav survive? I didn't want to predict that, but he wasn't the type to hide behind another dragon. He would lead his family from the front. I had no doubt.

"Help us." Ti stretched imploring hands toward me. "Help me free Ston'tareknor to take his spot as ruler on the gnomish home world again. He will tell his family what has been going on, and perhaps the Stormforge dragons will war on the Silverclaw clan. If Stormforge comes out ahead, they will return normalcy to the Cosmic Realms. If all the dragons end up killing each other... gnomes could go back to ruling themselves. Either way would be a win for my people—for all of the peoples of the realms. Yours too. Have dragons not recently started terrorizing this world?"

I started to deny that dragons had terrorized Earth—so far, the dark elves had done more damage than the dragons—but hadn't Velilah tried to light me on fire today? And what would have happened to Seattle if Dimitri and I hadn't gotten that stolen egg back to its owners in time?

"They've started to be a problem here," I said. "But what happens if neither of the two scenarios you suggest occurs? What happens if the Silverclaw Clan is pressed to make a frontal assault on the Stormforge dragons, and it turns out they're the stronger? They could end up solidifying their rule."

"I hope you will not let that happen."

"*Me?*" I pressed a hand to my chest. "How did that dwarf even hear about me? From that piece of paper from Belohk? How did you get his diary page? And why would you believe that a half-elf could be a dragon slayer and that my sword is special?"

I'd always known Chopper was special, but what was a *Dragon Blade*? How rare were they? And was it even right that I'd ended up with this one? When I had thought it a prize won fairly in battle, like the charms around my neck, I'd considered it mine fair and square, but now I had to wonder. Zav had said from the beginning that he believed I had a stolen blade.

"The dwarf who came to the caverns *was* Belohk. He is a traveler as well as a renowned smith and an old friend of mine. He knew I was a prisoner in the Crying Caverns. Years ago, when I was first captured, he tried to free me. Unfortunately, he failed and was almost killed. The booby traps in the caverns are deadly, and they are hidden everywhere along the route to the life cells. I told him to leave me and save himself, but he did not forget that I was imprisoned there. When he found out that Ston'tareknor was being brought to the caverns, he came to warn me and offer again to help me escape. He feared that the dwarves, who have similarly been ruled by Stormforge dragons, would face the same changes soon if something was not done.

"The dragons were distracted bringing in Ston'tareknor, and with Belohk's help, I was able to slip away. But Belohk was injured by the sentry creatures at the mouth of the valley, so I had to leave him with my people to be healed and continue on to your world alone. To find you. He believed *you* could help our people the way you'd helped him when he was imprisoned here."

"You do one good deed," I muttered.

Ti closed his eyes and slumped lower in the seat.

Nin frowned at him with worry. "Val, my grandfather must rest. Will you watch him while you consider if you can help him? I will go to my food truck and bring back hearty meals for him."

"We have food in the fridge here."

"Pop Tarts and breakfast burritos are not food. You do *not* eat properly."

"Hey, the Pop Tarts are Dimitri's. And your gnomish grandfather might like them. He'll think they're exotic."

"I remember from my youth that his favorite food is fish-eye soup."

"Then Pop Tarts should be a *big* improvement."

"The American palate is so strange." Nin shook her head. "You will watch him?"

"Yes, of course." I would make him Pop Tarts as soon as she left. He looked like he could use some sugar. "And I'll talk to Zav about all the rest of this as soon as he comes back."

"You expect him soon?"

"I hope so." I needed to get Zav a phone so I could call him if he was anywhere on Earth. Maybe he could keep it in the same extra-dimensional pocket that was now smeared with cake frosting.

Nin patted her grandfather's hand one more time and headed for the door. "I should be back in an hour."

"Maybe you should move your food truck to Green Lake so you'd be closer while he's convalescing."

She paused with her hand on the door. "That is a possibility. There are food trucks around here, I know. I will research the area and consider if it would be as profitable as my current spot."

"It might be okay if you made a little less for a month."

"You are *not* a good businesswoman, Val."

"No, but I'm going to let your grandpa stay here, so make sure to bring some takeout for me and Dimitri, please."

"Always." She opened the door but paused again. "Now that he is awake, do you wish me to move him to my house? There is not a guest bedroom, but he could use my room, and I could sleep on the couch." She nodded to herself, as if she'd already decided.

"No." I held up a hand. "Remember that someone is after him. Sindari and I would have a better shot than you at driving off another batch of orcs. And you don't want to get your roommates eaten by a monster dog from another realm. They wouldn't be able to make their rent payments then."

"You are sometimes wise, Val. I will bring you many meals and stock the refrigerator so you are not forced to eat substandard food out of boxes."

She waved and headed out.

"The burritos come in bags," I called after her.

"You are an uncouth cave woman, dear robber," came Zoltan's voice as Nin closed the door.

"Why? Because I don't like my sustenance fresh from a vein?"

"Among other reasons." He walked into view carrying a sheet of paper. My invoice, no doubt.

I glanced at Ti to see what he thought of discussions with vampires, but his head had lolled off to the side, and he appeared to be sleeping.

"Zoltan." I accepted the paper without looking—I'd try to get Willard to pay for his services before worrying if I could afford them. "Would the same formula you made to cure Ti work to fix up infected dragons?"

"I do not know. I would need to infect a dragon with the bacteria, wait for them to proliferate, and then dose him with my formula."

"Can't you just futz with the bacteria in a Petri dish or something?"

"Do you know nothing about science, dear robber?"

"Not much."

"You *are* a cave woman."

CHAPTER 15

After killing time with a workout of sword katas by the glow of the solar landscape lights in the back yard, I sat on one of the retaining walls near the fence and gazed at the moon.

Zav, if you can hear me, now would be a good time to come back for a visit. I didn't expect him to answer. Even if I was getting better at speaking telepathically to magical beings, my range seemed to be about a mile. And I had the niggling feeling that he had gone back to his world to discuss his dating problems with his mother.

Unfortunately, I didn't have a way to help Ti without Zav. I wasn't that interested in risking my life to solve Ti's problem even *with* Zav. It sounded like a suicide mission, and I had enough trouble protecting the citizens of Earth without wandering off to freedom fight on other planets. Still, if it would help the Stormforge clan—if it would help *Zav*—I would do it.

My phone buzzed, and I pulled it out of my pocket, expecting it to be Nin asking how much room I had in my fridge and freezer. But it was Thad.

Hey, Val. What's the name of Nin's food truck?

Crying Tiger. Why?

She told me about it when we met at your house. I thought I would visit it for lunch sometime.

You're going to drive from Edmonds to Pioneer Square for lunch at a food truck? Even without traffic, that was a long drive for some rice and beef, and Seattle was never without traffic.

I like to support local businesses.

Aren't the businesses in Edmonds more local to your house?

I like to support local businesses owned by people I know. She seemed nice. She gave me marketing advice.

Do you need marketing advice? The last I'd heard, Thad did business-to-business stuff and had a network of contacts and plenty of work.

No, but it was sweet. She almost convinced me of the need to have a YouTube presence and post regular videos to promote my Customer Relationship Management Software.

Nice and sweet. I eyed my phone, wondering if altruism was truly what Thad had in mind. Had he and Nin spoken for long enough to make some kind of connection? I'd been too busy fighting orcs to monitor my houseguests properly.

I texted him the address and added, *Ask her about her family and her dreams to buy a house here for all of them to live in. And about her plans for the coffee shop.*

Are those the things that excite her?

Yeah. As far as I know, she doesn't have any hobbies. She works all the time. So basically, she's a cuter version of you.

I'm offended that you don't find me cute.

You don't have blue pigtails. Do you want her number?

He hesitated before answering. *Do you think she would mind?*

Probably not. It's the same one she uses for her business and has listed on the website.

Okay. Sure.

When I put the phone away, I noticed that I sensed one less magical aura in the house than there should have been. Freysha was still in the kitchen studying those charms, and Zoltan was still in the basement, but… where was Ti?

I lurched to my feet. I didn't sense him. The only way he could have left the basement was through the door not twenty feet away from me. Had I been that distracted by Thad's conversation or my earlier exercises that I hadn't noticed him walking out? Or what if someone had sneaked in and used magic to *carry* him out?

Swearing, I sprinted for the basement. If he'd been kidnapped from under my nose after Nin had specifically asked me to keep an eye on him, I'd beat myself with my own sword.

Ti's chair was empty.

"Zoltan?" I spun toward the laboratory to find him puttering with a microscope. "Where did he go?"

Zoltan waved vaguely without lifting his face from the eyepiece. "He said he had to get something."

"Get something? Get what? He fled his world as a refugee."

"I didn't ask."

"You're a horrible babysitter."

"I didn't know that was a duty you wished me to take on. My hourly rate will go up if I must include gnome observation."

I swore some more and ran upstairs and into the house. I put on the magical vest Nin had made for me and grabbed Fezzik and my sword harness for Chopper. "Freysha, can you sense Ti?"

She yawned and leaned back from her chair at the table. "Isn't he…" Her gaze grew distant. "He's not here. I didn't notice him leave."

"Me either. Your range is better than mine. Can you sense him anywhere in the neighborhood?"

"I will check. But first take these and put them on your thong necklace." She handed me two of the charms that looked like they had been made by drunken goblins with crooked pliers. "My research tells me that is the one that will protect you from magical compulsion." She tapped the ugliest one of them all. "And that one will protect you from storm magic, such as lightning strikes. They're passive and don't require activation words."

"Can I just keep them in my pocket?"

She blinked and looked at me. "I suppose. You would not want to risk losing them."

"This one looks like an owl hawked it up after eating a mechanical mouse. I'm not putting it around my neck next to Sindari."

"As you wish." Freysha closed her eyes to try to locate Ti.

Where would he have gone and for *what*? Was it possible some enemy out there had magically compelled him to leave the house? Some enemy who didn't want to battle me, Sindari, and Freysha?

While she scoured the neighborhood with her senses, I pulled out my keychain and hung the ugly charms next to the house key. If they proved themselves invaluable, *maybe* I would paint them and move them to my neck thong.

As I stuck the keychain back in my pocket, I realized that I was taking Freysha's word on this. After being tricked by that first elf, maybe I shouldn't be so quick to trust another elf. But Freysha had helped me survive Velilah's wrath that afternoon and she was staying in my house and teaching me magic. If she'd meant to betray me, she could have done it already.

Logical thoughts, but I vowed to have Zav double-check the charms later.

"I sense him near the lake less than a mile away," Freysha said slowly, her eyes still closed. "He is moving about in the trees behind a fence on a hill."

I groped through my memories, trying to think of a fenced area near the lake. "The dog park?"

"I do not know. There are not dogs or people there now."

"No, because it's been dark for two hours. Okay, I'm going to go get him." And sling him over my shoulder, carry him back, and shackle him to that anvil in the basement until Nin got back.

"Do you wish assistance?" Freysha didn't manage to hide another yawn.

"Do you sense any dragons or orcs or anything else nefarious between here and there?"

"Not currently."

"Then I'll risk the trip alone." I grabbed the Jeep key and ran for the door. "If Nin comes, tell her that Gramps needed fresh air and we'll be right back."

Not exactly a lie. I hoped. Maybe Nin was busy flirting with Thad through text messages by now and wouldn't beat me back. I could hope.

When I pulled into the parking lot, the dog park was dark and empty. As I got out with my weapons, a raccoon scampered away from a garbage can. Frogs croaking across the street at the lake competed with distant traffic noise.

I sensed Ti up the hill and behind the fenced area, much as Freysha had promised. What the heck was he doing?

Trees grew densely in the area, and there weren't any streetlights in this part of the park. If not for my ability to detect magical beings, I would have struggled to find Ti. But my senses took me up the hill toward the clump of trees where he was hanging out.

Had he grown claustrophobic in the basement and needed some nature? If so, I might kick his butt. We had trees in the back yard he could have visited.

A faint rustle sounded as Ti whirled toward me. He crouched between two trees, and I could barely pick him out and wasn't sure if he had a weapon, so I stopped and lifted my hands.

"It's Val. What are you doing?"

"Val? The dragon slayer?"

"And hunter of wandering gnomes, yes." I worried he wouldn't get that I was joking and started to clarify, but he sighed in relief.

"Thank goodness. I am in such a weakened state that I am struggling to employ a levitation spell. I should have asked you to come along from the beginning."

"Yes, you should have. And you should have explained what you're doing."

Ti lowered his voice to a whisper and glanced around. "Getting your payment."

"Right. Withdrawing from the Bank of the Woods."

His English had been pretty solid earlier, if heavily accented, but maybe he had the wrong word now.

He hesitated. "I hid it here before I sought you out. I wasn't sure... Even though Belohk said you were a good person, I did not want to risk losing this after I scrounged from everyone I knew to get enough."

"Enough what?" I walked forward slowly, imagining him handing me an envelope of some gnomish currency that I would have to travel to Gnome Land to spend.

"Gold. It still has value here, yes?"

"Oh. Yeah."

"Good. That is what I heard. This is very heavy. Will you help me carry it?"

"How *much* gold are we talking?" I knew the metal was heavy—I'd been paid a few times in gold coins—but unless he had hundreds of ounces of it, I couldn't imagine it being that hard to carry, even for a three-and-a-half-foot-tall gnome.

"A small chest. I hope it is enough. I rarely worked with gold when I lived on this world before, and I am uncertain about how well it will convert to your currency."

A small chest sounded promising, but... "Look, you don't have to pay me. Your problem sounds like Zav's problem, and we're..." Saying we were mates always sounded goofy to me, even if all of the magical community seemed to find it a normal term. "We're dating. His problems have become my problems, however unwise that is. If this can help him, I'll do it."

"I wish you to do it whether it helps him or not. Please. That is why I brought gold. To pay you." Ti scrabbled at something in the dirt. "Here is the chest. Can you lift it?"

"I'm sure I can." I crouched down and patted around until I found the top half of what felt like an iron chest—no wonder it was heavy. "But I'm positive I can't do a thing to help your people or those dragons without Zav's help. I can't even make a portal."

"We can offer half the gold to him, if you wish, but I do not think dragons care about money."

"Not that I've seen. We'd have to exchange it for ribs." I tapped on my flashlight app for a better look, shining the beam over clumps of dirt on the top of a blue iron box. "I'd call that a medium chest, not a small chest, and I'm a lot bigger than you."

"Can you carry it?"

I spotted rings on either end and tugged at one. "Erg, what else is in here? Someone's change jar?" Having recently lugged mine from the old apartment to the new house, I could attest to the weight of spare change. "Anything we can dump out and leave?"

Or could we dump out the gold and leave the *chest*? It had to weigh eighty pounds. I levered it out of the pit of soft dirt and eyed the route through the trees back to my Jeep. This was going to be fun.

"Just gold," Ti said. "Many of my kin want to ensure the Silverclaws do not rule our people. They were all willing to chip in."

"Can I see it?" I didn't believe that the chest itself didn't account for most of the weight and snorted at the idea that it was a seventy-nine-pound chest with sixteen ounces of gold inside. Not that I would turn up my nose at sixteen ounces. Going by what the gold price had been the last time I'd looked, that would be more than twenty-five thousand dollars.

"Yes. It is right that you should see that I have funds before committing to the deal."

"There's no deal, Ti. If Zav wants to storm those Crying Caverns, I'll help him, but I wouldn't have a chance without him."

"There is often only one dragon there at a time." Ti touched his finger to the chest's lock, and I sensed a tickle of magic as he opened it. "You would only need to slay one if we timed it right. And I am intimately familiar with the Caverns. I can show you all the booby traps."

"Wonderful." I hadn't been thinking about booby traps, but now I remembered from his story that they'd almost killed his dwarf friend. A dragon *and* booby traps. Wouldn't that be a fun mission?

Ti pushed the lid open so I could shine my flashlight on the contents. On... okay, there were a *lot* of gold bars in there.

"Are those pure gold?" I picked one up. It was heavy enough to be pure gold, but I'd never seen blocks this large. Each one had to weigh ten pounds, and there were eight of them.

"Yes, of course. Gnomes are crafters. We do not cut our metal with inferior substances. The stamp ensures they came from the Official Miners' Mint."

I flipped over the bar. A dragon was stamped in the center.

"Is that Ston?" I asked, shortening the dragon's name.

"His predecessor and sire. The Stormforge Clan loved him. We chose to put his likeness on our money and metal."

"Sucking up?"

His brow furrowed. Maybe gnomes had another term for it.

I returned the bar to the chest and closed the lid. "We'll take this to the house, and Zoltan can put it under his coffin as a security measure." Only a loon would steal from a vampire. "If there's some way Zav and I can make this work, we can talk about payment then."

"This will not be enough?"

"This will be too much. You could hire me for ten years for this." And then some. Even putting aside half of it for taxes, this would likely be enough to buy our house and do all the home improvements Dimitri and I could dream of.

"It is yours if we can free Ston'tareknor and defeat the dragons who held me captive these last twenty years and took me from my family." Ti's voice had a forlorn note to it.

I patted him on the shoulder, then lifted the chest without throwing out my back. Barely.

As I waddled back toward the Jeep, I sensed powerful magic at the edge of my range. Familiar powerful magic. It was a portal like the one the orcs had opened above the house. And it was exactly back in the direction of the house.

"Shit."

I increased my waddle as quickly as I could with the heavy chest in my arms. If it hadn't been such a ridiculous amount of gold, I would have dumped it so I could get back to the house sooner, but with my luck, someone else would find it before we handled the orcs or whoever was opening portals this time.

Ti whispered something under his breath, and the weight of the chest decreased by half.

"Thanks." Turning my waddle into a sprint, I ran down the hill toward the parking lot.

Freysha had proven she could take care of herself, and I wasn't too worried about Zoltan, but Dimitri could make an easy target for orcs. He hadn't yet built and installed all the defenses he wanted to around the house.

As I reached the Jeep and flung the rear door open, a powerful aura registered on my senses.

"Dragon," Ti said.

"I know." Damn it.

It was Shaygor. I hadn't seen him since our showdown on Mt. Schweitzer, but I hadn't forgotten what his aura felt like. He was also back in the direction of the house—he must have come through that portal— and I worried anew for my friends. Even Freysha and Zoltan couldn't handle a dragon. Nobody could. Except for another dragon.

"Zav," I whispered as I levered the chest into the back of the Jeep. "Where are you?"

"I do not sense your dragon mate," Ti said.

"I know. That's a problem. Get in the Jeep." But even as I ran for the driver-side door, I realized that Shaygor was on the move. In this direction.

Of course. He hadn't come for our *house*. He'd come for his escaped gnome prisoner. And I was positive he wouldn't have a problem incinerating me along the way.

CHAPTER 16

"Here." I unfastened my camouflage charm for the second time that weekend and handed it to Ti. It was probably already too late—Shaygor was flying this way, so he had to have sensed Ti already. "Use this to cloak yourself while I…"

While I what? Slew the dragon? Hah.

"Try to convince him to look somewhere else."

Ti looked down at the charm, then toward the dark cloudy sky where Shaygor was sure to come into view any second. If not for the trees, he already *would* be in view.

"Just use it," I urged. "If you don't, I will."

Maybe that wouldn't be such a bad idea. If I hid, I could jump out and attack Shaygor while he was arrowing down to get Ti, but that wouldn't leave me with any options. I would be committed to fighting him at that point, and I couldn't beat a dragon one-on-one. No way.

Ti stepped back, activated the charm, and disappeared from my awareness, taking away the ambush possibility. It was just as well. Maybe I could come up with some crazy idea that would convince Shaygor to leave—and let me live.

The mighty silver dragon came into view, powerful wings flapping and bringing him toward me. I walked away from the Jeep, not wanting it to get torched.

On a whim, I hopped the fence and trotted into the dog park and halfway up the hill in the center. There were a few trees inside to hide behind if need be, but the packed earth was also relatively free of obstacles in case I had to run and dodge.

I summoned Sindari, though I knew how he felt about battling dragons. As any sane person would agree, it should be avoided.

Val, Sindari protested as Shaygor flew closer. *You should have called me sooner and given me time to prepare myself.*

Wouldn't you have just used that time to tell me how dumb it was for me to get into this situation?

Yes, but I like doing that.

Sorry. I'll be more considerate next time.

Do.

Shaygor dove for us, and I raised Chopper and whispered, "*Eravekt,*" so he would know I had the powerful blade. The *Dragon Blade* apparently. It had lopped off one of his toes once. I doubted that meant he feared it, but maybe it would at least make him pause.

Murderer of dragons! he roared into my mind as Chopper flared bright blue. *I am not surprised you are at the center of this.*

Center of what? I crouched, ready to swing if he came in close enough to reach, though I expected him to spew fire from twenty feet above me. *And watch yourself, dragon. I've been honing my skills since the last time we met.*

You've been holding Zavryd'nokquetal's tail and tysliir *like rabbits since last we met.*

Oh, did rabbits do that on other worlds too? Huh.

As I'd feared, Shaygor didn't come within reach. From twenty feet above, he opened his maw and spewed fired at me.

I dove behind one tree, and Sindari sprang behind another. Heat tried to broil the back of my neck as flames bathed the ground where I'd been standing. It was mostly dirt packed from the passage of thousands of dog paws, but a few timber steps embedded in the hillside charred. Tree branches caught by the flames singed and burned, and I hoped I wasn't about to get the local park burned down.

Do you have a plan to convince him to get close enough to strike with your sword? Sindari asked as Shaygor flew past, banking to turn around for another attack.

I'm working on it.

I wished Freysha were here to make some vines grow out of the ground and capture the dragon's foot, but having them shoot up twenty feet in the air might be beyond her skills.

Where is the gnome? Shaygor boomed into my mind.

What gnome?

He was beside you two minutes ago. Do you think I'm sense-dead? Shaygor arrowed toward my tree.

He told me he'd pay me if I gave him my cloaking charm and kept you busy while he escaped.

Where did he go?

This time, Shaygor came within fifteen feet of the ground as he opened his great fanged maw, smoke gathering in his throat. Maybe he wanted to make sure he struck me full on.

I darted toward another tree, zigzagging my path to try to throw him off. He could only adjust the trajectory of his descent so much now that he was committed, but he had no trouble swinging his neck around toward me while he was diving.

I was tempted to throw Chopper and hope to prong him in the stomach as he sailed past, but it was easy to envision him snatching the blade out of the air with his talons and flying off with it. Instead, I tried Freysha's fern trick as I ran, envisioning wet protective fronds filling the space between us as he breathed flames down on me.

This wasn't about mind manipulation, so I didn't expect it to work, but I only knew a few types of magic so far. To my surprise, as the flames spewed toward me, they were deflected by an invisible barrier where I'd imagined the fronds. The fiery gout bounced back up into the night.

That must have surprised Shaygor as much as it surprised me, because instead of coming around to attack again, he flew up and landed in a stout tree at the edge of the dog park.

Where did he go? Shaygor repeated, this time with compulsion in the words. He glowered down at me from the treetop, putting images of me spouting everything I knew to him while dropping to my knees and begging for my life.

Why did everybody want me on my knees?

Resisting him seemed easier than in the past—was the charm in my pocket helping out?—but I still felt the pull of his power. Before my body could think about obeying, I employed the fern fronds again, this time imagining them around my mind. As he glared at me, I could sense him summoning more power and directing it at me. My fronds wavered, threatening to dissolve, and one of my feet treacherously stepped out from behind the tree.

I dropped to one knee and pressed my fingers into the dirt, willing the earth to lend me its power. The fronds re-formed, steady and firm in my mind's eye.

I can kill you easily, Shaygor stated. *Even if you had not been responsible for my son's death, I would enjoy killing the mongrel toy that Zavryd'nokquetal plays with. I would enjoy it very much. Would he weep at your death, do you think? Our eyes do not have tear ducts, but I have seen dragons in elven or human form weep. They succumb to the weaknesses of the creatures they shift into, the fools.*

If you're trying to butter me up to get information from me, you suck at it.

Tell me where the gnome went, he boomed into my mind again, throwing a torrent of power at me.

I gasped and almost lurched to my feet, nearly overwhelmed by the urge to run out into the open and expose myself to him. But I willed the power of the earth and my own power to wrap around me and my mind, to protect me from his coercion. And the charm in my pocket warmed against my thigh, as if it too was contributing.

Once again, the urge lessened, and I glared defiantly back at Shaygor. *Look, asshole. If you want information from me, you better come down here and ask nicely, the same as anyone else. With a fistful of money for me.*

Not that I expected him to have money or wanted it. I just wanted him close enough for me to hit with my sword.

I glanced at Sindari, who crouched behind another tree, using his stealth magic to hide himself from Shaygor. I didn't speak to him, afraid Shaygor would intercept our telepathic communication, but I trusted he knew I would want him to try to distract our enemy if he came down. Just long enough for me to get close…

Shaygor snorted. *You are a whore. No wonder you find it so easy to hold the tail of such a weak dragon.*

Weak? Zav? I saw him kick your ass twice.

Shaygor sprang from his tree, and I braced myself for another attack, but he sailed to the bottom of the hill and landed next to a wooden bench. His big silver butt almost took out a large wooden sign with information about the park.

He is weak, and his family is weak. They will all be destroyed, and we will rule. Shaygor's outline blurred as he shifted into a smaller form.

I rushed out from hiding, hoping to attack while he was transforming, but he finished too quickly. The silver-haired elf version of him stood before me with a glowing sword in his hand. It was an imitation of Chopper, and I could tell from its aura that it wasn't as powerful. Unfortunately, *Shaygor's* aura was plenty powerful.

"Where do you keep that when you're in your dragon form?" I asked casually, slowing to a stop, as if I hadn't been trying to sprint over in time to mow him down. "It looks sharp for a keister stash."

"Does your idiotic wit please Zavryd'nokquetal?"

"It pleases him when I vex his enemies."

Shaygor snorted again. "That I believe." He gazed around the park while keeping the sword pointed toward me. "I believe the gnome is nearby, that you would not have given him your treasured trinket if you believed he would run off with it."

"Does it matter? You couldn't find him if he was five hundred miles or five feet away."

Taunting him is not wise, Val, Sindari warned me.

I didn't answer. I was prowling closer as I taunted him. If he was willing to fight me while in elven form, maybe I had a chance.

"Tell me where the gnome is." He glared into my eyes as he spoke, his own eyes flaring with light and power.

This time, I more easily resisted the compulsion. "Leave my planet alone, or I'll chop off another one of your toes."

"You *dare* threaten a superior being!"

"Of course I dare." I crept closer, close enough to spring. But I doubted a straightforward attack would be effective.

"Does Zavryd'nokquetal have any idea what a heathen he's rutting with?"

"We discuss it at length daily."

Ready to distract him? I sensed that Sindari had crept around behind the sign, behind Shaygor, but I knew he wouldn't be happy about attacking a dragon.

No.

But you'll do it anyway?

Yes, but only because I like Nin and want to see her grandfather live.

Shaygor extended his arm, using the sword to keep me from getting too close. "Tell me where he is." Compulsion again laced the words. "Tell me where he is, and I will spare your life."

"Isn't it against your rules to kill people in the Cosmic Realms?"

"Nobody cares if lesser species live or die." Shaygor gathered power and prepared to strike.

Willing the fern fronds to wrap protectively around my body, I dove under his sword and rolled toward him. A wall of pure magical energy swept at me, but it parted around my barrier, and I wasn't derailed from my attack. I whipped Chopper at his legs as I rolled past.

Shaygor let out a startled grunt, but he reacted quickly, levitating himself into the air to mostly avoid my swing. I'd been trying to lop off one of his legs, but I managed to slice through his pants and nick flesh.

He roared, the sound like a dragon's roar even though he was in elven form, and flung a second wave of power at me. This time, I was too slow getting my defenses up, and his magic struck me like a mallet. I tumbled head over heels all the way to the chain-link fence and hit hard enough to leave squares indented in my back.

Though the blow knocked the air out of me, I lunged to my feet to ready myself for another attack. Sindari sprang for Shaygor's back, claws slashing toward his head.

The dragon whirled and raised an invisible barrier. I ran toward him as Sindari bounced off, his claws never reaching Shaygor's flesh. He blasted power at Sindari, sending him flying across the bare earth and into one of the signposts. The wood crunched and gave, the sign toppling to the side.

Sorry, Sindari, I thought, but the diversion gave me enough time to get back to our foe and swing at the back of his neck. Unfortunately, the magical barrier extended all the way around him. Chopper halted a foot from his neck, but instead of bouncing away, the blade stuck, as if I'd swung it at a tree and it had lodged in the trunk.

As Shaygor turned slowly to face me, loathing burning in his eyes, I resisted the urge to pull back and instead leaned into Chopper. The blade inched through the barrier, drawing closer to Shaygor, but it took all my strength, and I knew I was vulnerable to attack. He didn't look worried in the least. The sword was ten inches from his throat now, but he didn't even step back.

"I *will* kill you," he stated, "but not until you tell me where the gnome is and why he fled here of all places."

He never lifted a finger, but pressure gripped my neck, as if he were wrapping his hands around my throat.

I kept leaning into Chopper, pushing it into his barrier. I was encouraged that it was creeping closer to his neck, however slowly, and stubbornly determined to land a blow that would do more than nick him. Even as I pressed the blade forward, I tried to use the magic Freysha had taught me to keep his attack from choking me, this time envisioning the fronds protecting my neck.

Chopper was only eight inches from his flesh. Had Shaygor lifted a hand, he could have punched me in the face, but maybe he couldn't do that through his barrier. Maybe he could only attack with magic. Magic that hurt—my airway was constricting, and pain coursed up and down my spine—but not as much as it had before when I'd faced him. If I could just get my blade to his throat...

You've stolen some new trinkets, he observed, switching to telepathy. *You have a ridiculous number of gewgaws for one person. How many beings have you slain to get them?*

Seven inches to his throat.

Out of the corner of my eye, I saw Sindari pulling himself out from under the sign wreckage and shaking shards of wood out of his fur. I didn't look at him. Shaygor was doubtless aware of him, but I didn't want to draw any attention to him.

What can I say, dragon? I had to reply silently since I couldn't suck in air. *I'm a girl, and I like jewelry.* Six inches.

His eyebrows drew together, jaw clenching, and I sensed him readying another blow. I pushed harder with Chopper and tried to add my mental power to what my muscles were doing to drive the blade toward his throat. Pain erupted in my neck as I shifted my magic away from defending myself and to attacking, but Chopper surged closer. Four inches. Three.

Sindari lunged in and I shifted my focus, willing the ferns to grow into Shaygor's barrier and create an opening for my ally. Sindari's snout slipped through, and he bit Shaygor in the calf, fangs sinking deep.

Shaygor roared in pain, the pressure on my throat disappearing, as he jerked his leg away. For an instant, his barrier was down, and I drove

Chopper downward. Because he'd moved, I didn't get his throat, but my blade sank an inch into his shoulder before he blasted Sindari and me with such power that we flew thirty feet.

I soared all the way over the chain-link fence and hit the ground in a hard roll that took me to the parking lot. Pain battered my body, but I forced myself to my feet.

Blood stained Shaygor's elven tunic, but any triumph I felt from landing a real blow disappeared when he sprang into the air and shifted into his dragon form. He would be stronger and harder to hurt again—harder to even reach. And he could attack us with fire from afar, as it appeared he planned to do. He flew up above the trees and banked. There was a hitch to his left wing—the side I'd struck—and it looked like I'd done real damage to him, but I feared it wouldn't be enough.

As I prepared to defend myself against fire, I sensed more auras in the trees across the road.

Orcs, Sindari warned. *Six of them. Similar to the ones we fought last time.*

I groaned. We hadn't stood a chance against a dragon to start with, and now he had reinforcements.

CHAPTER 17

Sindari and I only had time to scoot under the branches of trees—trees that would hopefully protect us from Shaygor's overhead attacks of fire—and position ourselves back to back before the burly orcs rushed out of the woods across the street. One fired a crossbow bolt that should have taken me in the eye, but I saw him squeezing the trigger and had time to dodge. The quarrel slammed into a tree over Sindari's head.

As he roared his disgruntlement, I pulled out Fezzik and fired at the charging orcs. My first few bullets ricocheted off magical barriers. Then, remembering how I'd burrowed through Shaygor's barrier with my magic, I re-formed the plant imagery in my mind and willed it to peel back the barriers of the two lead orcs. One grunted in what sounded like surprise. I fired right at him. Fezzik's magical bullets blasted into the orc's chest. Three more rounds hammered into his head, and he stutter-stepped before pitching forward.

More grunts of surprise came from the group, but the orcs kept coming. Shaygor screeched from the trees right above me. He didn't use fire, maybe because his allies were so close, but a magical hammer strike landed on me as if I were a nail. My knees gave way as his power forced me to the ground.

Sindari snapped at the orcs, trying to keep them at bay. Half of them tried to circle us and the others rushed at me, trying to take advantage.

Though pain and power battered at me from above, I rose to my feet and tried again to force the closest orc's barrier down. It was like attempting to focus with a nail gun firing into my head, and I couldn't summon the necessary imagery. I fired, but the bullets bounced off.

An orc with a crossbow fired at me. This time, he was too close, and I didn't have time to dodge the quarrel. It slipped past the edge of my armored vest and pierced my shoulder with fiery agony. Another orc sprang at me, a sword raised.

Fighting the pain in my shoulder, I swung Chopper up to block him. The force of the blow jarred my shoulder, and I couldn't keep a cry from escaping my lips. I gritted my teeth and thrust back, trying to drive him farther away. Behind me, Sindari snapped and slashed at his own opponents. He couldn't help me.

For the first time, I realized I might die tonight.

More orcs pressed in, and all I could do was defend, parrying axes and swords, barely managing to deflect blades before they pierced my chest or bashed my skull. I had to give ground, almost stepping on poor Sindari's feet as I backed toward the trees. I was too harried and in too much pain to focus on creating magic.

Overhead, Shaygor roared. His next attack would leave me on the ground and defenseless against the orcs.

But then I sensed another dragon. Zav.

Need some help, I cried telepathically toward him, though he surely already knew. He had been back at the house when he popped onto my radar, but he was flying fast toward us. Shaygor roared again, a frustrated roar.

Knowing Zav was coming helped me fight back the pain and gave me fresh energy to use against the orcs. Which was good because they weren't giving up. They must have also sensed Zav, but maybe they believed their dragon ally would best mine.

"Fat chance," I growled and found the concentration to focus on my magic once again.

I envisioned the fern fronds in my mind as if they were being batted by a wind, knocking into the orcs and hurling them back. Two of our attackers stumbled backward. It wasn't as impressive as when Shaygor had hurled me thirty feet, but it was something.

Once again, I tried to poke holes in the magical barriers protecting the orcs. One lifted a crossbow, but I fired with Fezzik first. A bullet took him in the eye, and he dropped his weapon as he pitched back.

Another of the orcs shouted what sounded like a warning. I didn't have my translation charm activated, but I hoped it was that they were in over their heads and should give up.

Overhead, Zav and Shaygor crashed together in the air. With the branches obscuring the sky, I couldn't see them with my eyes, but I sensed them and heard them. They fought with fang and talon and magic as they roared and shrieked like great birds of prey.

Meanwhile, I kept focusing on tearing down orc magical barriers with my mental attacks as I fired bullets into my enemies. When the three orcs who had faced me were all down or running back into the woods, I turned to help Sindari. Two of his foes were down, their throats torn by his mighty claws, but he continued to slash at a club-wielder determined to brain him. I shot him in the eye. He stumbled back, and Sindari sprang onto his chest, knocking him the rest of the way to the ground.

As Sindari finished off the orc, I slumped against a tree. In a moment, I would run out into the open and see if there was a way I could help Zav, but I was exhausted, and my shoulder throbbed so hard it was reverberating behind my eyes. Or maybe I had a fresh headache independent of the other wound, a byproduct of focusing so hard on using magic.

A thunderous crack sounded as something struck a tree not ten feet away. The trunk broke in half, and branches snapped off as a dragon plunged to the ground like a cannonball. A silver dragon. A second after he landed, the tree trunk fell on him.

Conniving vermin! Shaygor screeched into my mind as he found his feet, flinging the trunk off his back.

Magic burst into my awareness, and I raised my sword, thinking he meant to attack me. But he was forming a portal, the silvery circle appearing in the air next to him.

Next time we meet, you die! Shaygor pinned me with his fury-filled eyes before springing through the portal and disappearing from this world.

"Me? I'm not the one who dropped a tree on him." My voice sounded as shaky and weak as I felt.

Sindari came and sat next to me, also leaning against the tree for support. More than one sword had found him, and blood matted his silver fur.

I'm sorry you were hurt, Sindari.

This is the way of battle.

Thank you for your help. For the record, I didn't want to fight a dragon. I was trying to make sure he didn't get Nin's grandfather.

I know. Perhaps later, you will explain to me why one of our enemy dragons wants the gnome.

I will.

As the portal disappeared, Zav flew down and shifted into human form. He eyed the air where it had been, as if he was considering following Shaygor to wherever he'd gone and kicking his ass some more, but then he spotted me, our gazes meeting across the broken branches and dead orcs.

You are injured.

Fighting six orcs and a dragon will do that. I smiled, striving for nonchalance, though the realization of how close a call that had been refused to dissipate. My hands were shaking, and I was sure it wasn't only from the pain and adrenaline. I risked myself regularly for my job, but I didn't make a habit of picking fights I didn't believe I could win. *Thank you for your timely arrival.*

Zav strode toward me, barely glancing at Sindari. He rested one hand on my hip and lifted the other to my shoulder. The quarrel was broken off—I hadn't even felt that—and embedded in the muscle.

"I will incinerate this," Zav said. "It will hurt briefly."

"I know. Go ahead." I braced myself.

The flash of pain as he reduced the quarrel to ash was brief, especially compared to what I'd endured that night. He followed that by gently resting his palm against the gouge left in my shoulder. Soothing magic flowed into the wound, and the pain faded further.

Zav leaned in and kissed me as the puncture knitted itself back together. His kiss was gentle, but the telepathic words that accompanied it were determined. *I regret that you were hurt by another dragon. I do not know why he was here on Earth harassing you again, but I will find out.*

I already know. It's a long story, and I need to tell you. You're not going to be pleased.

You did something to goad him?

Yeah, I'm sheltering a fugitive gnome.

Zav drew back, the injury healed, and gave me a puzzled look.

I didn't know where Ti had chosen to hide, but I hoped he would show up again now that Shaygor was gone. Assuming he wasn't scared of Zav. Just because Ti thought Zav's uncle had been a decent ruler didn't mean he wanted to bump elbows with dragons in general. Most of the non-dragon species seemed to feel that way toward them.

"I'll let him explain it when we get back to the house. It has to do with you and your family, so it's a good thing you came back."

"My curiosity is fully piqued."

"Can you heal Sindari's injuries too?" I leaned over and patted him on the back, careful to avoid the gouges the orcs' swords had left.

There is no need, Sindari said. *I can return to my world and heal quickly.*

"Zav can heal you nearly instantly. As you just saw." I lifted my arm. The wound itched slightly but didn't hurt at all.

I saw that he kissed you. If that is part of his healing magic, I choose to reject it.

"You don't think he can resist putting his lips on you while he's healing you?"

Zav's eyebrows drifted upward, but he was looking at the spot where Shaygor's portal had been, probably wondering what story I would tell him that would explain this.

I will not risk it. If you have no further need of me?

"No. Thanks again for the help."

For our next battle, please do not involve dragons.

You didn't like biting Shaygor in the calf?

I didn't like being hurled into that sign and having all those little black baggies fall on me.

Black baggies? Oh. I realized some dog-poo collection baggies had been attached to the big sign. *At least they hadn't been used yet.*

As mist formed around Sindari and he faded from our world, Zav tensed and turned toward the road.

"It's me," Ti called warily, still far enough away to be invisible to my senses. "Is it all right to approach? Or do you wish to be alone with... your mate?"

"I enjoy being alone with him, but I also want my charm back and for you to tell him your story."

Ti came into view off to my side, doing his best to approach me without getting too close to Zav. He extended his open palm with my cloaking charm on it.

"Thank you for protecting me, Ruin Bringer." He bowed low over his extended arm.

"Call me Val." I accepted the charm and threaded it back onto my leather thong.

"You not only were unafraid to battle a dragon, but you are the mate of one." With his head still bowed, he glanced from me to Zav and back again. "Amazing."

Amazing, right. He must not have seen the part where I'd been getting my butt kicked by Shaygor and his orc underlings.

"It is most amazing when she vexes my enemies," Zav stated and turned back to me. "I detected that Shaygorthian was injured when I arrived. You struck a blow before he cowardly fled to the sky and sent his minions after you." Zav gave me that pleased, bedroom-eyes look of his, and I thought we might have ended up kissing again if Ti hadn't been there. Actually, he looked like he was thinking of kissing me, regardless.

I rested a hand on his chest. "Let's go back to the house. After you hear this story, you may want to do a lot more than vex Shaygor."

"I hope so." Ti rubbed his hands together. "It is time for the Silverclaw rule to be no more."

Zav eyed him. "I believe I am ready to hear this story."

CHAPTER 18

Zav listened in stony silence as Ti gestured expansively and shared the story he'd given me earlier.

We were in the dining room with Freysha, Dimitri, and Nin. Nin had returned with enough food to stock a Costco, and Dimitri had finally been able to close the shop and come home. Apparently, the goblins liked to stay late, swilling their coffee and playing board games that involved using a hand-cranked launcher to hurl dice across the room. The roll didn't count unless the dice hit at least two walls before landing.

While Ti relayed his tale, Zoltan wandered up to confer with Dimitri about which of his potions needed to be restocked in the shop. He slid into a seat at the table next to Freysha, where he kept eyeing her and Zav's necks. I remembered what he'd said about elf and dragon blood being extra appealing but assumed he wouldn't be foolish enough to try to claim any of either.

"If this is true," Zav said at the end of the story, "I must speak with the queen and my family's allies and come up with a plan to rescue my kin. *If* it is true." He squinted at Ti.

Ti lifted his hands. "I would not lie. I have risked much to come to the Ruin Bringer for help. I will succumb to a mind-scouring."

"Good. Come." Zav pointed to the back yard, and I detected a hint of compulsion to the order.

Ti followed him out.

Be gentle with him, Zav, I thought. *He's Nin's grandfather, and so far, he hasn't done anything suspicious. If we do what he asks, he's also willing to pay me enough gold to buy you all-you-can-eat barbecue ribs for life.*

We shall see. He gave me a long look over his shoulder as they walked out into the dark.

That made me wonder if I should have been more suspicious myself. But I trusted Nin, and she was certain this was her grandfather. Besides, Ti had been chased and almost died trying to get to me. It was hard to imagine all that being part of a ruse.

Dimitri mentioned being hungry, and Nin promptly led him into the kitchen.

I sat at the table next to Freysha and whispered, "Do you think Ti has been lying to us or holding anything back?"

"I did not get that sense from him, but like most with magical talent, he protects his thoughts from telepathic eavesdropping." Freysha peered out through the window. "If all this is true, it is a reason—if not an irresistible impetus—for Lord Zavryd's clan to go to war with the Silverclaw Clan. I am not aware of all of the nuances of the current dragon political situation, but such a war would affect people living all across the Cosmic Realms and cause a major upheaval for the dragons. Also, if the imprisoned Stormforge dragons could not be released and cured of that infection beforehand, Lord Zavryd and his kin would be at a disadvantage. The loss of so many family members during the last few centuries is the main reason that his clan's influence has been waning and that the Silverclaws and other dragons have claimed more positions on the Ruling Council and in the Justice Court. It is why they are so close now to staging a coup. We've all felt their maneuvering this last century."

"You haven't been alive for a century."

"I meant my kin." Freysha smiled. "Elves collectively. As well as the other intelligent species."

"Can't Zav's family rescue their kin without declaring war? Or will the Silverclaws consider that an opening volley?"

"It was in essence an opening volley for the Silverclaws. Once they know, the Stormforges will likely feel compelled to go to war over this massive affront whether they can win or not. Essentially, the Silverclaws have been secretly striking against them for centuries."

"Whether they can win or not? They better free the sick dragons first and cure them, so they can help the clan with the others."

"That is easier said than done. According to Ti—and I believe him—these Crying Caverns have numerous traps and alarms. I am certain the entire Silverclaw Clan would be made aware quickly if a flock of Stormforge dragons descended upon the area to mount a rescue. That might start the war right then and there, before any dragons could be freed, much less healed." Freysha looked toward Zoltan. "You created a formula to cure Ti of the bacterial infection. Would it work to cure a dragon?"

Zoltan folded his hands on the table. "As I told Val, I would need to inject a dragon with the bacteria and then give him the formula to see if it works. Do you think your dragon would volunteer, dear robber? I would be most curious to experiment on him."

"I'm sure he would love that," I muttered. "Are you ever going to start calling me Val? I paid your ludicrous invoice—I've paid several of them—and I've never stolen from you."

"The first time I encountered you, it was when you were breaking into my humble sanctuary and destroying my guard spider while holding a gun on me. I can think of less flattering things to call you than *dear robber*."

"You wouldn't worry about offending me and losing me as a client?"

"Not at all. My skills are in high demand. You need me."

Zav walked back into the house with Ti trailing behind him. The gnome's eyes were a little glassy, but he didn't appear harmed.

"Grandfather?" Nin came in and took his arm. "I made you some fish-eye soup when I was gathering beef and rice for the others. Come sit down and have some."

"You keep the ingredients for that in your food truck?" I'd only ever seen Nin serve one dish.

"I stopped at the store."

"What store carries fish eyes?"

"Any reputable Asian market. They are delicious, Val. Did your Norse ancestors not enjoy fish?"

"Yeah, the non-eyebally parts."

Nin gave me an exasperated look, then focused on preparing the meal for her grandfather.

He whispered something to her in Thai. She looked at Zav, shrugged, and whispered back.

"Everything okay?" I thought about tapping my translation charm—if Zav had been a bully, I wanted to know about it, so I could step on his foot the next time he wore sandals.

"My grandfather is feeling manly because he endured a dragon mind-scouring," Nin told me.

"Manly?" Dimitri asked.

"Just because someone is only half your size does not mean he can't be manly," Nin informed him.

Zav touched my arm. "I must speak with you."

He walked back outside, assuming I would follow. My curiosity ensured I would, but I lingered to examine Nin's dubious fish-eye soup and hear the rest of the manly discussion before joining him on the patio. I didn't like him to think he could snap his fingers and I would leap to obey.

When I stepped out and closed the door behind me, Zav was gripping his chin and staring up at the stars instead of huffing about my delay, and I felt guilty for worrying about making points at a time like this.

"What did you find out?" I asked quietly.

"The gnome believes everything he has said."

"Is that the same as he's telling the truth?"

"He is telling the truth as he sees it and has lived it. I am... inclined to believe there is some Silverclaw plan that has been in place against my family since before I was born, because they are cowardly and despicable and have no honor. This is what they resort to instead of fair fights. I have also found it strange that so many of my relatives have gotten sick and gone off to die, but this has happened to dragons from other clans too, so it seemed possible it was something natural. This suggestion that it is not..."

"I'm surprised you're not jumping up and down with fury and ready to charge off to war." I'd seen him get furious merely over an ogre picking a fight with me. This calmness now was almost eerie.

"I am seething with inner fury."

"Sounds uncomfortable."

"Yes." Zav stroked his chin. "I am attempting to weigh all the consequences and potential ramifications of taking action. As soon as I tell the queen, she will want to gather an army and strike. I admit that *I* want to do that. I would even volunteer to lead that army. But from what

I saw in the gnome's thoughts of this place, I worry that it's possible Shaygorthian or his ally could flip a switch and kill all of the imprisoned dragons. It is almost surprising that they haven't already. Why keep them alive when they could have killed them long ago and destroyed the evidence? It is hard to believe they care about obeying the tenets of our people about not killing other dragons. More likely, they feared reprisal. It is also possible they want to use them for bargaining—or blackmail. Will the Silverclaws try to force the queen to step down by threatening to kill our kin if she doesn't comply?" He shook his head slowly. "More than thirty members of my family have gone missing over the last few hundred years. Some I never knew, but I knew many of them. My uncle helped raise me after my father died."

"I'm sorry this has happened to you and your family." I stepped close and wrapped my arm around his waist.

"Yes." For a moment, he didn't move or acknowledge my embrace, and I wondered if he would prefer if I left him alone. Then he lowered his hand from his chin and rested his arm around my shoulders. "Another concern I must admit I have is that the queen might not be willing to listen to me right now. I visited her again to discuss Velilah'nav, and we had a heated argument. Our words were cross, and she told me not to come back until I've dissolved my claim on you and am willing to mate with one of my own kind."

I groaned. What crappy timing.

Before, I worried that he would succumb to his mother's wishes and walk away from me, but now, I worried about what would happen if he didn't. A lump formed in my throat as I wrestled the thought of losing him against the realization that it would be much easier on him if he left.

Even if I hadn't been on board with being *claimed* in the beginning, my feelings had changed. Now, I wanted to see where the relationship could go. The thought of him walking—flying—out of my life forever was heart-wrenching.

"Maybe you should do what she wants, so she'll speak with you and you can bring her this information," I made myself say, though tears threatened to fall.

Zav's arm tightened around my shoulders. "You wish me to dissolve my claim on you?"

"No, but if it's what you need to do to help your people…"

He grew still again and did not speak for several long moments. When he moved, it was to draw me closer and wrap both of his arms around me.

"No." It came out as a defiant growl, and he lifted a hand to the back of my head and stroked my hair. "You are mine. The queen will come to see your loyalty and value and that you *please* me, and she will accept it."

It sounded like he was describing a good hound, but by now, I was used to how he spoke and thought. Besides, I didn't feel like objecting to semantics tonight. I laid my face against his shoulder and hugged him tight.

"Can you tell your sister about all this and ask *her* to speak with your mother?" I suggested.

"Possibly." He started kneading the back of my head, and I melted against him. Then he kissed my ear. "It also pleases me that you wish to plan battles with me and assist my people."

"Well, I want to assist *you*. I'm not in love with the rest of your people. All the ones I've met have tried to flatten me or forcefully read my mind."

"Dragons are dangerous enemies."

"I've noticed."

"They are also dangerous family members."

"Sunday-night dinners at your house must be a blast."

"Sometimes, we fight over meat."

"Imagine my surprise."

He rubbed my head for a while before speaking again. I was happy to bask in the attention—and the delightful sensations flowing through my nerves—but I worried about his future. *Our* future.

"I am debating," Zav said, "if it would be possible to defeat the two Silverclaw dragons guarding that facility and sneak in and free my people before the rest of their clan figured out what was happening."

"Freysha thought they might have alarms that would go off if they sensed a bunch of dragons coming."

"That is likely, yes."

"Maybe they wouldn't notice a half-elf and a tiger. With a gnome guide."

Zav stepped back, his hands resting on my shoulders as he frowned sternly at me. "I am pleased that you wish to assist me, but this is a problem for dragons. It is too large for a half-elf and a tiger to handle."

"You forgot about the gnome."

The frown grew even sterner.

"*And* a vampire alchemist. Since Ti's predecessor—that gnome scientist who invented the bacteria—is gone, Zoltan may be the only one with experience eradicating this infection."

"He cannot accompany you to another world." His tone turned dry. "There is *light* there."

"He could prepare enough doses of his formula for me to take along. Assuming we can prove ahead of time that it works on dragons." I patted him on the chest. "That's where you would come in. How do you feel about lending your body to science?"

Zav's nostrils flared. "You want me to let him *experiment* on me?"

"If it'll get us a formula that can cure your family, isn't it worth it?"

He radiated distaste as he continued to gaze at me, but I could tell he was considering this.

I hoped it wasn't insane that *I* was considering this. It sounded like a suicide mission. My whole life had grown ten times more dangerous since Zav had come into it, bringing with him a whole passel of new dragon enemies. But did I truly regret that? I *liked* Zav. And maybe I was the tiniest bit tempted by the fact that Ti was willing to pay me enough to retire on if I actually managed to succeed.

"I would sacrifice myself so that my family could live," Zav said.

"I don't think you have to sacrifice yourself, just let a vampire poke needles into your veins."

"That sounds less palatable than sacrifice."

"Don't be overdramatic." I swatted him on the chest.

"If he is able to make a formula… and you are willing to go, I will go with you."

"Wouldn't the whole point be to avoid setting off the dragon detectors?"

"*If* I sense such a thing, and *if* I can't figure out how to mask my aura or otherwise elude the detectors, I will wait outside while you go in, but this will not be the case. I am cleverer than my more blunt kin. I can find a way to go in with you without setting off alarms."

"You're the non-blunt one in the family?"

"You do not believe me? You have met the queen. And my sister."

"This is true."

"Am I not more tactful?"

"I'm not sure if you're more tactful or I'm just more willing to find your arrogance charming because you're sexy and think I'm a great warrior."

His eyes narrowed as he gazed at me through his lashes. "You *are* a great warrior." His voice turned to a purr. "And I *am* sexy."

"I feel like I should object to such cocky statements, but I did see you earlier without your robe on." Smiling, I stepped in and kissed him.

Zav wrapped his arms around me again and returned the kiss, but there was a crease to his brow and tension in his mouth. He was worried. I was too. But if we could somehow make everything work out, it could return full power to his family and might solve problems for a lot of the innocent people in the Cosmic Realms. Maybe it would help my people, too, and keep dragon troubles away from Earth. So long as it didn't keep *my* dragon away from Earth.

My dragon whose hand drifted under my shirt, stroking his fingers across my bare skin. Little tingles of magic momentarily made me forget my worries. And everything we'd been talking about.

I might have gone on kissing him all night—or suggested we go up to the bedroom and finish what we'd started when Nin had interrupted us—but the back door opened, and Zoltan leaned out.

"Am I or am I not experimenting on your dragon tonight?" he asked without any apology for interrupting our kiss.

Zav glared coolly over at him, breaking the kiss but not letting go of me, neither with the hand on my butt nor the one that had found its way up to cup my breast. Why did I have a feeling Zav didn't care a whit about privacy and would be perfectly willing to have sex in a hot tub while a bunch of pervy goblins watched?

"I will allow you to use me to perfect a formula that will cure my kin," Zav finally said.

"Excellent." Zoltan practically skipped to the basement steps and down to his lab. Maybe he was fantasizing about sneaking a few more drops of dragon blood into his collection while he was working. He left the door open and his voice floated back. "I've already done the preliminary work with the bacteria, so I'm ready for you as soon as you can pull yourself away from your horny pleasures of the body."

"I do not like him," Zav stated.

"He's a vampire. I think most people feel that way."

He shifted his gaze back to me, letting his fingers stroke me a few more times. I almost suggested that Zoltan could wait a few hours, but Zav sighed and stepped back.

"The sooner we are able to act, the better. Shaygorthian will assume that you will tell me everything, and he may already be making plans to reinforce the facility." Zav's tone grew grim. "Or kill my kin so I won't have a chance to rescue them."

That bleak thought put thoughts of sex out of my mind, at least for the moment. If we somehow managed to succeed at this, I planned to kick everyone out of the house for the weekend and make the walls and floors shake with the vigor of our lovemaking.

Zav stepped toward the basement door, but he paused and looked over his shoulder. "You will not *pay* him for this. It is his honor to serve a dragon."

"Right." I was sure there would be an invoice on my desk in the morning.

CHAPTER 19

Work on the armored display cases in the shop was going slowly. I was distracted thinking of Zav back at home with Zoltan, letting the vampire experiment on him. I understood why Zav was willing to turn himself into a guinea pig to help his family—and I'd encouraged it—but it scared me. If the formula that had worked on Ti didn't work on him, and Zav ended up dying of some horrible bacterial infection, *then* what?

Dimitri caught my hand as I was about to swing my hammer. "You're supposed to hit that nail—" he pointed at the head of the nail I was holding, "—not that one." He pointed to the side of my swollen thumbnail, which I'd already hit once and had been about to clobber again.

"I knew I was doing something wrong."

"I assumed your half-elven agility would make you good at home improvements, but I guess it's only useful for slaying enemies."

"Ha ha. I'm distracted."

"You're lucky you heal fast."

"I know." I focused on the nail and hammered it in quickly. As quickly as I wished Zoltan's refining of the formula was going.

I'd hoped Zoltan would figure something out in a few hours the night before, but when I'd suggested that, he'd rolled his eyes and pointed out that the bacteria would take time to multiply in Zav's system and be substantial enough to register on his tests. There was no point to injecting the formula until then.

It was just as well that we had some time. I wanted to see Amber before I left, and say something pithy and wise to her, in case I didn't make it back. I wondered what she would think if I tried to impart everything I knew to her in two hours and then hugged her and cried in her hair before I left. She would probably flee to her room and bolt the door.

"You think these new cases will really keep ogres from trashing your breakables?" I asked.

"Once I magic them up, yes." Dimitri looked toward the full tables in the seating area. Nobody larger than a werewolf shifter chatting up a half-orc female was here now. The area was busy, though, with more than a few goblins—where did goblins get so much money for coffee?—mingling with kobolds and humans with mixed blood. People didn't seem to care that they had to stand or take their drinks outside where a few benches had been added around the side of the building. "I'm thinking of adding an electric buzz to deter anyone from touching them."

"I hear there's nothing better than a zap from a high-voltage current to excite someone about buying stuff."

"I'll put a sign on the cases, saying they need to get a manager to see them." Dimitri pointed a thumb at his chest.

"Why don't you sell LEGOs?" a young voice asked from the espresso stand.

It belonged to a scruffy troll kid with so much mud dried in his white hair that it appeared brown. His clothes were torn and grimy, and he was barefoot. It took me a moment to recognize him as the son of the deceased Rupert, the kid who'd wanted me to kill the dark elves who'd killed his father. Nin had said he'd stopped by the food truck a few weeks earlier looking for me, and she'd filled him in on the dark-elf story—as much of it as I'd told her—but I hadn't seen him again since then.

"We sell coffee and alchemy potions and yard art," Tam, the barista, said as she worked on orders, the steamer wand hissing.

"That's not an answer. LEGOs are better than any of those things."

As I walked over, I wondered what it meant that goblins and trolls and elves all liked the plastic building blocks. Probably that the manufacturer needed to expand to other planets.

"Do you have milkshakes?" the kid asked.

"I can make a Frappuccino," Tam said.

"What's that?"

"A milkshake with espresso in it."

"I don't think you're allowed to give eight-year-olds espresso," I said, coming up beside the blue-skinned troll kid. What was his name? Reb. He was even gaunter than the last time I'd seen him with his cheekbones far too prominent. I was positive all of his ribs would be visible if he took off that tattered shirt. "Better make him one without it."

I laid five dollars on the counter.

Reb gave me a mulish look, and I thought he might slink off, but the whir of the blender kept him in place as he alternated looking at that and the snacks on the shelf.

"I'm *nine* now," he said.

"Happy birthday." I grabbed a selection of nuts and string cheese that looked like something a kid might eat and that would be vaguely healthy—though he would probably eat anything right now—and set them on the counter for Tam to ring up. "How're you doing? You living on the streets?"

"Nah."

"Your people are taking care of you?" I couldn't keep the skepticism out of my voice. "Relatives of your father?"

Reb shrugged. "I'm staying with some other trolls in town, yeah. You have to scrounge and fight to get any food. It's okay. It's how it is when you're the littlest."

If he'd been a human kid, I would have tossed him in the Jeep and taken him to Child Protective Services, but they didn't acknowledge that trolls existed, much less find foster homes for them.

"You need a place to stay?" The idea of taking him home—the house was already weird and crowded enough—was horrifying, but maybe we could make it work until we found an appropriate troll who would take care of him. Who would take care of him and actually *feed* him.

He hesitated but shook his head. "Nah."

"You want a job?"

Tam placed a large milkshake on the counter in front of him, and his eyes grew wide with delight as he grabbed it.

"Am I supposed to charge you?" Tam whispered as she rang up the snacks.

"Oh, yes. Nin told me owners don't get special treatment and that we can only take out money—or coffee—after all the expenses have been calculated and we know there's a profit. Even then, we should roll the money back into the business." I was quoting her almost verbatim. Dimitri was lucky she'd approved a modest salary for him.

"She's a good business owner," Tam said.

"Yeah, I don't think we'll ever see her on any of those reality shows where gurus fix failing businesses. She could *be* the guru someday." I'd suggested that she take some time off and show Ti around Seattle. Instead, they were working together at her food truck today, crafting weapons and armor and whatever else excited gnome tinkerers.

I paid for the snacks and stuck them in Reb's soundest baggy pocket while he gulped from the milkshake glass.

"You want a job, Reb?" I repeated.

He eyed me warily over the glass, beige ice cream smeared all over his upper lip. "What kind of job?"

"Val?" Dimitri waved his hammer from across the room. "A word?"

"Picking up trash outside and cleaning up in here. Doing whatever grunt work Dimitri says to do. An hour or two a day when you can make it." Did trolls have the equivalent of school? I had no idea.

"You'd pay me in cash? Not those dumb pieces of paper?"

"Val?" Dimitri waved the hammer more vigorously, trying to summon me over.

I held up a finger.

"Cash," I told Reb, imagining he would get an odd look from a bank teller if he walked in and tried to cash a check.

"Can I start now?"

"Yeah. Finish up your drink, and then clean up the mess Dimitri and I are making building those display cases."

"Okay."

Slurping his milkshake, Reb wandered off to watch a group of goblins refining their dice launcher before their next game.

I dug into the cash I had left from my bodyguard gig and pushed some across the counter to Tam. "Stash that somewhere, please, and use it to feed him whenever he comes to work."

Tam nodded. "I would guess that Nin would be willing to send some extra meals over for us to keep in the fridge for him."

"Good. Thanks."

By the time I returned to Dimitri, his beefy arms were crossed over his chest and he was glowering.

"You can't hire people without asking me," he said. "Especially not people I'll end up having to babysit."

"I'll pay him on the side for his help."

"Help? You think a troll kid is going to be *help*?" Dimitri pointed his hammer at Reb. "The last trolls that were in here competed with the last ogres to see who could break the most stuff."

"Then it's a good thing we're beefing up the display cases. If he isn't useful, let me know, and I'll find something else for him to do."

Maybe he could pull weeds at the house. Though I didn't particularly want the troll community to know where I lived now.

"I'm glad *I* get to vet him."

"You're so grumpy. Do you need a Frappuccino?"

"No. I need my store to do well and for some of *my* goods to sell." Dimitri flattened a hand to his chest. "That was the whole point of this place. Not to employ trolls and make coffee."

"Maybe Nin will have some new marketing ideas for you at our next meeting. Have you managed to sell anything except the coffee yet?"

"Zoltan's under-eye cream is a big hit." Dimitri made a face.

"I'm sorry. I know selling your stuff is your dream." What I didn't know was if there was a big market for his recycled magicked-up yard art. Though we *had* sold some things at that farmers market.

His shoulders slumped. "I shouldn't complain, since the coffee shop I never wanted is already profitable. But it's hard not to feel..." He shrugged.

"I get it. Keep trying. The word should get out. It's a new location, and people may need to see some of your gizmos a few times before they want them. For instance, that..." I looked at one of the finished display cases, its shelves already laden with Dimitri's goods. "Is that a snail holding a toaster?"

"The snail *is* the toaster. It also opens beer bottles. See, there with its shell. That's the kitchen-appliance display case."

"Right. They may need to see that a few times before they realize they want it. Also, you may want to reconsider getting a liquor license."

Maybe he would get more impulse purchases if his visitors were drunk.

"I can't close before ten as it is. Why do goblins need to drink so much coffee and be up all night?"

"To tinker, I'd guess." I grabbed a few nails. "Hey, I'm going to leave some money behind when I go on this next mission. Will you buy some drywall, particle board, tiles, insulation, paint, and… whatever else the upstairs bathrooms need to have the floor, ceiling, and walls replaced? If we survive this, Zav said he'd help me eradicate the mold."

"How's he going to do that?"

"By eradicating everything the mold is growing on. Which could be most of the upstairs. Hence the need for supplies."

"You better leave a *lot* of money."

"If we survive this mission and it all goes as planned, I'll have plenty for home improvements." I thought the odds of us surviving and *anything* going as planned were low, so I didn't mention the gold.

"Do you think you will?" Dimitri frowned at me in concern. "From what I heard, it sounds nuts."

"Should I be concerned that the guy who treats building snail toasters as a normal thing thinks our plan is nuts?"

"Very concerned. Seriously, Val. Do you need to do this? I get that it would be kind of cool to go to another planet…" Did he look wistful? "But not to invade some dragon lair full of booby traps and piss off a ton of dragons. It sounds like they'll end up starting a war, and you'll be the little squishy human who could easily be trampled by accident."

"That's why I'm hardening myself with hammer blows to my thumb." I waved the tool.

"I'm serious."

"I know, and I don't disagree that it's unwise." As Sindari would be sure to tell me. "But Ti came specifically for me."

Dimitri lowered his voice, even though none of the coffee drinkers were paying a lick of attention to us. "Are we even sure that's *really* Nin's grandfather? The dude disappeared for twenty years—she thought he was dead. What if this is some shifter taking his form to mess with us?"

"He ate Nin's fish eyeball soup. That proves he's family."

"I'm still being serious, Val."

"Even if I couldn't detect it, I don't think a ruse like that would fool Freysha or Zav. Zav read his mind. Anyway, me going on this mission is more about Zav than Ti." I touched a hand to my chest. "I've come to care about him. You've probably guessed that."

"From seeing you two putting your tongues in each other's mouths here in our coffee shop? Yeah, I guessed."

My cheeks heated a few degrees. "Is that not allowed? I thought there were perks for owners."

"It gets the goblins excited."

"Yeah, but they're little pervs."

"True." Dimitri's frown faded. "Is there anything I can make you or give you to take along? I'd offer to go myself, but you've seen what kind of warrior I am."

"I actually haven't. Unless you're counting shooting a crossbow at that scientist in Weber's laboratory. Did you hit him?"

"I was ferocious and menacing. I scared him into fleeing."

I raised my eyebrows.

"Possibly it was all the naked vampires who scared him into fleeing."

"I think so. I doubt I need any yard art to take on my mission, but if I change my mind, I'll let you know." I *was* planning to stop by Nin's later to pick up a bunch of extra ammo. Maybe some grenades too. If this went to hell and dragons were waiting to attack us, I would make sure to give those Crying Caverns something to cry about before I got taken down myself. "If anything happens, would you mind checking on my mom from time to time? I'm sure she'll be fine, but she's getting older, and she doesn't really have anyone except Amber and me, and Amber's too young to go down there."

Dimitri's face grew bleak, and I thought he might protest my mission again, but he nodded. "I'll make sure she's doing okay. Help her find another van guy to rent her driveway if she needs it."

I snorted, not sure if Mom would appreciate that or not. But it did remind me that she'd mentioned that her property taxes had gotten high. If I survived this mission, I would give her some of the gold. Maybe I should update my will to leave her my ten percent of the coffee shop too. How horrified would Dimitri be if my mother moved up here to help keep an eye on things and imposed her opinions on how his business should be run?

It couldn't be any worse than one of the owners making out with a dragon in the main room.

"Thanks, Dimitri." I patted him on the shoulder. "You're a good guy."

"You're complimenting me? That means you're *positive* you're going to die, doesn't it?"

"No, it means I've learned to appreciate you."

He shook his head. "I don't believe you."

"I'll do my best to stay alive. Just don't forget to buy my drywall."

CHAPTER 20

Amber collapsed on the grassy lawn, letting her practice sword fall from her grip and moaning theatrically. "Why are you being so hard on me today? It's been *hours*."

"It's been less than two hours."

"That's a *ton*. I'm getting calluses." Amber thrust up her hand. "Swimmers aren't supposed to have calluses. Guys will think it's weird."

"Do you complain this much to your swim coach?"

"No. Swimming doesn't make me all sweaty and nasty." She glanced at her armpit and wrinkled her nose, then looked at her palm before letting the arm flop back down.

"You sweat when you swim. You're just in the water so you don't notice it."

"Gross."

"You're the one marinating in it." I crouched down beside her. "Before we finish, I want to go over a couple of defenses that are good against enemies with claws instead of swords and knives. You can rest for a few minutes first."

"Thanks *so* much." Amber lifted her head—we were in the back yard of her house, the grassy lawn framed by a large patio and fire pit on one side and tiers of retaining walls and perennial bushes in the back. The neighborhood was on a long hill that overlooked Puget Sound, giving most of the houses views of the water and downtown Edmonds below.

"Did you hear Dad's car pulling into the garage? If that's him, he might need me. He could have groceries or something."

"I didn't hear anything." My ears would have heard the garage door opening. I recognized an attempt to get out of training when I saw one. "We won't do much more. I promise."

Amber let her head flop back into the grass with another dramatic moan. "What's the deal, anyway? We usually only do an hour."

"I know, but I'm not sure... Never mind."

She frowned at me. "What?"

"I'm going on a dangerous mission. In case I don't make it back, I want to make sure I've taught you all the basics."

"You think you're going to die?"

"I hope not."

"Will you leave me your sword if you do?"

I snorted. Ah, the love and concern of teenagers. "I'm sure my sword will fall into whatever pit or chasm that I also fall into. If anyone gets it, it'll probably be a dragon or some heinous enemy."

"That sucks."

"Sorry. I'd get a magic sword for you if I could."

"A magic sword that could poke a dragon in the ass." A familiar flash of anguish haunted her eyes as she mentioned dragons—alluding to whatever Zondia had done when she'd been questioning Amber about me. Mind-scouring, probably. I hated all of the dragons that had bothered Amber, but Zondia seemed the worst, since she should have been an ally, not an enemy.

"Unfortunately, they don't sell them at 7-Eleven."

I thought of the magical swords those orcs I'd battled on Weber's property had used. And all the weapons in that stash. Willard's people had collected them, but I wondered if she would authorize one for Amber. I should have thought to simply snag one that day. It wasn't as if Weber had needed them after he died. But I hadn't known anything about them. I might have ended up with a sword that turned out to have a life-sucking soul trapped inside that constantly tried to take over its wielder's mind. I'd heard of such things. Possibly in fantasy books and not in reality, but I couldn't remember. The two tended to mesh for me.

"I'll see if I can get one for you. My boss has some in her vault. I'll put in the request before I go on this mission, so it'll happen whether I die or not. But only if you do these last exercises with me." I smiled and raised my eyebrows.

Amber sat up. "Do you seriously think you're going to die? Why would you go?"

"For Zav. For Earth. For Nin's gnomish grandfather who's going to pay me a lot if we succeed."

"Nin? Is that the woman with the *local business* that Dad keeps supporting?" Amber squinted at me.

"Uh, does he?" I wondered if Amber had gotten a vibe that Thad thought Nin was cute—or whatever had prompted him to ask me for her food truck name. And if so, what did she think? Amber had spent the summer trying to get rid of the last girlfriend. "He said he was going to go down there for lunch the other day."

"He's been down there three times this week. He keeps bringing back food wrapped in brown paper. Who puts rice in brown paper?"

"It's a traditional dish."

"And traditional brown paper?"

"Maybe."

Amber's nose wrinkle didn't have anything to do with armpit sweat this time. "Why can't he just be single for a while? Like until I go to college."

"Maybe he's lonely."

"*I'm* here."

And a delight, I was sure. I kept myself from saying that.

"I just don't want another bitchy woman in the house wandering around in his robe." Amber rolled her eyes. "So disgusting. And they're always angling for things from him. What is up with that? Dad isn't *that* rich." Another eye roll.

"I think it's too early to know if they're even going to date, but I'm positive Nin wouldn't angle for anything from anyone. She's determined to make her way in America on her own. And she is. Her business does very well."

"Does she have a BMW of her *own* so she doesn't have to ask Dad to buy her one?"

"I'm sure she could have one if she wanted one, but she's frugal. She's saving for a house and to bring her family to America." I decided not to mention how *large* Nin's family was, though I was tempted to torment Amber by saying that if Nin and Thad got serious, Nin's mother and grandmother and sisters might *all* end up in her house, wandering around in bathrobes.

My eyes must have twinkled at this thought, because I got another suspicious glower.

My phone buzzed, giving me a reason to step away without explaining my twinkle. It was Willard.

"Hey, Willard. Do you have any extra magical swords you don't need?" I wandered over and sat on the brick fire pit.

"That's not what I called to talk about."

"It's what I answered to talk about."

"Funny. I got your message about this mission you've decided you're taking. You left more details than usual. I'm not sure that's a good thing."

"I felt safe being thorough to your voice mail, since it couldn't interrupt me to tell me how unwise I am."

"I'm hoping the cell carrier adds that feature soon. Tell me you're not planning on going to this dangerous place on another planet to attempt to sneak past a passel of enemy dragons with nobody but Zav and Nin's grandfather."

"I'm not sure if Zav is coming. We think they'd detect him."

"Oh, even better. An ancient gnome is your only backup."

"Sindari is coming."

"And he likes fighting dragons?"

"No, he reminds me how dumb I am every time I do it."

"I'm starting to like him."

"Nin's grandfather isn't that ancient—gnomes live for centuries—and he says he knows the way in and where all the booby traps are."

"If that's somehow enough and you can sneak past all the bad guys, which one of you medical experts is going to cure the infected dragons so they can leave? I assume you don't plan to carry them out on a sledge."

"Zoltan's working on a dragon version of the formula that cured Ti."

"And you know how to inject it? And you're sure it'll work on dragons that have been in some kind of magical hibernation for years? And that there won't be complications?"

"No, but I'll ask Zoltan for instructions." Complications? I hadn't considered that. What if the dragons keeled over and needed a dragon doctor? "Possibly a flow chart."

"You should take a team of qualified personnel. I've called Dr. Walker to see if he's willing to go with you."

"I'm sure your handsome shifter doctor is lovely, but I don't want to take a stranger along, and I don't know why he would go with me on a dangerous mission anyway."

"Because I'd *pay* him. That's how it works."

"The government is willing to invest in this mission?"

"I'll figure something out. This sounds important and like it would be good for Earth if Zav's family came out on top." Willard sighed. "I'm tempted to come along with you. If this all goes sideways, maybe someone with a diplomatic streak could keep you from getting killed."

"And that's you?"

"I'm more diplomatic than you."

"That's saying amazingly little."

Willard snorted. "You're at least taking Walker. I insist."

"This isn't a mission that you assigned me. You don't get to insist." I was arguing more out of habit—and because I didn't know this doctor well—than because I thought it would be a bad idea to have someone with medical expertise along. A big feline shifter ought to be able to fight to some extent too.

"Consider it assigned. If you free all those dragons, and if we can strike up some kind of treaty with Zav's family to order dragon-kind to leave Earth alone, I'll pay you double your usual fee."

I thought about pointing out that Ti had already offered a ridiculous amount, but Nin would punch me if she were there and tell me that a smart businesswoman got paid twice for the same service if possible. Besides, Willard always paid. I didn't *think* Ti would swindle me, but there were no guarantees in life.

"You're the boss."

"How rare for you to acknowledge that."

"I'm sucking up so you'll get my kid a sword."

Amber had wandered over and was listening to my side of the conversation. She raised her eyebrows hopefully.

"Does she know which end goes in the dragon yet?" Willard asked.

"She's my daughter. She's smart enough to know about pointy ends."

"I'll have Corporal Clarke bring some weapons we've already researched over for you to pick from. Now that she's learning how to defend herself, I was actually going to ask if you thought she should have something magical, since she's a dragon magnet."

"So I didn't have to suck up?"

"Nope, but I appreciated it. Next thing, you'll be calling me colonel instead of *Hey, Willard.*"

"Now you're just getting delusional." I gave Amber a thumbs-up as I ended the call.

"Thanks, Val," she said. "I hope you don't die."

"So you get your sword?"

"Just 'cuz." She shrugged. "You know."

My daughter didn't want me to die. Was that considered a breakthrough? A ridiculous amount of emotion welled up in my throat, and I barely managed to keep my eyes from filming with tears.

I was positive Amber would freak out if I hugged her, so I kept myself to a casual return shrug and said, "Yeah. I know. Ready to learn the moves for defending against paw swipes from shifters in animal form?"

Amber rolled her eyes and slouched away with melodramatic weariness. "I *guess.*"

So this was motherhood. Huh.

CHAPTER 21

After checking on Zoltan in the basement—Zav was looming over his shoulder and watching him fiddle with a microscope—I went to bed early. Even though it had been a couple of days since my battle with Shaygor, I'd been tired all week. As usual, I wasn't sleeping well, with either insomnia or nightmares plaguing me most nights, but unlike usual, the weariness was palpable during the days. My edge was gone, and with this mission looming, that worried me.

I flopped into my bed, hoping for one good night of sleep.

Zav, his nights occupied by being poked and prodded—and infected—by Zoltan, hadn't suggested sexy times, but I wondered if that would help. A little stimulation and exercise before bed? I also wondered if we might miss our chance if we didn't do it soon. If one of us didn't walk away from this mission, would the other regret not having *truly* become mates? In all senses of the word?

With that bleak thought in my mind, I wasn't surprised when I had nightmares as soon as I fell asleep. A giant bee that breathed fire chased me through downtown Seattle, and I tried to escape it by riding on the monorail to the Space Needle, but a pack of werewolves wielding bows and arrows was waiting to jump me when I got off.

I woke up with sweat dampening my nightshirt and my braid wrapped around my throat. My phone told me I'd only been asleep for twenty minutes. I slumped back on my pillow exhausted and annoyed with the stupidity of my imagination. Bees? I was attacked regularly by dragons, and my brain conjured up giant bees?

My phone buzzed, and a text illuminated the screen. *Your dragon is being difficult.*

Zoltan? With the dream still fading from my mind, it took me a moment to gather my wits.

Of course, it is Zoltan. Who else contacts you in regard to your dragon?

More people than you'd think, but not usually people living in the same house.

I assumed you did not wish me to enter your bedroom uninvited.

I imagined waking up to vampire fangs in the dark—that would be as bad as the giant bee. *Right. I'm on my way down.*

I changed into a T-shirt that hadn't been maligned by nightmare sweat and went downstairs, pausing in the back yard to breathe in the fresh night air before going into the basement. The late summer air smelled of recently cut grass, a welcome change from the musty interior of the house's upstairs. If I survived this, I vowed to take a week off and get my new home fixed up.

As I turned for the basement steps, a dragon that wasn't Zav came within my range. I stopped and groaned, almost reaching out to him to tell him to deal with her.

But Velilah spoke into my mind first. *You have not told him to leave and return to his kind.*

No, I haven't. He doesn't take orders from me. Or you.

Unless he is incredibly foolish, he will take orders from his queen. She wishes that he mate with me.

Look, he's here in the house. If you want to discuss it with someone, discuss it with Zav. I suspected this attempt to circumvent him meant she already had and hadn't found him receptive. Good.

His clan is at risk from political machinations among the dragons.

No shit.

The Stormforges need an alliance, and my clan is willing to offer it, but only if he mates with me and promises them preferential positions in the Ruling Council.

Not my problem. Go talk to him.

I was about to warn Zav that she was pestering me, but she stopped speaking and also stopped flying closer. Interestingly, she was over by the dog park where we'd battled Shaygor. Could she sense some remnant of the fight? Did she know anything about the Crying Caverns or that the

Silverclaws and Stormforges might be at war soon? If Zav were to mate with her, would his family have enough allies to win that war?

That same uncertainty that I'd felt in the elven sanctuary returned, bringing to mind the decision my father had made to leave my mother and go back to marry someone he didn't love because it could help his people. Then, I'd been afraid Zav would do the same. Now that I suspected he wouldn't, I was afraid again, afraid he was making a big mistake in picking me. I didn't want him to go mate with some bitch that only wanted to use him to better her family's position, but… what if she had twenty dragons in her clan, twenty dragons who would help Zav's clan against the manipulating Silverclaws?

I shook my head. No. *I* was going to help Zav. Me, along with Sindari, Ti, and Willard's rich shifter doctor. We would sneak in, heal and free Zav's relatives, and then he wouldn't need to bow to the queen's pressure. He could stay with me or choose whoever he wished because it was what he truly wanted, not because of politics.

I told her to go away, Zav spoke into my mind. *Come join me.*

Will she listen to you this time? Or do we need to get a restraining order?

What is that?

Our court would order her to refrain from stalking you and arrest her if she doesn't comply. I imagined a plucky young police officer walking up to a dragon and delivering that order. That would go well.

Vermin laws do not apply to dragons. Come join me in the vampire's abode. He is being rude.

That's the basement in my *abode. Zoltan doesn't even pay rent, despite being richer than the rest of the people living in this house.*

So, he is an unsatisfactory ally to all. I will inform him thus.

The female dragon flew out of my range. Good. We had enough to deal with without a dragon stalker.

Another text buzzed on my phone as I descended the steps.

Your dragon is still being difficult, Zoltan's message read. *Where are you?*

I opened the door instead of answering, worried about what Zav might be doing to our unsatisfactory ally. Our unsatisfactory ally that we were depending on to concoct a formula to heal Zav's kin.

Zav was inside the lab, his arms folded over his chest, and glowering. His powerful aura buzzed with threatening magic. Zoltan glowered back while waving a needle around, but he was keeping a good six feet away.

"Are you being difficult?" Ignoring Zav's glower and his dangerous aura, I slid up to his side and patted him on the butt.

"He has already taken a sample of my blood. I do not believe he needs more of it. He wishes only to retain dragon blood for his nefarious alchemical purposes."

"Untrue," Zoltan said. "I need to check your blood again to see if the signs of infection are gone."

"You can see from looking at me that I am hale and not diseased." Zav gestured from his face, down his robed form, to his feet.

My gaze snagged there. I didn't know when he'd found time to acquire new shoes, but he had. Sort of. These were brown shoes with teal highlights. They had thick soles and ventilation holes all over. It looked like a hiking boot and a water shoe had gotten drunk together and had babies. Someday, I would ask Zav to take me to the shoe store with him. I had to find out if the merchant was messing with him or genuinely trying to find the right footwear for this frequent and fussy client.

"That's not how it works." Zoltan gave me an exasperated look and flung a hand toward Zav. "Tell him."

"I don't know how it works either. What are you looking for? Antibodies that would show he fought off the bacteria?"

"I am simply looking to see if there is still evidence of bacteremia— bacteria in the blood stream—as there was before. He should be relieved, because many bacterial infections are focused in the gastrointestinal tract, which would have required he give me stool samples for analysis."

"He should be relieved, or you are?"

"I should think we both would be." Zoltan lifted his needle toward Zav. "Now that I've thoroughly explained myself *twice*, will you allow me to take your blood?"

"Do not imply that I am unintelligent, vampire."

"Do not be so uptight and paranoid, dragon."

"Lesser beings concoct all manner of plots against my kind. We are rightfully suspicious of them."

"What if you stick around, watch the test, and incinerate the blood after he's done checking it?" I suggested to Zav.

"That's hardly necessary," Zoltan said.

His protest made me wonder if he did indeed plan to keep some of Zav's blood for his experiments. I gave him a hard look.

"Fine, fine." Zoltan lifted his hands. "I care not what he does with it after I examine it."

"Very well." Zav lowered his arms and looked at me. "If the vampire tries anything shifty, I will give him to Velilah'nav to eat."

"Are vampires palatable?"

"No. But Velilah'nav wishes me to go somewhere with her so she can sample the food of this world."

"She's angling for you to feed her? I knew there was a reason I wanted to kick her ass."

Zav's eyelids drooped contemplatively. "I do not believe such a battle would go well for you, but you *did* wound Shaygorthian."

"Yes, I did." I quirked an eyebrow at his speculative bedroom eyes. "Are you fantasizing about me battling her right now?"

"Possibly. I do not care for the way she is attempting to manipulate me, and you know I like it when you vex my enemies." He wrapped an arm around my waist.

Zoltan cleared his throat before Zav and I ended up kissing over this shared fantasy of ass-kicking. "I am prepared to take the blood sample."

Zav glowered at him but lifted his forearm and shook the voluminous sleeve of his robe so that it fell to his elbow. "Do so. Know that I am watching you."

"And contemplating eating me apparently." Zoltan came warily forward with his needle.

"No, I wanted to give you to another dragon to eat."

"*Much* better."

As Zoltan finished taking a small vial of blood, a distant dong sounded. The doorbell? I didn't sense anyone with a magical aura standing on our porch. I glanced at the time on my phone. It was after eleven.

The ceiling beams creaked as someone walked to the door. Maybe Dimitri had ordered pizza. He usually got back late from the coffee shop.

"Running the test will take some time." Zoltan headed to his centrifuge.

"I will wait." Zav wasn't taking his eyes from his blood sample.

"I won't. I'm going back to bed. If this works, I assume we'll be able to leave soon." Even though I'd been bracing myself for this for days, a fresh twinge of nerves assailed my gut.

"I have already prepared doses of the formula," Zoltan said, "as

I am quite confident this will have worked. You can go tomorrow if you wish."

"I'll let Willard know."

A knock at the basement door startled me.

It opened, and Dimitri leaned his head inside. "Val, are you down here?"

"Yeah."

"Did you order barbecue delivery?"

"No. I assumed you ordered a pizza."

"A pizza is what I *would* order... if I had ordered something. But I didn't." Dimitri stepped in and held up two large, bulging paper bags. "This came already paid for though. The guy just left it on the porch. It was a delivery car from one of the local restaurants. If it wasn't you, was it a mistake? Maybe some neighbor ordered it. Or Freysha? Do elves eat barbecue?"

"Barbecue?" Even though Zav was in human form, his twitching nostrils reminded me of a wolf. "Those bags are full of meat."

"I would ask if *you* ordered barbecue," I told him, "but I doubt you've set up a Paypal account."

"I have ordered nothing."

"Would it be wrong of us to eat it?" Dimitri sniffed the bag. "It smells really good. Maybe one of the neighbors thought one of us is cute and had it sent as a housewarming gift."

"People send plants for housewarming gifts, not bags of barbecue." I eyed them. "Unless you can have Zoltan test it for poison, I wouldn't touch it. I have enemies, remember."

"Enemies who know you adore barbecue?" Dimitri sounded disappointed and like he truly wanted some neighbor who thought he was cute to have sent it to him.

"Actually, *Zav* adores barbecue." I liked it, but I wasn't the one who'd eaten eight servings of ribs on our first date. Not that anyone except the staff at that restaurant would know that. And his sister. Zondia had been spying on us that night. But would she send poisoned ribs to her own brother? That didn't make sense. She cared enough about him that she'd been determined to save him from *me*. Maybe this was just someone's guess. It couldn't be a secret that dragons liked meat. "Does someone want to poison you, Zav? Like one of those Silverclaw dragons?"

"No dragon would resort to such a cowardly way of attacking a rival," Zav stated.

"Are you sure? Because we're planning a mission to rescue a whole passel of dragons who were poisoned and stored in a magical cavern."

Zoltan lifted a finger. "It's a bacterial infection, not a poison."

I walked over and took the bags from Dimitri—I had to tug because his fingers were slow to release the prizes. "Test these for signs of the bacteria, Zoltan."

"That is a menial task for an alchemist of my caliber."

"Does that mean I'm going to have to pay you to do it?"

"You're a much swifter robber than I guessed when we first met." Zoltan smiled and took the bags.

"You thought I was a dummy? I'm offended."

"You did barge in looking like the female version of Rambo as you assaulted my guard tarantula."

Hm, Amber had also compared me to Rambo. Maybe my wardrobe needed an overhaul.

Zav watched as Zoltan unwrapped racks of barbecue ribs from tinfoil, and the delicious scents of smoked pork filled the basement. He wasn't drooling, but he had to be close.

"We have food upstairs if you want something," I told him. "Nin brought all that beef and rice. Same goes for you, Dimitri."

He also appeared to be on the verge of drooling. "I know. I'll heat some up." With a wistful look toward the bags, he headed back upstairs.

I patted Zav's arm. "Do I need to drag you out for your own safety?"

"No." He folded his arms over his chest again. "I will wait for the results of the test before consuming anything. And I will make sure my blood sample doesn't get secreted away in a vault."

"Blood samples go into refrigerators, good dragon," Zoltan said. "I'll text you the results of the test, dear robber."

"Great." I headed back upstairs to sleep while I could.

Freysha stepped out of her room as I passed it. It wasn't dark as one would expect at this hour. A desk light was on and books filled the area, along with some charms from the Weber collection.

"Val? I believe I've identified what another one of these trinkets does. I suspected from the beginning, but I wasn't able to activate it, so I wasn't sure. It's one of the dragon-crafted ones."

"So, it's super powerful and would allow us to defeat a horde of dragons?"

"Not quite. But I believe it could allow you to *hide* from a horde of dragons."

"I've already got a charm that lets me do that." I waved to my thong.

"I know, but I thought you might want another one for your mission, so Ti or someone else can also hide."

"Ah, good thinking. And yes, I'm sure that would be useful."

"It may even be able to hide more than one person. The activation term I tried that finally worked roughly translates as *let us disappear. Us.*" She stepped back into the room and grabbed a note with a word written on it.

"So, our whole group could be camouflaged from dragons?"

"From everyone, yes. A small group. I believe everyone has to be touching the charm for it to work."

I imagined Ti and Dr. Walker advancing through a cavern, clasping hands with the charm pressed between their palms. Very intimate for near-strangers. Though I supposed that since Walker had inserted a catheter for Ti, they'd already trodden the path of intimacy.

"Are you sure one person can't just grip the shoulder of the person holding the charm?" I asked.

"I am not. It didn't come with instructions." Freysha handed me the charm and the paper.

"Hence the research. Right. This is what I say to activate it?" I tried it and mangled the word. Naturally, anything in the dragon language was unpronounceable.

It took more than ten tries and corrections from Freysha before she said it was working. She took several steps back and nodded. "At this distance, I can no longer see or sense you."

"Good. Thanks for doing all this research. I know that wasn't part of the deal."

Freysha shrugged. "You are my sister. Also, I like research and books of all kinds."

"As much as you like plants?"

"Equally. Books *about* plants are my favorites. Also books about engineering. And oh, books about engineering *with* plants." She clasped her hands in front of her chest and oozed adoration for this notion.

"I'm guessing there aren't a lot of those."

"They are rare, usually written by half-bloods. Elves who married dwarves or gnomes and wanted to help others bridge the cultural divide. Half-bloods do have purpose." She smiled encouragingly at me.

"Does that mean I'd be more welcome in Elf Land if I wrote books?"

"It could. Helping the Stormforge dragons and defeating the Silverclaws would likely also earn you a place of honor in the city."

"Sounds like less work than writing a book."

"More dangerous though." Freysha lowered her hands. "I am worried about your mission."

"Me too."

"Do you want me to come to help? I am not a warrior, but I have a few tricks, as you have seen." She wriggled her fingers.

Yes, the fire-retardant plant barrier had been handy, as had been the vines that had grown up and grabbed that creature's feet. I was sure she could help on this mission, but...

"Are you like the heiress to the elven kingdom? Would Eireth be pissed if I let you get killed?"

"He would be distressed if I died, because he is my father. I am his only full-blooded child at this time, so it is likely I would one day be considered to rule after him, but blood is not everything among our people. Positions can be hereditary, but if the people don't agree that the heir or heiress is a good leader, that person will not be chosen. Also, the ruling dragons on their council have a say these days in who they want to deal with as the leader of the elves."

"So, he'd miss you, but the elven kingdom wouldn't necessarily fall apart without you."

"Correct."

I closed my eyes, imagining myself returning to Veleshna Var and telling Eireth that I'd survived but that Freysha hadn't made it. The thought was horrible, and given my luck, it was exactly what would happen. I'd survived before when people close to me had died. I already hated the idea of taking Dr. Walker and risking his life.

"You better stay here." I opened my eyes. "This isn't really your fight."

"Is it yours?" Freysha raised her eyebrows.

"Since those Silverclaw dragons are a threat to Earth, and since I want to shag Zav, yes."

"What is... shag?"

"You better look it up in one of your books." I squeezed her shoulder and waved goodnight. "The Urban Dictionary, if you have a copy."

"Colonel Willard did not give me that book," Freysha called after me. "Strange."

CHAPTER 22

I managed to sleep until almost dawn, when the creak of my bedroom door opening and the aura of a powerful dragon entering woke me. My lungs were tight, and my first instinct was to reach for the inhaler in the drawer of my bedside table, but my ongoing reluctance to use it in front of others—in front of Zav—kept me from making the move.

He came in and sat on the edge of the bed and stroked the side of my head. Did he have randy thoughts in mind? Maybe not. His touch was gentle, not provocative, and the sweetness of the gesture, especially coming from my haughty dragon, warmed my heart. It also made me wonder if he had bad news, since he didn't usually pop into my bedroom before sunrise.

I reached up and laid my hand on his. "Is everything all right?"

His face was shrouded in the pre-dawn gloom. "The meat was tainted. Infected with the bacteria."

I sat up and swore.

"You were wise to question it," he added.

After all the times I'd been called unwise this summer, I should have been delighted at the compliment—and I wasn't unappreciative—but I was too busy being concerned to bask in it. Someone had tried to take out Zav.

It was possible the tainted meat had been meant for me, but two racks of ribs were surely designed to tempt a dragon more than a half-elf. Maybe our enemy had hoped everyone in the house would eat from the free meal and die.

No, not die. At least not right away. But if we'd gotten sick and passed out, we would have been easy targets for whatever whims our enemies had in mind.

The swirl of emotions made my chest even tighter. I was going to have to use the damn inhaler if I didn't want to end up wheezing in front of Zav.

"I'm glad none of us ate it." I leaned against Zav's side and surreptitiously tried Mary's 4-7-8 breathing technique to try to calm my body—and my lungs—while he wrapped an arm around me.

"Yes. I believe Shaygorthian was responsible."

I debated whether I agreed. It *did* seem like a scheme one of the dragons would have arranged, since their kind wouldn't be fully familiar with how food delivery worked on Earth. They wouldn't have known that we would be suspicious of pre-paid food arriving late at night out of nowhere. If nobody else had been in the house, would *Zav* have been suspicious? Or would he, taking for granted that dragons were superior beings destined to be served by lesser species, have believed it normal for some admirer to send him a gift?

"Have you sensed Shaygor since we drove him off at the park?" I asked between breaths.

"No. But he could be on Earth and hiding himself from me, as Dobsaurin did when he was plotting against me."

"True. But we did both sense your would-be girlfriend last night. Maybe she didn't truly come for a date."

"Velilah'nav?"

"Do you have other would-be girlfriends?"

"Dragons do not use that word. Nor is there *dating*. Once our potential mates have proven themselves worthy, we choose them decisively and promptly."

"And without always telling them first." I nudged him with an elbow and smiled, though I eyed my drawer again. The breathing exercise wasn't doing that much, maybe because I was trying to have a conversation in the middle of it.

"That is rare, but sometimes it is for their own good."

"Uh huh."

"You are fortunate another dragon did not choose you first."

"That *would* have been a nightmare." I doubted there had been any danger of that, since most other dragons I'd met wanted to kill me, not date me.

"I know this."

A part of me wanted to stick a pin in his bubble of pomposity, but not now. I wrapped my arms around him and hugged him, glad we'd caught the ruse and glad he was okay.

"If I die, you will not mate with that Starsinger oaf," Zav stated firmly.

"You're not actually worried about that, are you?"

"He has informed me that he wishes to *tysliir* you." Zav pulled me into his lap and hugged me.

It was a possessive hug, and I almost teased him, but again, it didn't seem like the time. Had he been worrying about his own mortality all night while he'd been watching Zoltan test the food and his blood?

"He was trying to vex you," I said. "If you were dead, he wouldn't care about me. You dragons are big-time into vexing each other."

"In older, more civilized days, we settled our differences with duels to the death."

So civilized. "Deaths are much better than vexation, I'm sure."

"Yes." He missed my sarcasm and sighed wistfully. "I've often wished I'd been born back in those times. The backstabbing and manipulating that modern dragons do is wearisome and immature."

"Then you never would have met me."

"That would have been unfortunate." Zav lifted a hand to thread his fingers into my hair and kiss me.

Normally, I would have found that a good way to start the morning, but I was still preoccupied by the tightness in my chest. The last thing I wanted was for us to finally have sex only for me to collapse in an asthmatic fit.

Besides, as silly as it was in comparison, I also worried that I hadn't brushed my teeth yet. Not that Zav seemed to mind. Funny how he never smelled like body odor or morning breath. Magic was a wonderful thing. It kept a man from stinking and needing to shave.

That thought made me pull back, realizing I'd never seen for myself if the spot he'd shaved had grown back. "I have to see it."

"It?" Puzzled, he looked down toward his crotch.

"Not *that*. Unless you shaved a lot higher up than I guessed."

"Ah." He shifted me to the side so that he could lift one of his legs and prop it on the opposite knee. "Making it magically grow back has not been as simple as I expected."

"No? What's the problem?" It was still dim, so I leaned over and turned on the bedside lamp. I used the movement to casually open the drawer and slip out my inhaler, covering it with my palm so he wouldn't notice it. In a moment, I would slip off to the bathroom to use it in private.

Zav pushed up the hem of the robe, showing off a nicely muscular calf and shin. A three-inch-long, half-grown-in stripe of bristly hair the width of my razor was right on the shin where it was hard to miss.

Zav prodded it. "The strands are going straight up instead of lying in the same direction as the other ones."

I laughed softly and rested my forehead on his shoulder. "That's just how it works as it grows out. They'll lie down once they're longer."

"Hm."

I pushed his hand aside and stroked my fingers down his shin. "By the time we get back from this mission, it'll probably all be the same length. If you ever want to experiment with razors again, I'll get you some articles on manscaping."

"Manscaping?" he murmured, his eyes closing to slits as he watched my hand on his leg.

"Never mind. I like you with a natural look."

He reached for my hand and removed it from his leg. "I must stop you from touching me, or I will forget to tell you my plan. We may have little time before it must be enacted."

I'd been about to tell him I had to go to the bathroom, but I paused. "Plan?"

"Remember how we spoke of how difficult it would be for a dragon to sneak into these Crying Caverns?"

"Yes, but oh. Freysha identified another of the charms, and it's for camouflaging someone. We might be able to sneak our whole group in."

He frowned thoughtfully. "That could work, but I am certain the Silverclaws designed this compound specifically to deter other dragons, so I may have trouble sneaking in, no matter what magic I employ."

"We'll find a way in. We've got Ti to guide us."

"I am considering letting them take me in."

"Them? Shaygor?"

Zav nodded. "I could pretend that I fell for the ruse and place myself somewhere nearby where he would be certain to find me. He would take me back to the caverns, and when he attempted to imprison me, I would rise up and battle him. It is possible that another Silverclaw dragon would be there—the gnome mentioned a second one, correct?—so it would be desirable for you and your allies to attempt to reach the caverns at the same time. You could assist me with the second dragon. I have no fear of surviving a battle against Shaygorthian, but even cowardly dragons are powerful, and fighting two at once would be difficult, especially in the confines of a cave."

"I see you've been thinking about this all night."

"Glaring at the vampire was not mentally taxing."

"Maybe not for you. I bet he spent time being taxed by it."

"What do you think of my plan?" Zav genuinely seemed to want my opinion.

This touched me as much as his proclamation that I was wise, and I reached up and stroked the side of his face.

His eyebrows twitched. "I am uncertain whether this is a gesture of adoration or pity."

"Do dragons often get pitied by lesser beings?"

"You may believe I am going to die and therefore feel sorry for me." Dying was definitely on his mind.

"I'm adoring you, but I do have concerns about this plan. Three that I can think of right away. First off, how do you know it's going to be Shaygor and not the female? I'm more suspicious of her since she was on Earth—in my *neighborhood*—when the food was delivered."

"Her clan should not be plotting against mine. Over the years, they have been aligned with the Stormforges, not the Silverclaws. The queen promised her a favorable position if she mated with me."

"What if she's secretly mating with Shaygor and has been promised an even better position on your Ruling Council if his clan succeeds in taking over everything?"

"They have not magically marked one another to let other dragons know they have claimed each other."

"If it's a secret plan, they wouldn't. Or couldn't they be working together without all the mating stuff?"

Zav sighed, his gaze dropping. I made sure my other hand was still positioned to hide the inhaler.

"None of this would be honorable," he said.

"But you've admitted that times have changed and not all dragons *are* honorable anymore, right?"

"Correct. Very well. I will not dismiss the possibility that she is involved. If she is, I will resume fantasizing about pinning her down while you poke her in the backside with your sword."

"Kinky."

He mouthed the word, then asked, "Twisted or curled?"

"I think the dictionary updated on you again."

"Humans change the meanings of their words extremely frequently."

"Sorry." I held up two fingers. "Second potential problem with your plan. What if they have a way to tell if you've been infected or not? Could a dragon that knows what he's looking for see into your body and tell if the bacteria are present?" All this talking was making me breathless and more aware of the need to use my inhaler. I needed to break away from this soon, but I hated to interrupt his planning session.

"Possibly. That is why I asked your vampire to prepare some of the bacteria to infect me again. Last night, he confirmed that his curative formula worked on me. I will take a dose of it with me to use once they've taken me to their prison."

I shivered at the idea of him dosing himself with the bacteria again. It had been one thing when it had been in the relative safety of Zoltan's lab and we'd known Zoltan had successfully cured Ti. But... "What if they search you when you're pretending to be unconscious—or you're *actually* unconscious—and find it?"

"I can magically store it in another dimension where they won't see it."

"With the crumbs from that cake?"

The night after we'd returned from the elven sanctuary, I'd been amused to find the smooshed and battered lump of cake resting on a drip tray in the conservatory. It seemed Zav didn't know that the kitchen was the appropriate place to store baked goods. Even more surprising had been that the cake had still tasted good. Very good. I'd dragged Dimitri out to sample some and told him to get the recipe for the shop.

"I cleaned those out." Zav's lips pinched together. Maybe that had been a challenging task, even for dragon magic. "What is your third concern?"

"As far as I know, you're the only one in our group who knows how to make a portal. If they take you, how do we follow you to the gnome home world?"

"It is likely the gnome crafter is capable of creating a portal."

"Ti?"

"He came to your world."

"Maybe he had help. He had time to chat up his people and collect a chest of gold."

"Ask him." Zav shifted me to the side and stood. "There is not much time. Shaygorthian—or Velilah'nav—will expect that I ate the meat right away and that I'll feel the effects soon. They will come check. You must leave before then."

"*Before?*"

"Shaygorthian knows of you and our relationship." Zav clearly felt that Shaygor was the mastermind behind this. Maybe he was right. "He may anticipate that you and your allies would learn that I'd been captured and come after me, and he may set a trap. But if you were already in that world and ahead of them…"

"I see your point." I got out of bed and grabbed my phone, fumbled it, and almost dropped my inhaler.

Zav frowned at my hand. Had he noticed I was holding something besides the phone?

I really didn't want to explain my medicine—or the need for it—to him. Not now. Later, after we'd dealt with his problem, we could sit on a beach somewhere and I could open up about my weaknesses.

"I already picked up grenades and extra ammo from Nin. I'll text Willard to have Dr. Walker grab whatever he needs and meet us over here." I checked to make sure I sensed Ti in the house and that he hadn't wandered off to the park again. Yes, he was sleeping in one of the guest rooms. "It occurs to me that you could open a portal and send us through beforehand. If you're willing."

"I would be willing, yes."

"Good. If Ti can't do it, then we'll plan on that." I sent the text, an uncharacteristic tremble to my fingers and my stomach under a butterfly assault as I realized we could be going to another world to take on dragons in scant hours. And that I would have to leave Zav behind to pull off his scheme by himself. What if that scheme didn't work? He would be stuck facing at least one dragon but potentially even more— and without any backup.

A return text came in from Willard saying she'd already ordered Walker to pack and that he would be here in a couple of hours. I thanked her and put my phone on the bedside table.

"My small but effective team will soon be ready to go free some Stormforge dragons and make the Cosmic Realms a better place." I smiled at Zav. "And maybe make one Lord Zavryd's life a little less fraught."

"I am pleased that you wish those things." Zav watched me through his eyelashes, and a little shiver went through me as he eased closer, the magic of his aura firing along my nerves. "How long is soon?"

I glanced at the time again. It was still early, the sun barely creeping over the horizon outside. "Two hours."

"Barely sufficient," he murmured, lifting his hand to my head again, fingers slipping through my hair to massage my scalp as he gazed intently into my eyes. Intently and intensely. Teasing tendrils of magic flowed from his fingers, and pleasure curled through my entire body.

That felt so good, but...

"I have to go to the bathroom," I blurted.

I caught a puzzled look on his face as I hurried out. Or was that a suspicious look at my abrupt departure?

Maybe I should have explained, but surely even dragons understood biological needs. After closing the door and taking two deep inhalations of my medicine, I brushed my teeth and used the facilities so I wouldn't be lying to him. But when I returned to the bedroom, my heart was pounding from the stimulating medicine, and I realized I was still clutching my inhaler. Why hadn't I left it in the bathroom?

"Sorry about that." I ambled toward the bedside table, intending to return it to the drawer.

Zav intercepted me, slipping his arm around my waist and pulling me against him. "We must not delay further. As I said, our time is barely sufficient."

"Sufficient for what?" I was aware of my heart pounding as our chests touched and thought about tossing the inhaler on my bed. I could feel the contours of his firm pectorals through his robe, and now that my lungs were loosening, thoughts of sex crept into my mind. It would be a shame to waste these two hours, especially if they might be our last ones together for a while.

"Me to show you how pleased I am to have you for my mate."

"I've been hoping you would," I admitted and leaned in to kiss him.

I know, he spoke into my mind, lips meeting mine with fervor.

Cocky dragon.

Yes. He frowned against my mouth. *What are you holding?*

Nothing. Without breaking the kiss, I tossed the inhaler toward the bed. Of course it bounced off and clattered to the hardwood floor on the other side.

Zav broke the kiss. *You are being dishonest with me?*

He sounded puzzled, as if he couldn't believe it, and that stung me. I didn't want to be dishonest with him.

"Sorry. I'm just..." What? Embarrassed. Afraid to admit my weaknesses to him? Yes, both of those things.

Your heart is racing.

"Yeah." As I took a breath, intending to finally explain, the inhaler floated back over the bed and toward us. As Zav caught it, his face went stony, his body rigid.

"What is this?" His voice had cooled to a startling degree, and his frown deepened as he looked down at the inhaler.

Only then did I realize that he might be remembering the elven lover who'd tried to assassinate him. What if he believed it was some poison that I'd been manipulated into applying against him? And that my heart was beating quickly because I was nervous about attacking him?

"It's medicine," I said, my heart racing from more than using the inhaler now. What if I finally confessed, but because I'd done it so poorly, so *sneakily*, he didn't believe me?

"Medicine." His tone was flat as he stared down at his hand. The stupid inhaler didn't have a prescription label on it—that had been on the box it came in—so there was nothing to explain to a dragon what it truly was. For all he knew, it was for delivering an aerosol dosage of poison.

But Zav hadn't exploded yet. He looked into my eyes, as if probing them for the truth.

"Yes. For my lungs. I've developed something we call asthma. When it gets bad, the airways in my lungs close up, and I struggle to get enough oxygen into my body to function properly. The medication is kind of a stimulant—a bronchodilator, I think is the term. It helps me breathe when I need it, but right after I take it, sometimes I get a little shaky and my heart speeds up for a bit."

His gaze shifted back to the inhaler, and he turned it over in his hand, studying it. Before, all I'd worried about was revealing my weakness, but now, I hoped I hadn't screwed up and put a wall between us. Or worse.

"You wished to hide this from me." His tone was still flat and hard to read.

"I didn't want you to think I'm weak because I have this health problem. I'm working on it, and most of the time it doesn't bother me that much, but it's been worse in this house. Remember when I told you about the mold?"

"Yes." He was talking to me still. That was promising—I hoped.

"That makes it worse. So does smoke and pollution and any kind of bad air quality. Remember how I could barely breathe in those ice caves with the volcanic gas?"

"I do." Zav held the inhaler end away from us and squeezed it. He observed me out of the corner of his eye as the aerosol puffed out. Watching to see if I sprang away?

I waited patiently, hoping he would see that I had nothing else to hide, and wishing I'd told him the full truth when we'd discussed the mold.

His nose wrinkled. "It smells foul."

"It's not that appealing when it hits the back of your throat either. Too bad they don't make a meat-scented version." I tried a smile, though I didn't know where I stood with him.

He hadn't yet accused me of trying to poison him, nor had he demanded to scour my mind to know my true thoughts, though I would have let him.

"You did not want me to know of this because it is a weakness?" Zav lowered his hand and returned his gaze to mine.

"I worried you'd think I was... not as great a warrior as you seem to believe. And that you wouldn't want me to stand at your side when we go into battle if you knew my lungs might turn against me in a crucial moment."

Why was it that being open about one's vulnerabilities was so hard? I trusted him, but… he was so powerful and perfect that he might not understand. Or he might reject me for my lack of perfection. But it was better that he know about my faults than believe I was planning some treachery.

"You care about my opinion of you," he said, his tone softening.

"Yes." I didn't trust my voice to say more.

"I already know you have weaknesses. You are half human."

"A terrible crime, I know."

"It is not your fault. But humans are frail. That you are a great warrior *anyway* is what impresses me."

I'd been on the verge of feeling insulted on behalf of my species, but that last sentence, and the gentle little smile that came with it, stole my burgeoning ire.

"You're impressed by me?"

"I am impressed by you." Zav tossed the inhaler into the air, and it floated over to the nightstand. The drawer opened, and it settled down into its original spot, making me realize he'd noticed me slip it out in the first place. He must have been wary and alert the whole time I was holding it, wondering what it was and if it was a threat.

I slumped against him, disappointed in myself for being afraid to tell him the truth.

"I am impressed by you," he repeated, lifting my chin with a finger and gazing deep into my eyes. "And I am aroused by you, great warrior who vexes my enemies."

There wasn't any disappointment in *his* eyes, so I smiled and told myself to get over it. If he could forgive me for lying, I could forgive myself. Besides, this was cutting into our two hours.

"I'm glad," I said and kissed him. Or maybe he kissed me first. It was hard to tell, but I melted into his embrace and wrapped my arms around him, relieved he believed me and relieved he didn't care about my lousy lungs.

We shall mate now, Zav stated into my mind, his aura wrapping around me, claiming me as my senses tingled with intense awareness of him. *When we complete our mission, I will incinerate your mold.*

Will you? I smiled against his mouth. *Damn, now I'm getting aroused.*

I know. Now you are hiding nothing.

I hope you approve.

I approve of you very much, he purred into my mind, sliding his warm hand under my nightshirt.

His open appreciation of me threatened to bring tears to my eyes. I was relieved he knew all my secrets now, even if I wished I'd been less clumsy about revealing them. Leaning into him, I pushed my hands into his short hair, the soft strands cool and lush against my fingers as I rubbed his scalp. I deepened our kiss, wanting to hold nothing back, wanting to give myself to the moment—to *him*—fully.

Zav responded to my passion with a pleased growl deep in his throat and pushed my nightshirt over my head. He tossed it onto the bed and cupped my breasts, breaking the kiss to look down at them, his gaze heated and possessive. It made me feel like a sexy goddess, not a forty-something mongrel with health issues. Sparks of desire rocketed to the core of my being as he explored further, bending his head to stroke me with his tongue.

I kneaded his shoulders, searching for the clasp for his robe. I wanted to explore *his* body too, but I couldn't find a zipper or button. How did his magical wardrobe work? I opened my mouth to ask, but his ministrations were *very* distracting.

Once, he'd promised me I would enjoy it if we mated, and as magic blended with physical touch to make my nerves zing, I had no doubt he'd spoken the truth. I was already enjoying this—a *lot*.

His tongue brushed my nipple, and I gasped and tugged at his robe, wanting the cursed thing off him, wanting nothing between us.

"Strip, Zav," I said. "I want to touch you."

My mate presumes to give me orders? He sounded amused rather than indignant and he caressed me with his mouth.

I arched toward him, unable to hide how amazing that felt. *Yes, she does. She's as cocky and demanding as you are.*

It is fortunate she pleases me so. His mouth slid lower, and he ran his finger along the waistband of my pajama bottoms. He slid them down my legs and lifted me out of them and onto the bed.

His own robe finally came off with a whisper of magic, floating across the room to drape over a chair, and leaving his magnificent form open for viewing. The gentle lamplight cast shadows between the swells of his lean, powerful muscles, and I thought of the first time I'd seen him naked, when we'd pretended not to be interested in each other in the hot tub. This time, there was nothing but honesty between us.

I reached out, running my hands over his torso and then lower as our gazes locked. I had the pleasure of making him gasp as I explored. The gasp turned into another growl, and he climbed into bed with me, his hungry violet eyes reminding me of the predator he was. He paused to gaze at my naked body, his eyes as appreciative as they were aroused. That appreciation excited me almost as much as his touch. I liked knowing that he valued having me as a partner in battle as well as in bed.

"How weirded out are you going to be if I pull out a condom?" I whispered, reluctant to break the spell, but I doubted dragons worried much about safe sex. "And do you know what one is?"

"A sheath of rubber or animal intestine worn over the penis to prevent conception or venereal infection."

I laughed. "Your dictionary knowledge is excellent, but a little tip: mentioning venereal infections doesn't get a woman excited."

"You *are* excited." Zav's lashes drooped as he slid his hand over my bare stomach, sending one of his magical tingles flaring through me. "I can tell."

He was right. I couldn't keep from writhing with pleasure under his expert strokes.

"Also, condoms are unnecessary. I am free of disease, and dragons cannot produce offspring with other species. That is why there are no half-dragon mongrels wandering your world."

"I suppose that's good." I pushed up into his touch, reveling in it, and in the way he drank me in with his eyes. "I can't imagine giving birth to something with a tail and talons would feel good."

"Female dragons lay eggs."

"Makes sense." Those tingles were making me breathless, and I felt silly squirming on my back as he gazed down at me.

This discussion had gone on long enough. I wrapped my arms around him and pulled him down, kissing him hard and with all the need coursing through my body. I didn't want to delay any longer, no matter how much I enjoyed his teasing touches. I grazed the hard muscles of his back with my nails, willing my meager magic to fill *him* with tingles.

It must have worked, because his eyes flared with inner light, and he lost his measured control as his kisses grew more demanding, almost wild. His power crackled around me, flooding me with tangible desire. His? Mine? I wasn't sure, but we were in sync as our need built together. I opened myself to him, wanting what we'd both wanted for months. Finally, he trusted me enough to allow himself to be naked and vulnerable in my bed, to let loose his reserves and lower his defenses to fully enjoy this moment. As we came together, venturing to places I hadn't known I could reach, conscious thought scattered from my mind, and pure animal instincts overtook us.

Pure, beautiful animal instincts. And he'd been right. It was *very* enjoyable.

It was light out by the time we collapsed together to rest, and I wished we'd spent the whole night together, that we could stay here and spend the rest of the week—the rest of the year—together. But that couldn't be unless we survived this next mission. I rubbed my cheek against his and kissed him. We would. Both of us.

You are an excellent mate, Val, Zav murmured into my mind.

I'm glad you think so, because I'm kind of falling for you.

He lifted himself onto his elbows, gazed into my eyes, and stroked my hair. *This means you love me, yes?*

Yeah. Too bad you told me dragons don't have a concept for love in your language.

I may have been mistaken. He smiled and kissed me.

CHAPTER 23

A cold creepy mist wrapped around me as I stepped out of the portal onto the gnomish home world. At least that was where Ti had promised to send us. It was my third trip through a portal and my first to somewhere that looked like Mordor. A *chilly* Mordor, with clouds and mist keeping the visibility to a quarter mile despite the flatness of the fissure-split gray earth.

I wore my duster, but it had been a warm late-August morning back in Seattle, and it hadn't occurred to me to bring gloves and a scarf. Or, I amended as I stared around the bleak black-and-gray landscape, maybe the perky pink Hello Kitty mittens that a client had once given me as a gag gift. This place needed color. *Any* color.

Ti and Dr. Walker stepped out of the portal behind me. Even they seemed gray in this place, their skin taking on a colorless pallor.

Ti wore the same cloak and overalls he'd first arrived at the house in, but he'd added a backpack—maybe he'd had it stashed in the park with the chest of gold—and it was stuffed with tools and magical items that I could sense but not identify. He also wore a magical dagger belted at his waist.

A little surprisingly, Walker was also armed. He had a medical kit filled with basic first-aid supplies as well as most of the vials of Zoltan's formula—I carried a few in one of my ammo pouches—but he also carried a rifle on a strap over his shoulder, one that looked to be Nin's work, and a short sword at his hip.

Even though I'd been hesitant to bring along a near-stranger and worried he would be a hindrance, I was reassured that he appeared comfortable in the gear. Willard had said he'd been in the army, and he was a full-blooded shifter, so he ought to be able to take care of himself. Against modest threats, anyway. If we ran into the two dragons Ti had said might be here, we'd all be in trouble. Especially if Zav was busy with his own scheme—or if something happened back on Earth and Zav didn't come.

Walker eyed our surroundings. "Back home, this is what we call being out in woop woop."

"Isolated and far away from anything?" I asked.

"You got it."

"I'm a little sad that we can't see Mount Doom off in the distance."

"It could be behind all the fog."

"True."

Ti raised a finger. "Allow me a moment to get my bearings."

"You can have two." I jogged in place to warm up and thought about summoning Sindari, but we might be walking for hours to get anywhere. Or days. I would rather save him for when a battle was imminent.

"Don't think I'm having a whinge, but we should have brought my SUV." Walker spun a slow circle as the portal faded, gazing into the misty bleakness that stretched in all directions. "I don't sense anything nearby. We could have a long trek ahead of us."

"Can you drive cars through portals?" I asked.

Ti was standing with his eyes slitted and unfocused, gazing off in one direction. I couldn't tell if anything was out there, but as a full-blooded gnome, his range for sensing magical items and beings would be greater than mine.

"Sure." Walker shrugged. "Why not?"

"I see a dearth of roads and gas stations."

"I've got extra petrol cans I could have brought. And my ride doesn't need roads. It's a rugged beast."

"I heard the seats have massaging butt warmers."

"They're rugged massaging butt warmers."

"That sounds like a driving distraction."

Walker eyed me. "Are you going to be like Willard?"

"A sarcastic smartass? Count on it."

I wasn't sure how he would react to that, but he snorted and quirked a half smile. "I guess I won't get homesick then."

"I didn't get the impression that you two were that close."

"No, but I do work for her office on occasion. I don't get a lot of sarcastic smartassery from my clients, so I have to get it from her. If I go too long between visits, the lack of it leaves my stomach with a forlorn emptiness."

"Do antacids help with that?"

"Yeah, but long-term use of those causes micronutrient deficiencies."

"Your life must be difficult."

"It's why I have the butt massagers."

Ti turned to us. I wondered if he would be the kind of guide to object to pointless banter. I hoped not. This place had a bleakness that permeated the skin, and cracking jokes might be the only thing that kept me sane, especially if we had to stay here a long time. I'd brought three days' worth of food and water—Mom would have been proud—but if this mission took longer than that, we would need to find local sources.

"I have brought us into the world three miles from the opening to the Crying Caverns," Ti said. "It was the closest that I dared use magic, lest we trigger the detectors and alarms around the perimeter of the entrance canyon. As it is, since we are all carrying magical items and have magical blood, we will have to use the camouflaging trinkets and hope for the best."

"I love missions that depend on hope," I murmured.

"The dragon creators of the facility were most worried about rival dragons invading it, so the detectors might not go off at the approach of lesser species—I sneaked past one without triggering it on the way out—but we should not depend on that. Also, the booby traps will go off for all, even a mouse. They are hidden throughout the caverns. I know what to look for and will do my best to lead you around them."

Hope for the best. Do my best. Why did I already have a bad feeling about this mission and our guide?

I glanced skyward, as if I might see Zav flying through the misty gray clouds, but I didn't sense him and didn't expect to for a while. If his ruse went according to plan, we might see Shaygor magically dragging him to this canyon, but that likely wouldn't be for a while.

"Lead the way," Walker said.

"Wait." I handed him a chain that I'd put the camouflage charm Freysha had identified on. "You two should both be able to use that, but I think you have to be touching."

"Touching?" Walker raised his eyebrows, then put a finger on Ti's bald head.

"However you want to walk. Freysha and I discussed hand-holding."

"That's difficult when there's a three-foot height disparity," Walker said. "I could carry him."

Ti stepped away from the finger on his head and fished into a pocket. "I have a trinket of my own with similar power. It is good that we all have one. They will help us evade the detectors."

"And the booby traps?" I asked hopefully.

"No." Ti activated his charm and wavered in my vision, growing half-translucent and fading to my senses. "Weight will trigger those."

I stepped closer, and he solidified. Our group would have to stay close on the trek if we didn't want to lose each other.

"Walker, if you put that on your neck—" I pointed to the chain and goblin charm, "—will it stay with you when you shift into your animal form?" I didn't know if he planned to do that on this trip, but canine and feline shifters all seemed to get furry when it was time for a serious fight.

"It would stay with me even if it was in my pocket. Any halfway decent shifter knows how to magically store his belongings while he's in his alter form. Otherwise, you'd see a lot of them running around naked afterward."

"Nobody wants to see that."

"No?" His brows rose.

Ti and I shook our heads.

"Disappointing," Walker said.

"This way." Ti led off across the black, porous terrain.

It reminded me of the bare lava rock areas around my mother's hometown in Oregon, where trees had never grown back after the last eruption, but this place was damp and dreary instead of sunny and dry. If there were any trees here, I couldn't see them.

"This isn't how I imagined the gnomish home world looking," I told Ti as we maneuvered across the lumpy terrain, no hint of a road or paths making the way easier.

"We are far to the south of the continents where my people evolved and still live. This continent has little native life, and our people rarely visit it, except on quests for treasure."

"There's treasure here?"

"There are stories about gold and magical artifacts being hoarded by the golems and volcano monsters that make their homes here." A moaning that might have been caused by the wind punctuated Ti's sentence.

But I didn't feel a breeze, and nothing stirred the mist.

Ti pointed to something off to our right. Two white, feathered creatures reminiscent of vultures sprang into the air, squawking as they flew away from us. They'd been perched on a small humanoid form in metal armor that had blended in with the rock. My senses told me that he or she was dead even before my nose caught the scent of decomposing flesh.

"Did he run into a booby trap?" I asked.

"Probably one of the packs of predators that scavenge here," Ti said. "Some chased me when I came out of the caverns. I was able to find a nook in the rock and hide until I gained strength enough to create a portal and escape. The magic of the Crying Caverns gets in the way of creating portals from inside. I had to get out first."

"So, once we're in there, we'll be stuck?"

"Unless you are a dragon, yes." Ti led us onward. "Their power is so great that they can create portals even with magical interference. I have witnessed it."

"Too bad we didn't bring our dragon."

"Yes."

When I'd told Ti about Zav's plan, he hadn't been enthusiastic. He'd wanted to return to the caverns with me *and* Zav at his side. I hoped Zav's idea didn't turn out to be a mistake.

As we traveled farther, I sensed magic in the distance, a *lot* of magic. It didn't feel like a being or an artifact, but instead magic that somehow infused the terrain ahead. I hadn't encountered anything like it before.

"This place is strange," Walker murmured.

"You're just now noticing?"

"At first, I thought it couldn't be any rougher than the Outback. That's where I grew up and lived until I was twenty. But it didn't have all this magic."

"But the insects and snakes are probably deadlier there, right?"

"Maybe. We don't know what got that explorer."

"True."

"This is my first time visiting another world," Walker admitted. "I may have underestimated how dangerous this mission would be."

"I'm a little surprised you were willing to come along for whatever Willard pays you."

"It's not a lot," he admitted. "Not compared to what I make in my practice."

"So why are you here?" I wondered if Willard had told him anything about the possible threat to humanity if the Silverclaw dragons ended up on top.

His eyebrows lifted. "Willard told me it would be dangerous, involve scads of dragons, and might get us all killed."

"Natural selling points."

"She was pretty sure I wouldn't do it."

"You're not answering my question."

"No? Huh."

I guessed that was the only answer I would get. So long as he didn't plan to betray me, I didn't care why he was here, but his reticence to give me the truth made me wary.

"We are almost to the canyon," Ti whispered over his shoulder as he headed around a stack of black boulders that looked like they'd been vomited up by a giant. A few balanced precariously, as if a stiff wind could send them tumbling down onto us.

As we followed Ti around the boulders, the mist cleared enough to see a vast chasm. In the poor visibility, it was impossible to tell how far it stretched or even see all the way down to the bottom.

Walker peered over the edge, nostrils twitching. "There's water down there."

"Under the fog?" I asked.

"Yup."

A predatory squawk came up from the mist, and he leaned back. Something similar to a giant pterodactyl flew up out of the canyon toward us, and I drew Chopper.

Four others flapped out of the mist, but they all headed in different directions. The one coming our way flew over our heads without glancing at us.

I started to return Chopper to its scabbard, but then I sensed a dragon. No, *several* dragons. One was Zav. I also sensed Shaygor, and a couple of the others seemed familiar, though they weren't close enough yet for me to be certain I knew them. The magic emanating from the ground also interfered with my senses.

"Take cover," Ti whispered. "They may be able to see through our trinkets."

He trotted back toward the boulders and ducked into a nook between two of them.

I squeezed into a gap near him. "You said you'd never seen more than two dragons in this place, Ti."

"Yes."

"I sense more than two dragons coming."

"So do I."

As the dragons flew into sight—black, silver, and blue shapes against the gray sky—Walker shifted into his animal form for the first time since I'd met him. As Zoltan had suggested, Walker was more exotic than the lion shifter I'd originally thought him. He was a heavily muscled, three-hundred-pound, tawny-furred predator that looked like nothing I'd seen before, like some creature out of prehistoric times. His face was vaguely feline, and he crouched on four muscular legs, but his body was thicker than a lion's, and his tail was as broad as a kangaroo's.

Walker eyed the dragons as they flew closer, clearly intending to face them in his animal form rather than with guns and knives.

I fingered my feline charm and considered summoning Sindari, but I was hoping Ti was wrong about the dragons sensing us. The three—or four—of us together would be lucky to take down a single dragon. But there were *four* of them, not including Zav. There was no way. Even if Zav was conscious and able to help, that would be an iffy fight.

As the group flew into view, I decided he didn't appear conscious. His head drooped on his long neck, his tail hung limp, and some magic was flying him along rather than his own wings. Two dragons flew to either side of him, keeping him prisoner. One was Shaygor, and—I sucked in a startled but angry breath—the other one was Velilah.

I'd been right. She must have been the one to arrange the delivery of the tainted food.

A blue dragon trailed after them. I'd seen a couple of blue dragons among the Starsinger Clan that had mobbed Weber's house, but this one didn't have a familiar aura. Maybe he was another Silverclaw dragon that I hadn't met before.

I drew in another startled breath as the final dragon came into view and solidified to my senses.

"That's Zav's sister," I breathed, staring at the lilac scales, a pop of brightness against the drab sky.

At first, I thought she must have been captured too, but she wasn't unconscious. She was flying along of her own accord, violet eyes alert as she scanned the ground. I froze as her cold and reptilian gaze raked across the boulder pile.

She didn't seem to see us, and the dragons continued past our hiding spot, but that was the only thing good about this scenario. Zondia's presence among Zav's enemies could only mean that she'd betrayed him. Maybe she had been betraying him all along and passing information to enemies of their clan.

But why? Because she, like the cousin Zav had once mentioned to me, had switched sides, believing the Stormforge Clan was doomed?

I slumped against the nearest boulder, feeling defeated on Zav's behalf. If most of his family was against him, how could he succeed? Would Zondia stand back and allow her brother to be imprisoned here? Or worse?

And did this also mean that neither Zav's mother nor any other dragon in his family who might be legitimately on his side knew about this mission? And that his kin were all trapped in these caverns? He had said he'd told Zondia to relay the message to the prickly queen.

Any chance any of those dragons are on our side? Walker asked telepathically as the dragons dove and disappeared into the canyon.

The one in the middle is, I replied.

The one that looked half-dead and was being dragged along by magic?

Yeah.

I should have asked Willard for more money. Are we going ahead with this? Walker looked toward Ti and me.

"We must," Ti said. "Now more than ever. We're the only hope for my people and for the Stormforge dragons."

Walker, who probably didn't have a reason to care about gnomes or dragons, focused on me.

"We have to," I said with quiet determination.

We were also the only hope for Zav.

CHAPTER 24

The bad news was that we had to rappel to get down to the bottom of the canyon and the entrance to the Crying Caverns that Ti promised was there. The good news was that our gnome guide was the MacGyver of gnome guides and had crafted magical devices to aid us with the rappelling.

They looked like round napkin holders with slender twine unraveling from spools inside, and they made me wonder if Ti had trained at the same tinkering academy as Gondo, but they proved effective. They allowed us to descend several hundred feet at a time before pausing on ledges to reset the devices. At a whispered word from Ti, the napkin holders detached from the rock wall and floated slowly down to us on parachutes, sucking in the twine along the way. When we caught them, they were ready to be put to use again.

On a ledge halfway down into the vast canyon, I stopped to wait for Ti and Walker, who had needed to return to his human form to grip the holder basket, as Ti called it, and use the rappelling device. For the first time, the ground below was visible through the mist, and I searched for the entrance. We'd sensed the dragons fly down and into some entrance on the canyon wall opposite us, but so much magic oozed from the terrain itself that I could no longer tell where they were. Presumably, they'd flown deep into the caverns.

I spotted a dark opening that might be the entrance, but from the ledge, I couldn't see how deep it went back into the canyon wall. It was shaped like a lightbulb, narrow down by the ground and wider up above. Wide enough for dragons to fly through.

I itched to hurry the rest of the way down, cross the stream that was also now visible, and check it out. Worry for Zav made me impatient at any delays—I hadn't expected him to arrive so soon.

A pack of large, four-legged, shaggy gray creatures browsing at spiky vegetation in front of the opening convinced me to wait. Even though they were nipping at foliage, they might be omnivores and interested in attacking a half-elf who wandered past. Given the dearth of foliage I'd seen so far in this world, it seemed unlikely such large animals could survive here on leaves alone.

"Those are sentries," Ti whispered when he joined me. "They have very good noses and eyes and are sensitive to magic. I barely got past them on my way out. I was saved by the fact that they don't climb as well as gnomes."

"We don't want to climb. Will they follow us inside if they spot us?"

"I believe that's likely."

"Wonderful."

There had to be close to a hundred of the creatures. Far more than I wanted to try mowing down with Fezzik. Besides, if we started shooting up the canyon, our chances of sneaking in would plummet.

Walker hopped down, landing in an easy crouch as he whispered Ti's word to release his rappelling device. "Can we sneak past them with our charms?"

Ti hesitated. "Possibly. But I also have a plan in case we have to deal with them."

He patted his pack, but he didn't explain further, leaving Walker and me to wonder as we descended the rest of the way. We picked our way across the stream, the ashy gray water making me glad I'd filled my canteen back on Earth, and approached the cave opening from downwind. A scent reminiscent of stables drifted from the pack of animals. There were a dozen creatures near the entrance, some standing halfway inside, so sneaking past them seemed unlikely, even with the charms.

"I wonder what they taste like," Walker mused.

"Sh." Ti held a finger to his lips, then crouched and pulled metal pieces out of his pack.

While he assembled something similar to a crossbow, I summoned Sindari. If we ended up in a fight, his help would be invaluable.

After constructing the crossbow, Ti pulled out two familiar brown paper packages. He loaded a giant quarrel into his weapon, then pierced the packages in the middle as he slid them onto the tip like shrimp on a kebab.

You've called me forth for lunch? Sindari asked.

I hate to dine without your company. I patted him on the back.

As Ti advanced ahead of us and we trailed slowly after, I explained the dragon situation to Sindari.

We were about twenty feet from the opening when one creature lifted its head to sniff the air and peer around. The animals looked like crosses between horses and panthers, and when one opened its mouth, sharp fangs were visible. Others caught the scent—were they smelling us through our charms or Ti's borrowed rice-and-beef meals?—and turned toward our group. A few sank into half crouches and prowled toward us.

Ti waited longer than I would have liked before lifting the crossbow. Not certain what he meant to do, I drew Fezzik. Making noise wouldn't be a good idea, but the creatures appeared powerful and dangerous enough that I would prefer to shoot them from afar rather than getting in a sword fight with dozens at a time.

Ti fired his crossbow. The meal-laden quarrel shot over their heads, over the stream, and landed in a crack in the rock wall on the far side, twenty feet above the ground.

One of the packets came partially open on the flight and littered pieces of beef and rice across the canyon floor. The creatures surged for the prizes, snapping up the meat. Others that were too slow to get pieces of beef lapped at the rice. As soon as the food on the ground was gone, most of the pack ran across the creek to the rock wall. They had hooves rather than paws, and their attempts to climb up to get the dangling treat did not go well. Some sprang, trying to snap at the packet, but they fell short by several feet.

"Now," Ti breathed, pointing at the entrance.

A few of the pack lingered in the area, sniffing the air suspiciously, but he was right. This was our best shot to get inside unnoticed.

Sindari took the lead, and I jogged beside Ti. Walker shifted back into his feline form to guard us from behind.

We made it to the opening, and though the pervasive mist from outside curled inside and hazed the view, I could see back far enough to guess that we'd reached our cavern.

Company is coming, Walker warned telepathically.

We'd gone only ten feet into the cavern.

Run? I asked as two of the creatures ran into view, heading straight for us.

"No!" Ti blurted aloud. He lowered his voice to add, "We can't run into the booby traps."

"Right." I aimed Fezzik and fired at the creature on the right as Sindari and Walker bounded for the one on the left.

Though my senses were overwhelmed by magic that seemed to ooze from the rock itself here, no barriers or magical defenses kept my bullets from sinking in. The creature was tough, however, and I slammed six bullets into its chest before it faltered. I lifted my aim toward one of its eyes.

Sindari and Walker tore into the other one like the powerful predators they were, but it was by no means an easy fight. A hoof clipped Walker in the shoulder hard enough to hurl him into the cavern wall ten feet away. The creature's fanged maw snapped for Sindari as he lunged around it to sink his fangs into its muscled neck.

My bullet landed true, taking my target in the eye. Finally, the creature pitched to the ground.

I started to shift my aim to help Sindari with the other one, but two more of the sentry animals rushed through the opening. I fired on them instead.

"The rest are returning." Ti had dropped to his knees and was rummaging in his pack. "Delay them, please."

Even as I fired at the newcomers, I glimpsed the rest of the herd across the creek. Dozens had given up on the bait and were turning to rush toward us. Walker and Sindari finished off their first target and charged at one I'd wounded but not yet taken down. They were fast and deadly and worked well together, but we wouldn't survive if dozens of the creatures poured into the cavern.

"Delay them. Right." I dug into my belt pouches and pulled out a couple of Nin's magical grenades. "Get back, guys! Toward me!"

Sindari and Walker glanced back, saw me pulling the pin for the first grenade, and ran back to my side. Two of the creatures raced after them. Trusting them to keep our foes from taking me down, I threw the grenade, not at the animals directly but at one side of the opening. As it rolled to a stop next to the rock wall, I chucked the second one toward the opposite side. The lightbulb-shaped opening was narrow at ground level, and as I resumed firing at the surge of creatures, I mentally crossed my fingers that the grenades would do the job.

The first one blew up, smoke filling the opening, and the sound of a rockfall filled our ears. I backed farther away, pausing when I reached Ti, because I didn't want to leave him vulnerable. He was still digging for something. The second grenade went off. A creature squealed in pain as more rocks clattered and thudded, some hitting the far wall, some slamming to the ground.

I finished off one of the sentries that had made it to our side of the smoke as Sindari and Walker tore two others to pieces. With Fezzik aimed into the smoke, I waited to attack any more that rushed toward us, but as the rocks and dust settled, all movement ceased.

Sindari and Walker, standing shoulder to shoulder like furry brothers, turned from their dead foes and faced the opening. Misty light still filtered through from above, but I'd succeeded in caving in the lower portion of the entrance. Rocks had tumbled from the sides but also from above, and rubble piled more than ten feet high blocked the bottom of the opening.

Beside me, Ti rose to his feet with a magical glowing blue ball in his hand. He looked from the cave-in to his ball, back to the cave-in, and then to me. "We had similar plans." He dropped the ball into a pouch he could more quickly access next time. "You were faster."

"I have a lot of practice with grenades."

"Nin made yours?"

"Yeah."

"Excellent." He smiled, the gesture alleviating the usual graveness of his face.

Clunks sounded as a boulder rolled from the top down to the bottom on the far side of the cave-in.

"Think they'll climb over?" I kept my gun pointed at the entrance, not knowing if gravity had caught up to the boulder late or if the creatures were disturbing the rubble. They weren't magical, so I couldn't sense where they were, though a few noises halfway between moans and goat bleats sounded on the far side.

"Let us hope not." Ti returned his pack to his back. "It would be inconvenient if they ran up behind us as we were navigating the booby traps."

"Among other things." I walked backward for a while, following Ti as he headed slowly into the cavern, scrutinizing the floor and walls as he went.

We will guard the rear, Sindari informed me, walking side by side with Walker.

Made a new buddy, did you?

We slew several creatures together.

You better make him the godfather of your kids if you have any.

Amusing. I sense dragons ahead.

I know.

A lot of them.

I know that too.

It is likely they are close enough to have heard the noise we just made.

I grimaced. If that was true, we had a problem. All this depended on us sneaking in and freeing and curing the captured dragons before anyone knew we were here. Unfortunately, that cure would take time to work. A day? Two days? I had no idea, but if we had to fight four dragons at any point, we were screwed.

CHAPTER 25

The booby traps weren't as bad as I'd feared, but probably only because Ti carefully led us around them and we hadn't triggered any. Yet. We'd swung across pits on ropes, followed two-inch ledges along the wall to avoid the ground, and now we were swinging through a forest of stalactites like kids using monkey bars. Monkey bars that dangled us over a pool of molten lava with only a scattering of small islands and stepping-stones in it, all of which Ti assured us were unsafe to land on.

I'd had to dismiss Sindari for the acrobatic activities, and Walker had shifted back to his human form. He weighed more than Ti or I did, and one of the tips of the stalactites crumbled when he grabbed it. In an impressive feat of agility, he managed to lunge in the air and grasp another one before he plummeted into the lava steaming below. I'd been too far away to help and had envisioned having to explain to Willard how I'd gotten the doctor who liked her snark killed.

Sweat streamed down his face, but he recovered and made it the rest of the way across. Ti swung down first, landing in a carefully chosen spot at the edge of the pool, and he pointed to the ground right next to him.

"Here is safe and only here," he informed us.

Walker nodded for me to swing down first.

I was glad that there was natural light here, if only from the orange glow of the magma. For large parts of the trek, when I'd needed my hands and couldn't have the blue-glowing Chopper out, I'd been using my night-vision charm to navigate. But it had its weaknesses and didn't allow me to pick out fine details—like trip wires. According to my teammates, gnomes and feline shifters could naturally see in the dark. Lucky them.

Almost an hour had passed since we caved in the entrance, and I was beginning to think that the dragons had miraculously not heard the noise—or had not been worried enough about it to investigate—but as I landed in a crouch, I sensed one of their powerful auras up ahead. Shaygor.

Ti frowned in that direction. "Trouble comes."

Walker landed next to us, brushing our shoulders as he took care to drop down exactly where Ti had pointed.

"We have to hide." Ti touched his charm to refresh the magic.

Walker and I also made sure ours were still active, then followed Ti as he picked a careful path toward the wall. On the ground here and there, I sensed more magic than in the surrounding area and thought the spots might represent traps, but I was glad we had Ti. I doubted my ability to navigate through without him. All I could tell for certain was that Shaygor was getting closer.

There weren't any nooks to squeeze into or ledges to duck under. All we could do was flatten ourselves against the rock wall and hope the dragon wouldn't see through our camouflaging magic. I summoned Sindari again in case that didn't work.

Shaygor's silver form came into view, sailing through the cavern, flapping his wings when there was room and tucking them in close to glide when the passageway narrowed or the ceiling lowered. His nostrils sniffed as he flew, and his reptilian eyes scanned the passage. As far as I could tell, he didn't see or sense us, but I held my breath and willed my heart to beat quietly as he neared.

Shaygor flew past, tucking his wings to glide below the stalactites and above the lava. Near the end of the steaming orange lake, his momentum slowed, and he had to flap his wings. One of the tips brushed one of the rocks I'd been thinking of as stepping-stones, and a gout of flames burst from a crack in the nearby wall to bathe him. His magic either protected him, or dragon scales were resilient to fire, for he flew on without a peep to indicate pain. Had that struck any of us, we would have been charred to husks.

I believe he's going to check on the mess at the entrance, Sindari spoke into my mind as Shaygor flew out of sight around the bend.

At which point, he'll know that visitors have arrived. I wondered how far we were from Zav.

Since I couldn't sense him or the other dragons, I feared we still had miles of booby-trap dodging ahead of us. And what happened when we made it? If our enemies knew we were here, they would stay and guard their prisoners and search for us until they found us.

Not an appealing thought.

I looked at Walker and Ti and spoke silently to them. *Can either of you guys sense the other dragons? The four we saw fly in? And Zav?*

I *hoped* Zav was still alive with an aura that could be sensed. It had taken longer than I wanted to get to this point. Who knew what they had done to him in the last hour?

That thought sent a jolt of worry through me. I had to resist the urge to sprint down the cavern with Chopper drawn and ready to hack at any booby trap or dragon that got in my way. That would get me killed, and I knew it. And it would probably get everyone on my team killed too.

I took a deep breath, striving for patience as Ti and Walker closed their eyes to check with their senses.

Walker shook his head and replied telepathically with, *Just the one that flew past. He's at the entrance.*

But Ti nodded. *I sense all five living dragons. We are not yet close enough for me to sense the ones in their cells, but that is not surprising. Their auras were always very subdued.*

Are the living dragons in the same place as the imprisoned ones? I asked.

No. The living dragons are in the first chamber. There is another chamber farther back where the life cells and hibernating dragons are located. Unless something has changed in the weeks I've been gone, but that is unlikely. The cells involve complex magic and complex machinery, and I do not believe the dragons are ever moved once they're put into hibernation. In the twenty years I was here, none were relocated.

So, we need to somehow sneak past the living dragons to get to the cells and release them all and inject them without anyone noticing.

That will be difficult at this point.

I know. I regretted lobbing the grenades, but Ti had planned to do something similar. We'd failed in our attempt to sneak in undetected and hadn't had much choice. *Someone is going to need to distract the dragons, I think.*

Someone. Walker raised his eyebrows. *That sounds like a suicide mission.*

He and Ti looked deeper into the cavern, then pressed their backs against the wall again.

Another one is coming, Sindari warned me.

I sense him. It was the blue dragon I hadn't met before.

We waited in silence as he zipped quickly through. Why did I have a feeling Shaygor had called him to look at the mess we'd made?

I have an idea, I thought to the others once he was out of sight.

We may need to retreat and try another day, Ti said. *They will be highly alert and suspect trouble. As soon as the first life cell is opened, if they are paying attention, they will sense it.*

We're not retreating or waiting. I thought of Zav—who knew if they would keep him alive another day? *You guys go ahead, sneak past the dragons, and start freeing the other ones. Once you dose them all with the cure, you can leave. I know they're not going to recover right away, but I'll do my best to distract the other two.*

Distract? Tigers didn't frown, but Sindari managed to convey great disapproval with the glare he gave me.

They know someone is here. Once they capture me, they won't continue looking for you. As long as I could keep them from scouring my mind. I grimaced. Could the trinket in my pocket and the tricks Freysha had taught me keep that from happening? What if all four dragons combined forces to dig into my mind?

Why would they capture you? Ti shook his head.

Because I'll let them. I've got some of Zoltan's vials. I patted the ammo pouch that I'd dedicated to vials instead of cartridges, and while it was on my mind, I prepared a needle for Zav. *I'll try to get them to drop me down next to Zav so I can dose him.*

Drop you down? Sindari asked. *You're going to—*

He stopped, and we all turned toward the molten lake again, sensing the two dragons flying back. Flying *slowly* back. One sailed high, checking out ledges and cracks near the ceiling. One sailed low, eyes scanning, nostrils sniffing the air. If chance brought either of them close, they would detect us through the magic of our charms.

They flew past, not quite close enough to our wall to spot us, but the slow methodical way they searched suggested they would continue to hunt, and it would only be a matter of time before they found us.

I'm going to let them find me, I silently told the others. *You guys keep going and free the dragons. I'll say I'm alone.*

They will force the truth from your mind, Ti warned. *They are dragons!*

Then you better free the others quickly. I nodded at them and stepped away from the wall. *Dr. Walker, I'm counting on you to nurse those dragons back to health as fast as you can. If they rouse themselves enough to fight on Zav's behalf...*

I had to hope they would, that Zondia wouldn't tell them some lie that they would believe. And that Zav was still all right and able to speak with his uncle and anyone else back there he knew.

Val. Walker lifted a hand, his fingers nearly translucent since I'd moved away. *It could take days for them to revive. If not months. I have no idea how much damage this infection will have done to them over the years, not to mention possible side effects of being locked up in whatever these chambers are.*

Do the best you can, and I'll tell Willard what a badass you are when you get furry.

I expected a sarcastic response, but he lowered his hand and raised his eyebrows. *Promise?*

So that was it. They hadn't dated. Willard hadn't been interested. But it seemed like Walker was. Did Willard even know? Or did she know and not care because she thought he was pretentious?

It was something to ponder another time.

Yeah. I gave him a thumbs-up and stepped farther away from the wall.

Thanks to our link, I could still see Sindari, but Ti and Walker disappeared from my awareness. I pointed for them to continue deeper into the cavern, even though I could sense Shaygor and his buddy again. They'd turned around and were flying back this way.

I crouched near the edge of the molten pool and debated my options. If I let them find me in an obvious spot, that would be suspicious, but if I did my best to stay hidden, the dragons might chance across the others before me.

Plan, Val? Sindari asked.

Have the others left?

Yes. I'm staying with you.

They might find your help useful, I pointed out.

They are not the ones intending to expose themselves to irritated dragons.

We don't know the dragons are irritated. Maybe this place is catnip to them, and they're in delightful moods.

Even if that were true, they would grow irritated as soon as they started talking to you.

Funny.

I wish it were.

I'm going to lead them on a wild goose chase. Will you go with the others and find out if Zav is… all right? I couldn't bring myself to suggest the possibility that he might be dead. If my mind strayed in that direction, tears would start dripping from my eyes. This wasn't the time for crying—or thinking about how much I'd started to care for my pompous dragon this summer. For Zav.

Very well. Do not get yourself killed. Even if it is my fate to one day serve dragons, I would be most put out to serve these *dragons.*

Would you serve Zav? Willingly?

I don't know. He doesn't rub my ears, as a good handler should.

I see. You want to serve Dimitri.

As Sindari headed off after the others, I slipped a cartridge out of one of my magazines. I held it, breathed on it, and buffed it under my armpit. If that didn't convey my scent, I didn't know what would. Then I stuck the cartridge in my pocket and sprang back into the stalactites to carefully retrace the route Ti had led me on before.

Heading in the opposite direction of Zav bothered me, but it made sense to try to lead the dragons away from my allies. Maybe Zondia and Velilah would also join the hunt for me, and it would make it easier for Walker and Ti to sneak into that far chamber.

As I landed on the far side of the molten lake, Shaygor and the blue dragon came into view again. I scooted to the wall, flattening myself against it. As the dragons sailed under the stalactites, I drew the cartridge and threw it as far down the cavern in the direction of the entrance as I could.

Whatever tink it made when it landed on the rocky ground was too far away for me to hear, but Shaygor shifted from his slow methodical flying into swift wingbeats that blew at my face and stirred my braid as he passed. The blue dragon picked up speed right behind him.

Shaygor halted near one cavern wall, landing right on top of the fallen cartridge. His great silver head lowered to the ground, nostrils sniffing it.

His mate is here, Shaygor boomed.

Up until then, they'd been using pinpoint telepathy instead of broadcasting, but maybe he was pissed now and didn't care who heard him. Or maybe he *wanted* me to hear him.

The blue dragon dove down behind him but landed on a booby trap. An explosion roared, and the walls shuddered. Pebbles bounced down from the ceiling, hitting my shoulders before falling to the ground. Greater boulders tumbled down where the dragons were. Shaygor erected a magical barrier to keep the rocks from falling onto him. His buddy wasn't as swift and took a bruising boulder to the wing before he furled them in and created magical protection around himself.

Shaygor looked back at the blue dragon as the smoke cleared. *Fool.*

I've never been here before. How am I supposed to know where the booby traps are? What did you see anyway?

This.

As the smoke cleared further, and the last of the rocks fell, they crowded around the cartridge to examine it. It was ridiculously small in comparison to their huge bodies.

The dragons turned slowly, sniffing the air.

His mongrel mate is here, Shaygor said. *She dropped this. We will find her.*

They would. It was inevitable, but I planned to make sure it took a while. Hopefully long enough for my allies to do their work.

It worried me that the female dragons hadn't come out yet, but maybe they would. At the least, maybe they were paying attention to this hunt and not to anything else. The idea that they might be torturing Zav came to mind, horrifying me as my imagination ran wild. I could only hope that Zondia didn't truly hate her brother that much, but the fact that she was here made me fear I couldn't make that assumption.

CHAPTER 26

Thanks to my camouflaging charm and a lot of running, ducking, and climbing walls—being careful only to tread places I'd gone before and that Ti had pointed out as safe—it took the dragons another hour to surround me and trap me.

Shaygor landed in the middle of the cavern on one side of me and the blue dragon on the other. They spewed fire at the same time, filling the space between them with flames, and I had to tap-dance to keep from being roasted alive. If not for my fire-resisting charm, no amount of dancing would have helped. Even with its protection, the intense heat seared my lungs and made me feel like a hot dog dropped into the embers.

Were they trying to slay me without asking any questions? I'd been sure Shaygor would want to ask about Ti again, and interrogate me for everything else I knew, but maybe they simply wanted to kill me.

I had Chopper in hand, the blade flaring blue and the grip growing warm against my palm, and was about to sprint in and attack Shaygor when the flames stopped. I put my back to the wall, so I could see both dragons staring at me as gray smoke curled up from their nostrils. I had a feeling the attack had knocked out the camouflaging ability of my charm for the moment.

Murderer of my son, Shaygor boomed into my mind. *You are the stupidest mongrel in existence. You were the stupidest mongrel in existence. No longer.*

He inhaled to breathe fire again, and I crouched, debating whether to rush him or rush his buddy in the hope of getting them in each other's crosshairs. But the blue dragon spoke and interrupted the attack before it came.

Wait. This vermin female is marked as Zavryd'nokquetal's mate and must have come to find him. How did she track him? And how did she get here? There is no way someone so weak could make a portal.

The escaped gnome went to her and told her everything. He wanted to hire her to kill us. Shaygor sounded a lot more pissed than the other dragon. Of course, he hated me with the fiery intensity of a thousand suns.

But how did she get here? The blue dragon squinted at me, and I felt him trying to probe my mind.

In the past, such an act would have filled my head with pain, but I felt only an unpleasant tickle today. Maybe it was my imagination, but the goblin charm on my keychain in my pocket seemed to warm against my thigh.

I cannot read her mind, the blue dragon said.

"Zondia is the only one who's managed that." I threw that out, hoping they would take me to her—and that she was with Zav. Then, afraid the comment would be too obvious, I added, "Too bad I couldn't read *her* mind. I would have warned Zav that she would betray him."

I hoped they would verify—or deny—that, if only so I would know if there was any possibility that Zondia had been coerced to join them and that I might have an ally. But they didn't.

She speaks of Zondia'qareshi? The blue dragon looked at Shaygor.

Yes. Her feeble mind is incapable of remembering our names.

Shall we take her to the females? Let them read her thoughts. We must know how she got here. Was it the gnome? Or another ally that we need worry about? It could be disastrous that he escaped if word gets out about this place. We would have to move the dragons and start all over again.

Or kill them and be done with it. Shaygor squinted at me, and I sensed him raking at the barrier of my mind, making his own attempt to read my thoughts.

It was a more forceful attack than the other dragon's had been, and I resisted the urge to stick my hand in my pocket and wrap it around the charm for support. The last thing I wanted was to draw attention to it. Eventually, they would think to remove my charms and my weapons, but maybe they wouldn't know what the trinkets did and would believe my power to resist their mind-reading was innate. In case it helped convey that, I formed the mental fern fronds in my mind, wrapping them protectively around my thoughts.

There would be no going back from that, the blue dragon replied softly.

There is no need *to go back.* Shaygor's eyes flared with inner light. *We have succeeded, cousin. The Justice Court and Ruling Council will be ours as soon as the queen is dead.*

Do not speak of this in front of the vermin.

The vermin we are about to kill? Shaygor issued the telepathic version of a scoff. But they fell silent after that—or switched to pinpoint telepathy. At least for several minutes. Then Shaygor spoke to me again. *Drop your weapons. We are taking you to the females.*

"I don't want to see them. I've met them, and they're bitchy."

Magical power wrapped around me, hefted me into the air, and flipped me face-up and parallel to the ground. My braid dragged along the rock as invisible energy propelled me deeper into the cavern. The magical grip tightened, constricting my lungs and keeping me from moving my muscles.

The dragon's mental compulsions and attempts to read my mind might not work, but none of my charms could protect me from being manhandled. And judging from the way Shaygor glared at me as he followed, he was contemplating all the ways he could use his power to kill me.

A jerk of power ripped Chopper out of my hand. I tightened my grip too late, not that I could have held it against that much power regardless. Fezzik flew out of my holster. This time, I was ready for it, but it didn't matter. The power wrapping around my body kept me from grabbing for the pistol as it floated away.

I've located Lord Zavryd, Sindari whispered into my mind, as if he knew I was surrounded by dragons who might overhear our telepathic communications.

And they very well might. Zav had heard my responses to Sindari before. That might have been because I'd been a neophyte telepath then, thinking my words for anyone with magic to pick up. The problem was I was *still* a neophyte.

I did my best to imagine Sindari and send my thoughts only to him. *Is he with the other dragons? Is he okay?*

He is in a large chamber with the two females. I have been inside for about fifteen minutes, and they seem to be discussing something—I cannot intercept their telepathic communications. He has not moved and is, I believe, unconscious, but I sense his aura, so he cannot be dead.

Neither Shaygor nor the blue dragon gave any indication that they were listening in as they flew—and levitated me—deeper into the cavern. A faint blue light had grown visible, coming from crystals in stalactites that stretched down from above.

Is the plan carrying on? I asked Sindari vaguely. If the dragons were listening and were hiding it, I didn't want to risk giving away everything.

I do not know. I fell behind and had to advance on my own. Only my superior instincts and agility allowed me to pass the booby traps without significant damage to myself.

We humans call that luck.

Because you are not superior.

I guess I can't argue that.

No. Sindari paused. *I sense you approaching. I also sense two dragons approaching. You have been captured?*

I've strategically placed myself into their grasp.

You have been captured.

Hold tight, and don't show yourself unless they try to kill me. I didn't know what poor Sindari could do to stop that. *Don't show yourself even if they try to kill me,* I amended. *Help the others if you can. If all those dragons are freed, maybe it'll be enough.*

Maybe. Sindari didn't sound like he agreed with my suggestion for him.

Brighter blue light came from somewhere beyond the lead dragon. With the power still wrapped around me, I couldn't lift my head to peer in that direction, but I sensed the cavern walls opening up.

A plop of water dropped onto my forehead, and I flinched. Condensation from the cave? We were still passing under stalactites, so I supposed that made sense.

I sensed Zav up ahead, but I also sensed Zondia and Velilah. When the two females tried to scour my mind, would I be able to resist them?

I don't suppose you're awake? I attempted to funnel the words toward Zav's aura but didn't get a response.

How many hours had passed since he'd been infected with the

bacteria? It seemed soon for him to have fallen unconscious. Ti had managed to round up gold and supplies from his people and travel to Earth before succumbing to the bacterial infection and passing out. Why had Zav's infection progressed more quickly? Had Zoltan given him a much higher dosage?

Droplets of water spattered my face and hands as we flew into a wide chamber within the cavern system. More crystals glittered from the stalactites in here, and they also seemed to be the source of the moisture. A droplet splashed onto my lips, and I tasted salt, as if they were tears instead of simply water.

I figured out how the Crying Caverns got their name, I thought to Zav, wishing he were awake to advise me on how to deal with these dragons—and to see that his sister had betrayed him. If he *had* been awake, maybe he could have talked her back to his side.

A clatter came from behind me. Shaygor had dumped my weapons unceremoniously on the ground. Too bad Fezzik hadn't gone off and shot him in the ass.

You will read the mongrel's mind and learn where the gnome is, Shaygor stated, broadcasting his thoughts again.

Puny male, you will not tell us what to do. That was Velilah, as lovely as I remembered.

I have brought you into my alliance and my plans, Shaygor boomed in return. *Your sex does not make you worthy of superior treatment. You will do as I say if you wish that place on the Ruling Council that you covet.*

My sex makes me your superior, *you cowardly, conniving frog of a dragon.*

Shaygor dropped me, and I hit the ground with a startled, "Ommph."

He almost took my head off as he flew over me and arrowed toward Velilah with his fangs bared. I was so surprised that I sat on my butt and gaped for several seconds as Velilah sprang into the air to meet Shaygor. Not as allies but as enemies. They breathed fire and raked and snapped at each other, tumbling across the chamber in a frenzied wrestling match. Someone drew blood, and it spattered in several directions, dark red droplets landing beside the salty puddles wept from the ceiling.

The blue dragon was to my right and issued something that almost sounded like a sigh. Zondia, her lilac scales glistening from the water, sat on her haunches farther back in the cave. She also watched, though I caught her looking at me. No magic was wrapped around me at the moment, but I doubted I could sprint out of the cavern without being noticed. Besides, if I ran off, I would be in as much danger from those booby traps as the dragons.

I was more interested in getting to Zav's side and injecting him with the formula. His black form lay crumpled behind Zondia, his head in a puddle on the ground, his eyes closed. I hoped they hadn't hurt him beyond whatever the bacteria was doing to him.

Sindari was at the far end of the wide, blue-lit chamber, sitting on a ledge that looked to lead deeper into the cavern. Hopefully, Ti and Walker were back there now, using this time to free the other dragons.

Zav was the only dragon I might be able to help from here. But how did I get over there without the dragons who *weren't* fighting noticing?

Shaygor and Velilah rolled past, tails flapping against each other and the ground as they continued to fight like cats in an alley. I would have wondered if this was some kind of foreplay, but there was a lot of blood for that.

I slowly pushed myself to my feet. The blue dragon and Zondia looked at me. The other two might be distracted—it was delightful of my enemies to fight each other—but these two were probably the level-headed ones who wouldn't be easily fooled.

A tail slammed down a few feet away from me, spraying water everywhere and shattering an innocent rock. Pretending I was afraid for my life—it wasn't that hard to pretend—I ran several steps in Zav's direction while looking back at the wrestling match.

Zondia watched me like a hawk, but she didn't stop me, so I grew bolder and turned my back on the fighting dragons and strode to Zav.

She stepped toward me, as if to intercept me, but a pained screech echoed from the fighters, and she stopped to look at them. Velilah had ended up on top with Shaygor on his back underneath her. Sadly, he was not dead. His chest heaved with his labored breathing, and he glared up at her, his talons sunken into the scales of her chest. But she had clearly won, her weight settled atop him, two of his legs pinned under her as she leered down at him, face to face.

This gave me a chance to hurry the rest of the way to Zav's side. The blue dragon was watching me from across the chamber, so I didn't yet lunge for the ammo pouch with the needle and vials inside. Instead, I flung my arm across Zav and collapsed at his side. Feeling his cool lifeless body made it easy to pretend I was distraught and defeated, but I made sure to arrange myself so I could hide my movements as I slid a hand down to unfasten the pouch.

You are weak, old dragon, Velilah announced to the entire chamber, though she was glaring down at Shaygor.

He glared back up at her, eyes blazing with indignation. *I have strong allies, and you risk yourself with this immature display, female.*

I watched them as I remained slumped against Zav's side and did not look down as I slid the already-prepared needle slowly out of the ammo pouch.

Zavryd'nokquetal bested me when we tussled the other day, Velilah said. *You are fortunate I seek power and position instead of a mate, for I would much rather take him into my nest. It is amazing that you ever found a female to mate with you and give you sons.*

The indignation in Shaygor's eyes turned to fury, and he hurled power at her even as he bucked up, throwing her off him. She rolled away, and he sprang after her, their wrestling match momentarily blocking the blue dragon's view of me.

Needle in hand, I turned toward Zav, reaching for what Zoltan had promised me would be the tender scales under his armpit. Sort of tender. He'd had to make a special needle for this that looked more like a nail gun than a medical instrument.

As I leaned in to inject him, I sensed Zondia looming behind me. Even though I feared she'd spotted me, I tried to finish the task. But just as the needle touched his scales, power knocked me back. Power followed by a massive taloned foot. I tried to roll away, but her magic pinned me down as her foot came down on my chest, great talons slicing through my jacket and brushing my ribs.

Crushing weight leaned onto that foot, and her long neck flexed and lowered her head until she stared into my eyes. Her maw parted, sword-like fangs revealed, and I saw my death in her violet eyes.

CHAPTER 27

top, a new voice sounded in my mind as Zondia's fangs lowered toward my throat. It was Zav.

He still lay unmoving with his eyes closed, appearing half-dead with his head in that puddle, but there was no mistaking his voice. Zondia must have heard it too, for she paused, her reptilian lips peeled back and saliva gleaming on her fangs. A droplet splashed my forehead, and I thought it was saliva at first, but another tear from the weepy crystals had found my face.

She was going to stab you with something, Zondia replied.

Yes. Zav's tone managed to be dry. *The cure to the infection.*

I sensed Sindari halfway from the ledge to Zondia. *Stop,* I thought to him, realizing he'd been charging down to rescue me.

Stop? he asked.

Yeah. We're having a discussion.

You are certain?

Technically, she and Zav are having a discussion. He's feigning being unconscious. Hold tight.

Are you positive it is a cure and not some poison, Brother?

Of course, I am positive. We planned this ruse ahead of time. She is my mate and devoted to me. She will never betray me. Zav shared an image of us having sex that would have made me blush with embarrassment if a dragon foot hadn't been smashing my chest. He carefully selected a moment of ardor, of me writhing naked underneath him and shouting out that he was amazing. I would have been less embarrassed if he had been making it up, but I remembered the moment. It was decidedly weird seeing it through someone else's eyes, though a feeling of pleasure and contentment oozed from Zav as he shared it.

That's disgusting, Zondia informed us.

And private. I barely resisted the urge to roll my head to the side and shoot Zav a dirty look. We probably had an audience. Even if Velilah and Shaygor were busy with round two of their battle, the blue dragon was likely watching from across the cavern. *You're not supposed to share thoughts of us in bed with others, Zav.*

She is my sister, he said as if that explained it. *And you are magnificent and loyal, Val. All shall know.*

All? What did *that* mean? *We're going to have a discussion later.*

I look forward to many *discussions similar to that one.* He oozed thoughts of nudity and sheet wrestling again, hopefully just to me this time, since Zondia still looked disgusted. And like she might eat me.

What's going on, Zav? I asked. *I thought your sister turned sides on you.*

As do Shaygorthian and Iyenathor. Was that the blue dragon? *It is a ruse. But we did not expect that Velilah'nav would be here and that we would have to fight against more than two. There are also four Silverclaw dragons flying outside of the cavern. Because the gnome escaped, they are wary that my clan will find out and come attempt to free their kin.*

Don't you still need the cure to the infection? My arm was as pinned as the rest of me, so all I could do was twitch my fingers. I'd managed to keep hold of the needle.

I do not. I tricked them. Zav sounded very smug for someone lying forlornly in a puddle and looking dead. *I studied how the infection appeared in my body when the vampire experimented on me, and when the treacherous dragons came to get me, I made them see what they were looking for.*

That means you're not infected right now? You're fine? And here I'd been worried about him and on the verge of tears several times.

I am very fine.

Yes, yes, he's terribly clever. And cocky. Brother, what do you want to do? I do not know if my message to the queen made it through or if it was intercepted by their spies. These may be the best odds that we get.

I concur. Shaygorthian is injured, and Val will fight with us.

Yes, your mongrel female is sure to turn the tide.

I glowered up at her, but it was hard to look convincingly threatening while pinned by a dragon's talons.

What is the mongrel doing? The blue dragon strode toward us. *Are you questioning her? Can you see her thoughts?*

Zondia lifted her head to look at him. From my back, it was hard to see what the other two dragons were doing, but I sensed that they'd broken apart. I could hear their ragged breaths from across the cavern, but I couldn't tell if they were watching us or glowering at each other while contemplating round three.

Of course I can read her thoughts. Zondia glared haughtily at the blue dragon. *She is a simpleton. Any idiot could see into her mind.*

Thanks so much, Zondia. I glared up at her, but she ignored me.

She came to try to rescue my foolish brother. She is a mindless slave besotted by him. Human vermin are so pathetic.

Are you sure *she's on our side?* I directed the thought to Zav.

She has a thespian streak.

The blue dragon continued closer. *How did she travel here from her world?*

Your escaped gnome opened a portal for her.

Is he here? He gazed around the cavern. *Or is he attempting to rally forces for a rescue?*

The forces are here, Zav told me grimly. *I am preparing to spring. Go for your weapons and assist us as soon as you can.*

I will.

Is your feline here?

Yes.

Sindari was still poised and ready to help me.

Good, Zav told me. *We must vanquish them as quickly as possible. Before their allies outside learn of this and fly down here to help them.*

The blue dragon stopped ten feet away, eyeing Zondia and then Zav. *I believe Zavryd'nokquetal has regained consciousness.*

He has not, Zondia stated.

For the first time, the blue dragon looked suspicious as his big head swung from Zondia to Zav and back.

Perhaps it is time for you to prove your loyalty to us, he said, *by killing your brother.*

Yes. Velilah crooned from across the cavern. *You will kill his mongrel mate and then kill the fool who rejected me for her.*

Zondia did not hesitate to glare down at me, as if to obey. She made a show of lifting her foreleg, talons gleaming with dampness in the blue light, and growled and leaned down, fangs ready to bite into my throat. The power that had gripped me earlier disappeared, and I rolled toward Zav to avoid the blow.

An explosion boomed in the back of the cavern, startling us all. I gaped back in time to see Sindari rolling away from a burst of red magical flames firing up from a triggered booby trap.

I didn't know if he'd done it on purpose to create a distraction or by accident, but all of the dragons sprang into action, starting with Zav.

With amazing agility, he went from a prone position on the ground to springing for the blue dragon. Zondia charged across the cavern and leaped into the air, flying full speed toward Velilah, who screeched and flung herself to the side. Zondia adjusted her course and crashed into her. Shaygor rushed to join the blue dragon against Zav.

I scrambled out of their way and skirted the chamber so I could grab my weapons. But my weapons were on the ground under the spot where Zondia and Velilah were wrestling.

"Great," I muttered.

As roars echoed from the walls and Zav hurled magic at the two dragons attacking him, I hoped he truly was completely uninjured and well.

Sindari avoided their battle and rushed toward the two females. He leaped and slashed at Velilah's back, then sprang away as they rolled and thrashed. I couldn't tell if his claws did any damage against her scales, and the females were too busy fighting each other to notice, but luck took them away from my weapons.

I rushed for Fezzik and Chopper, but Velilah flung a wave of power before I reached them. The attack was meant for Zondia, but the edge of it caught me. Just as I was about to grab Chopper, the magical blow knocked me ten feet.

I rolled, trying to protect myself from injuries as the hard rock battered my sides. Fortunately, Nin's vest armor kept my ribs from cracking.

As soon as I slowed enough, I leaped to my feet and rushed back for the weapons. A lilac tail slammed inches to my side. These crazy dragons would kill me completely by accident.

Finally, I snatched up my weapons. *Help me with Zav,* I told Sindari.

Since Zav battled two enemies, Zondia would have to fend for herself. That was my thought, but as I backed away from her, Velilah hurled her into a cavern wall. She struck so hard that the ground quaked. A huge stalactite that might have been loosened in the earlier explosion plunged down and slammed into Zondia's back. She must have been too busy attacking to create a shield around herself, for its point hit hard enough to gouge into her scales and draw blood. Zondia's head drooped, as if the blow had dazed her.

Velilah crouched to spring. I held down Fezzik's trigger to fire round after round at her. The bullets didn't bounce off a shield, but they also didn't pierce her armored scales, not the way Chopper could. Still, the irritation was enough that she whirled toward me.

Zondia, who wasn't as dazed as she'd pretended, charged at our enemy. I fired again to keep Velilah distracted—or at least try. She saw the greater threat and spun back toward Zondia, but she was too late. Zondia's powerful jaws snapped around her neck.

Trusting she had all the advantage she needed, I turned to help Zav.

Shaygor lay groaning on the ground between me and Zav, who was wrestling and hurling magic at the blue dragon now. Had Zav already defeated Shaygor?

I was on the verge of running around his prone form to help with the blue, but Shaygor rose to his feet and shook off like a wet dog. His chest heaved, though I didn't know if he was out of breath or seething with anger. He started toward Zav to jump back into that fight, but then he sensed me.

His eyes gleamed, not with fury this time but with the hatching of some idea, and he prowled toward me. He didn't have to say anything for me to know he wanted to use me to make Zav surrender. Well, that wasn't going to happen.

In my arrogance, I believed I could keep him busy while Zav and Zondia finished off their foes, and then they could come handle Shaygor. I hoped that arrogance wasn't misplaced. If he hadn't already been injured, I might not have thought that way, but he was limping, and blood dripped from talon gouges on his flanks and fang marks in his neck.

Use your charm to disappear, Sindari encouraged me.

I pointed Fezzik at Shaygor. "Are you ready to get your ass kicked for a *third* time today, you big silver cream puff?"

Vaaaaal, Sindari groaned into my mind.

If I disappear, he can gang up on Zav. I'm keeping him busy.

Shaygor roared and charged at me. He flung magic ahead of him. As I dove to the side, I envisioned some of Freysha's fronds rising up to deter the magical blow.

It didn't completely work, but at least his power didn't hurl me all the way across the chamber. It might have been more that he was weakened than that my attempt at a magical defense worked, but I only stumbled a few steps before I was able to recover. I spun back and opened fire.

Unlike Velilah, Shaygor had the wherewithal to get a magical barrier up. The bullets ricocheted away. When my magazine ran out of rounds, I returned Fezzik to my holster instead of reloading. Shaygor was crouching to spring. Chopper was the weapon for this job.

He flew at me like a panther leaping, his talons outstretched to tear my head off. Before, I'd dodged to the side. Since he might expect that again, I ducked my head low and rushed toward him, rolling under those swiping forelegs and jumping up under his belly. I slashed Chopper upward, the blade slicing into Shaygor's scales.

He jerked and scrambled away, lashing out with a hind leg. The abrupt attack surprised me, but I managed to dodge those deadly talons.

As Shaygor spun back, he opened his maw wide to attack with fire. Once again, I sprinted toward him instead of away. Flames bathed the ground all around me, and my skin screamed with pain as I took far too much of the heat, but I managed to get under his body again where the fire couldn't reach me.

He bent his legs to jump away, but I leaped up, stabbing for his armpit this time. If it was a vulnerable spot to a medical needle, it ought to be vulnerable to my blade too.

The point drove in more easily than it had at the belly, gouging several inches into flesh, and Shaygor shrieked like a dying pig. He might have intended to leap straight into the air and fly out of my reach, but he ended up pitching over, jerking his legs away from me.

Knowing he would recover if I gave him time, I rushed for him, leaping onto his flank and clawing my way up to stand on him. His head came up and around, jaws snapping for me. Hatred and fury flared in his eyes, and I knew he'd kill me if he could. Maybe he'd wanted to use me before. Now, he wanted me dead.

But I stood my ground in a balanced crouch on his flank. As his jaws snapped for me, I swept Chopper into the side of his maw, the blade digging deep. As I cut into him, I dropped low, evading his bite. Wounded again, he pulled his head back.

I rose up and shifted my grip to use Chopper like a spear. With all my physical strength and all the magic that might lie within my blood, I thrust the blade down point-first into his flank. It sank deep, and his entire body jerked, limbs twitching spasmodically.

Had I struck his heart? I had no idea. I yanked out the blade and drove it in again.

His head and neck flopped to the ground, and the limbs stopped jerking about. I tugged Chopper free, ready to drive the sword in again if needed, but his powerful aura slowly faded from my awareness as the life seeped out of him. I'd done it. I'd defeated him.

The other battles had fallen silent, and only the sound of dripping water remained. I looked around and found Zondia and Zav staring at me—gaping at me?—from opposite ends of the chamber. Their opponents lay unconscious or dead at their feet. But as they stared at me, at the dragon blood dripping from Chopper's blade and Shaygor dead under me, I couldn't tell if they were pleased or horrified. The last time I'd killed a dragon, Zav hadn't reacted well at all… Would he blame me for this? Believe I should have somehow subdued Shaygor so he could be taken in for punishment and rehabilitation?

While Zondia was still staring at me with a stunned expression on her dragon face, Zav strode toward me. As he walked, he shifted into his human form.

When he drew close to Shaygor's body, he lifted an arm, his eyes flaring with violet light. "Come to me, my mate."

Though I was still wary about what their reaction would be, I didn't want to spend the rest of the day standing on a dead dragon. I slid down Shaygor's flank and walked to Zav. Usually, when his eyes glowed, it was a sign of danger, but neither his expression nor his aura seemed angry. If anything, as I stepped close to him, the power of his aura crackled around me with sexual intensity that shifted my thoughts from battle to much more intimate things.

Zav wrapped an arm around me and pulled me against him, kissing me with intense desire that weakened my knees and almost had me dropping Chopper. Though I doubted we were out of danger, I wrapped my free arm around him and kissed him back. It seemed appropriate given that we'd defied death together. Or at least dragons.

But when his hands started roaming, I rested my palm on his chest. *I believe we have a mission to complete and enemies to worry about.*

Indeed. Zav smiled against my mouth without taking his lips from mine. *But I am overcome with pride and desire for my ferocious warrior mate.*

I'll take the pride now, but let's save the desire for later, huh? I pulled my mouth away—not surprisingly, Zondia stood nearby doing the dragon equivalent of rolling her eyes—but I didn't want him to feel that I didn't care or wasn't glad to have him here with me, so I hugged him and patted him on the butt.

Yes. We will mate when we are done. He stroked the back of my head and gazed into my eyes, that pleased smile tugging at his lips. *You are mine.*

Fine, but you're mine too, dragon.

Obviously. He snorted, as if he'd been waiting all summer for me to figure that out.

And you're taking me on a date before we mate again. You can't just show up at a girl's bedroom door and expect sex.

What do humans do on dates?

Lots of things. Walks on the beach. Ferry rides. Dinner and a movie.

Dinner?

Trust you to focus on the thing that involves eating.

His eyes glinted. *You will feed me?*

Yes, I will feed you. If this all works out and I get Ti's gold, I'll even be able to afford your ten portions of ribs more than once a month.

Excellent.

CHAPTER 28

Sindari and I rode on Zav's back as he and Zondia flew deeper into the cavern, avoiding booby traps by soaring over them. A convenient way to travel. I hoped we would find that Ti and Walker had already freed the other dragons.

Sindari tensed, claws digging into scales as Zav banked to follow a bend in the narrow passage.

It is not wise to prong a dragon with one's claws, Zav informed us.

Sindari loosened his grip. *My apologies, Lord Zavryd. I have not flown on a dragon before. It is unnerving.*

You accidentally stepped on an explosive booby trap earlier, I pointed out. *By comparison, this should barely faze your nerves.*

I intentionally stepped on that because I believed you were in danger and needed your enemies diverted.

What made you think that?

The lilac dragon was crushing you with her foot.

That's Zav's sister, and it was a ruse. I suspect she secretly adores me. I glanced over my shoulder to make sure Zondia was still following us—and wasn't glaring at the back of my head with plans to send beams of magical energy through my brain.

It didn't look like much of a ruse.

Zav says she's a thespian. I patted Zav's shoulder. *How did your sister convince Shaygor she was on his side?*

It has been fashionable for a long time for Stormforges to defect, Zav growled into my mind. *I gather it didn't take much convincing, but in truth, she's been keeping an eye on him for the queen for some time. Because she's been loitering around with Silverclaws, the arrogant ass thought she wished to curry favor and have a position with him in the event that they defeated us. Which they will not. Not now, not ever.* Another blue-lit chamber came into view ahead, and Zav flapped his wings harder to reach it. *We don't have much time. One of the dragons outside the caverns has realized he lost touch with Shaygorthian and believes something is wrong. He's questioning my sister.*

With luck, Ti and Dr. Walker have already started freeing your relatives.

A lot of luck, I reluctantly admitted. It had been at least two hours since I'd parted ways with them, but I hadn't realized how much farther back this second chamber was. For people who had to walk to it, dodging booby traps all along the way, it couldn't have been an easy journey. It was a simple matter for dragons to fly through these caverns, and if the four Silverclaws that Zav had said were outside decided to pop in for a visit, we would have another fight.

My body ached at the thought. I'd hit my back and hips hard when Shaygor had thrown me around, and Zondia and Zav had wicked gouges on their sides where talons had raked deep.

Zav landed at the entrance to the new chamber, and a surge of protective magic wrapped around us. An explosive boom erupted from the ground under Zav's belly, and fire burst up on either side of him. I tensed, but I didn't feel the heat through his barrier.

Sindari gave me a flat look, perhaps not agreeing that riding dragons shouldn't faze one's nerves.

I patted Zav's back. *Did you know that was there?*

No, the booby traps are cleverly hidden. They don't even give off a noticeable magical signature, but I felt a slight click under my toes.

"Walking around in here will be fun," I muttered, then raised my voice enough to softly call, "Ti? Dr. Walker?"

A bead of water plopped down on Sindari's ear from above. He hadn't suffered many wounds in the battle, but he was damp from the weeping ceilings. So was I. My body had cooled off since the battle, and I shivered in the perpetual chill and dampness of the caverns.

I do not sense the others, Sindari said as Zondia landed next to us—she managed to do so without setting off a trap. *It is possible they are still camouflaged. I do sense the dragons, though their auras are muted.*

For the first time, I could sense them too. Dozens of dragons were hibernating inside sunken cells—I would call them caves within the larger chamber—along the walls to either side of us.

Zav strode toward one of the nearest cells, where a black dragon was visible curled in a ball on the ground. I could barely sense his aura. Instead, I sensed magic inside and all around the cell. More than that, alien cords and conduits snaked along one wall and ran to a mechanical box mounted near the entrance. Gnomish handiwork?

Another booby trap went off as Zav neared the cell, but again, his magic protected us. It worried me that Ti and Walker hadn't called out to us. It wasn't as if they could have missed Zav's entrance. His flagrant indifference to the traps reminded me of his landing at Weber's house when he'd deliberately set off all the alarms and fireworks there.

My dragon. I smiled and patted him on the shoulder again.

This is my uncle, Zav shared grimly, gazing at the unconscious black dragon.

He reached out a talon, but a silver force field appeared, preventing him from reaching in. Judging by the way he jerked his limb back, it also zapped him.

"It doesn't bode well that he's still in there." I looked around again for the rest of my party. "Ti worked here for twenty years. He should have been able to get the cells open, and Walker should have been in here already injecting these dragons…"

I'd almost sacrificed myself to buy time for them. They should have used it, damn it. Unless…

They may have triggered a booby trap, Sindari said. *A deadly one. Perhaps they never made it back here.*

"No." I shook my head. "We would have seen their bodies if they'd been mangled by a trap."

Would we have? Some of those gouts of fire and explosions had been powerful. It was possible they could incinerate people without leaving sign.

They are coming, Zondia told us.

Zav had been contemplating the force field, but he looked back at her. *The other dragons?*

Yes. I tried to allay their suspicions, but they know they can't sense Shaygorthian and Iyenathor anymore, and it didn't work. It's also possible that one of the dragons we battled said something to them before we defeated them.

Are all four coming?

Yes. Zondia was as grim as Zav. *I am willing to fly into battle with you again, Brother, but I do not think we can win. It is also possible there are more dragons on this world that are too far away for us to sense or that are hiding themselves.*

I know.

What do you want to do?

We must not let any of Shaygorthian's allies back into this chamber. Once they see that we are here and know about this heinous crime, they may try to destroy the evidence. Destroy our kin.

I agree, Zondia said, *but how can we be certain to stop them?*

I will go confront them and keep them busy while you fly home. Tell the queen what is happening—tell the whole family. Get as many allies as you can and bring them back. We must free and heal our people.

Zondia stared at him. I was staring down at him too, though he couldn't see it when I was on his back.

You cannot fight four dragons alone, Brother.

I will be crafty and merely keep them busy until you return with reinforcements.

I do not believe you.

Zav did not answer her. Instead, he looked back and levitated Sindari and me off his back. He lowered us carefully to the ground, to a spot he'd already trod on and that shouldn't have more booby traps. I appreciated that, though I worried what would happen once he left and I tried to move three feet in any direction.

Be careful, Val. Zav didn't switch forms again—he was poised to fly back out—but he rested a wingtip on my shoulder, and my eyes threatened to tear up. Did this propensity for getting weepy worrying about Zav mean I truly was falling in love?

"Don't get yourself killed," I said, making my voice gruff to hide the quaver that threatened, "or I'm going to be pissed."

Because you will not get a chance to feed me again? His humor didn't usually come through in his eyes when he was in dragon form, but there was a hint of it there now.

"Yeah. That's the reason."

I knew that excited you as much as it does me.

I snorted but didn't deny it. I stepped in and hugged his foreleg before backing up and letting him fly away.

Zondia had formed a portal while we were talking—probably not wanting to witness our mushy goodbye—and she sprang through it as Zav flew back the way we had come.

The magic faded, leaving Sindari and me alone in the cavern with stalactites dripping salty water on our heads.

CHAPTER 29

I was gazing through the force field at Zav's unmoving uncle, trying to figure out how I could get through the barrier to dose him with the formula, when a call came from the far end of the chamber.

I whirled, Fezzik in hand before my brain caught up to my instincts. That voice was familiar.

"Dr. Walker?" I peered in that direction but couldn't see or sense anyone.

"Sorry, Val." Walker appeared in front of the last cell in the cavern, lifting an arm. "I wasn't sure how to deactivate your cloaking charm. I also wasn't sure if it was safe to."

"I called out to you when we first came in," I pointed out, though I was relieved to see him. I hoped Ti was there too and that he knew how to lower these force fields.

"Yes, but you and the familiar dragon looked like you might be a prisoner of the purple one. Since we saw her fly in with the others earlier, I assumed she was on their side and was forcing you to come back here and look for us."

"No. That was a trick. She's Zav's sister. Is Ti with you? Have you figured out how to unlock the dragons?" I felt silly shouting across the chamber to him, but those explosions were fresh in my mind. I had no delusions that my feeble magical powers would be sufficient to protect me from booby traps.

"Yes. He's done half of them, and I'm administering the formula."

Walker pointed toward cells that I couldn't see into from my end of the chamber. "We were hiding back here, worried the purple dragon would sense that the magical barriers were down and know where we were."

"The dragons that captured Zav are dead. Can you come get this one out? This is his uncle."

Walker looked back, though I couldn't see anyone. "Ti? Want to get him now?"

The gnome appeared, not looking any worse for their adventures, and I breathed a sigh of relief. Ti led Walker across the chamber, zigzagged in particular spots, and reached Sindari and me.

"I recognized him and wanted to free him first." Ti knelt in front of the cell and stuck a tool that reminded me of a giant Allen wrench into a small hole in the ground. "But since he was the closest to the front, we knew anyone coming back to check would notice if the cell field was down."

With a pulse of magical energy, that field disappeared.

"Go ahead, Doctor." Ti waved Walker inside and then picked a careful route to the next cell with a dragon in it. "I'll open the rest of them."

"How many have you already dosed?" I asked as Walker worked.

"Ah, ten or twelve."

"Have any of them woken up?" I assumed not, or I would have sensed it. The dragon auras in the chamber were so subdued that they were barely noticeable. A few of the auras in the back seemed a little stronger, but it might have been my imagination.

"I don't think so. Given how long some of these dragons have been here, it could take days or months for their metabolisms to ramp up and clear the infection, and for them to be able to walk or fly out of their own accord."

"*Months?*" I doubted we had hours.

Even as I asked that, I sensed a dragon flying by somewhere above the underground cavern. A second soared into my range behind that one. They seemed to be heading toward the entrance of the cavern. I hoped Zav was out there distracting them without being hurt himself.

"It's possible this one will wake up sooner." Walker finished injecting Zav's uncle under the armpit and stepped back. "He should only have been in here for a few weeks, right?"

"I think so."

"If we got one to wake up and regain his faculties—his powers—he could make a portal and take the rest through to somewhere safe."

Wherever that was. With schemes and plots flying through the air like migrating geese in the fall, I wondered if even the dragon home world—wherever Zav's family lived—would be safe. The last thing I wanted was to invite them back to Earth to hang out at my place. Zoltan would have a fit.

Ti moved on to open the next cell, and Walker went to dose the next dragon.

"Is there anything I can do to help?" I shifted from foot to foot, feeling unhelpful.

"Just let us know if trouble is coming."

Val? Zav spoke into my mind from beyond my range. *Are you all right?*

So far. Are you?

A long moment passed before he answered, which amped my worry up to ten.

I had to fight one to keep him from going into the caverns, Zav finally said, and I wondered if he was fighting—or fleeing—now. *Two more are coming this way, and I'm trying to lead them away, but I'm not sure where the fourth dragon is. He might have used some magical stealth to slip past me and go inside.*

Lovely.

I'll keep an eye out for him. Stay safe, Zav.

Tell your people to stay camouflaged.

Right. Thanks.

"Reactivate your stealth charms, guys. We may be getting company."

"Dragon company?" Walker asked.

"I'm afraid so."

"I am not afraid," Ti said. "You will slay any dragon that attempts to interfere with our noble mission. Have you not already done so today? I detect dragon blood on your blade right now."

"I cleaned that off."

"The magical taint of dragon lingers."

I made a note to loofah my sword when I got home.

I thought about pointing out that Shaygor had been badly injured after battling both Zav and the female dragon, but Ti might feel better if he believed I could handle whatever enemy flew in here. So long as he camouflaged himself in the meantime…

The sensation of someone looking at me crawled up my spine. I looked toward the nearest cell—and jumped. Blue dragon eyes were looking at me. Zav's uncle was awake. And as far as I knew, he didn't know I was a friend.

"Hello." I waved cheerfully, resisting the urge to grab Chopper. A dragon recovering from a deadly bacterial infection shouldn't be perky enough to spring immediately for my throat, right? "Are you Uncle Ston? We're here with Zav. We're trying to get you and all the other dragons here out and healed."

He hadn't yet lifted his head, and only his nostrils moved. Inhaling the air—or checking out my scent.

You bear his mark, Ston spoke into my mind. *You are his mate.*

"Yup. And he's my dragon." Somehow, it seemed less demeaning to be called *his mate*—all of these guys said it in the way one might say *his property*—if Zav was also *my* dragon.

You are cheeky.

He didn't know the half of it yet.

It figures that he would like you.

I almost fell over. This was the first of Zav's family not to glare daggers at me for presuming to allow myself to be claimed by him. I wasn't sure he was ready to fall in love with me yet, but this seemed a promising start.

I vex his enemies.

Good. Ston closed his eyes. *I am very weak. What happened to me?*

No sooner had I started to explain it to him than Sindari spoke into my mind. *The trouble you promised to watch for is coming.*

Before I could ask for details, the aura of a new dragon came within range of my senses. It wasn't flying high above the underground cavern system; it was down here with us.

I groaned and drew Chopper, but I also activated my camouflage charm. Fighting a dragon in a chamber full of booby traps sounded like a bad idea.

A silver dragon that reminded me all too much of Shaygor flew into the chamber and landed where Zav had landed earlier. Unfortunately, the booby trap Zav had triggered didn't go off a second time. It was probably useless to hope this dragon would be less swift at getting up his defenses if he stepped on one.

He peered around the chamber, yellow eyes glowing. They skimmed over Sindari and me without seeing us. Ti had stopped lowering barriers, and I assumed Walker was crouched behind a dragon and not doing anything.

After the newcomer scanned the whole chamber, his gaze turned back in my direction. No, in *Ston's* direction. Maybe he'd figured out that Ston, who had his eyes closed again, was free and that some of the cells were open.

The dragon prowled toward us. Though I was reluctant to leave Ston open to attack, I eased to the side so this new threat wouldn't get close enough to see through my charm's magic. It would be better to spring on the dragon from the side when he wasn't looking.

His focus remained on Ston, his eyes icy cold. Smoke wafted from his nostrils, and his jaw parted, revealing fangs. Did he mean to attack old half-dead Ston? What an ass.

I crouched as he drew even with me, willing my muscles to stay loose and ready for action. Maybe it was my imagination, but eagerness seemed to flow from Chopper, as if the sword had tasted dragon blood once today and was ready to do so again.

Too bad I wasn't. This guy was as large and muscular as Zav and didn't show any indication of being wounded.

You are awake, the dragon boomed, his voice old and stern in my mind.

Ston lifted his head slowly on his long serpentine neck and smacked his lips—inasmuch as dragons had lips. *Yes, I am. Who are you? Have you brought me a refreshing morning beverage?* Ston looked around. *I'm not sure where I am, but I believe I've been asleep for a long time.*

Bring you? I am not a servant! I am Dhorasmusnost of the Silverclaw Clan.

Are you? How fabulous.

I would have snorted if I hadn't been fifteen feet to the side of a dragon who would crush me if he realized I was there. No wonder the gnomes preferred Ston to rule their world to one of the stuffy Silverclaws.

Unfortunately, Dhor-whatever didn't appreciate the comment. He roared, the noise echoing from the walls of the cavern, and opened his maw to breathe fire. Poor Ston probably couldn't stand up, much less fight.

Anger surged through me, and I ran and slashed at Dhor's flank. I wished I could have leaped onto his back, since I'd had good luck attacking dragons from behind, but he was standing and too tall for that.

He recoiled in surprise at my appearance, but he reacted swiftly. Magic flowed around him, and Chopper met the resistance of a barrier before it reached his scales. Damn. I'd hoped I would get in a free cut before he got his defenses up.

The fire he'd intended to breathe at Ston went toward me. I sprinted around behind him as it splashed the damp rocky ground, and I slashed again, this time willing my magic to part his barrier so I could stab his flank. Chopper slid through the dragon's defenses and nicked him.

That elicited another roar as he leaped into the air, a wing almost smacking me in the head. I rolled away and came up facing him with Chopper ready to defend.

A burst of magic came from the center of the chamber. A portal opened, and the big dragon flew farther away from me instead of attacking again. A huge black dragon flew out of the portal, followed by three more black dragons.

I scurried back, flattened myself to the wall, and tapped my camouflage charm to hide myself. If these were Zav's family members, this could be a good thing, but if they were Silverclaw reinforcements, we were dead. All of us.

A big female screeched and flew toward Dhor like an eagle arrowing in to snatch up a field mouse. The Silverclaw dragon tried to fly for the exit to escape, but she caught up with him. It was the queen, I realized, remembering her aura from our encounter in Idaho.

She plowed into Dhor, bearing him to the ground and smothering him with her magic as she bit into his neck with her fangs. The other dragons piled on as even more flew out of the portal. Earlier, the huge chamber had seemed vast. Now, it felt crowded.

Lilac-scaled Zondia came out at the end of the line of dragons. She flew around the cavern, looking at the fight as if she wanted to join in, but there was no room. Nor was there a need. The others were tearing Dhor to pieces. Literally. Some amendment must have been made to their no-killing-other-dragons rule. Either that, or the queen was royally pissed.

Ston shambled slowly out of the cell, looking weak and wobbly, but at least he was on his feet. *Where did you go, mate of young Zavryd?*

I wasn't positive I should reveal myself. The queen, who was clearly in the mood to kill, hadn't been my biggest fan, and who knew what all these other dragons would think of me? Hiding and letting them handle everything seemed like a good idea, but Ston was peering around as the fight wound down.

I'm hiding, I answered telepathically without revealing myself. *Your kin seem angry.*

A bloody chunk of Dhor's tail splatted down three feet in front of me. *Do they? Hmm.*

With her enemy slain and dismembered, the queen sprang into the air and flew for the exit. Her posse—what was the correct term for a bunch of dragons?—flew after her.

Young Zavryd has been injured, Ston informed me. *They hope to reach him before the others kill him.*

"Kill?" I blurted, no longer caring if I remained camouflaged.

Zondia flew toward me, landing in a crouch. *Get on. I'll take you to him.*

Normally, I would be wary about climbing onto another dragon's back, but if Zav was hurt, I needed to go to him. I needed to help. Somehow.

Without hesitating, I scrambled up her tail and onto her back. *Sindari? Are you coming?*

He eyed Zondia's back. *Dismiss me, and I'll rejoin you out there if you need me. The ride in was that bad?*

Worse than in your vehicle.

Are you sure? There isn't a tree air freshener hanging around Zondia's neck. I smiled, though my heart wasn't in it. All I wanted was to find Zav and for him to be okay. I didn't know if Zondia was waiting for me before taking off, but I patted her back so she would know I was ready.

I will remain here and assist the invisible people in freeing the others, Ston stated.

As Zondia took off, I glanced back toward where I'd last seen Ti and Walker.

We'll be fine and able to finish now, Ti spoke into my mind. *Go help your mate.*

❖ ❖ ❖ ❖ ❖

I clenched Chopper as Zondia flew us through the cavern, the wind from her wings whipping my braid around. It wasn't as smooth a ride as when I flew with Zav, but I hardly cared. I just wanted to get out there and help.

As we flew over the lava lake and neared the entrance, I sensed him. He was up on the top of the cliff near that pile of boulders where Ti, Walker, and I had hidden. A battle raged nearby, the queen and her followers tearing into the three dragons that had been ganging up on Zav.

Rage tightened my chest, and I was glad when I could see the scene for myself, could see that Zav's family was beating the crap out of them. They deserved to be ganged up on in return.

But Zav. He wasn't moving. He lay on the ground, one of his legs turned out at an angle that had to indicate a break. Blood spattered the gray rock all around him.

Fear replaced my rage as I checked with my senses to make sure I could still detect his aura, that he wasn't dead. He *looked* dead.

Zondia must have decided her family had the battle in hand, for she flew straight to her brother. Before she even touched down, I sprang from her back. I ran to one side of Zav's head and touched his cheek. His eyes were closed, and he didn't stir.

"Are you conscious?" I whispered as the shrieks and growls and snaps echoed from the other side of the boulder pile as the dragons continued to battle. "Zav?"

I told myself that he was still alive and that his family was here, so he would be fine—dragons had powerful healing magic, after all—but that didn't keep me from leaning my cheek against his with tears leaking from my eyes. I stroked the side of his snout, his scales cool.

"If you don't wake up and heal yourself, I'm not going to be able to feed you," I whispered. "I have a meal of a whole roasted chicken and barbecue ribs planned, so you would be super foolish to die and not get to eat it."

Only then did I realize that the sounds of the battle had faded. Several dragons had landed nearby and were staring at us—at me crying all over Zav's snout.

Step back, mate of my son. The queen was one of the dragons standing and watching. I mulishly wanted to resist, to stay there with Zav, but she added, *We will take him home and heal him.*

"Right." My throat was raspy, and I switched to telepathy to ask, *He's not too injured, is he? Will he be all right?*

We shall see.

A portal formed near the boulder pile, and one of the dragons levitated

Zav's inert form into the air. I wiped my cheeks as he was floated through the portal, followed by several other dragons.

The queen, a dragon as large as any I'd seen, walked toward me. When Zav had been lying helpless on the ground, all my thoughts had been for him, and I hadn't worried that I was a very small half-elf surrounded by more than a dozen very large dragons, but now I grew aware of how vulnerable I was.

If they were all Zav's kin and loyal to the family, they *shouldn't* have a reason to harm me, but it wasn't as if all the dragons I'd met had been reasonable beings. Or even *most* of them.

The queen lowered her head to scrutinize me. I abruptly worried that I had pit stains and hadn't flossed before leaving the house and might have food lingering in my teeth.

I objected to my son claiming you as a mate, she said.

Yes, I remember. I clamped down on my tongue to refrain from saying something sarcastic. This wasn't the time. Given how huge and imposing the queen was, I had a feeling it would *never* be the time.

I retract my objection. With that, she sprang into the air and flew through the portal.

I stared after her, almost too stunned to feel relieved. Or was I supposed to be grateful? If that meant she wouldn't try to keep us apart—or send more female dragons to try to woo Zav away—I decided I could manage gratefulness.

Huh. Zondia was the only living dragon remaining.

"Surprised?"

Yes.

"Does this mean she'll send me a Christmas present?"

I do not know what that is.

"Just tell her I could use a chest freezer full of meat, now that Zav is visiting the house more often."

Zondia swished her tail and looked at me like I was odd. What was new?

I will return you to the others and assist in reviving the imprisoned dragons, Zondia said.

"Any chance you can take me to your home world so I can keep an eye on Zav?" I doubted I could do anything to help Ti and Walker. I couldn't do anything to help Zav either, but I would prefer to be with him when he woke up. And *until* he woke up.

Humans are not welcome in our world. The portal faded, and Zondia lowered to the ground. *Come.*

Reluctantly, I climbed onto her back to return to the caverns. I had to trust that Zav's family would take care of him and that he would recover.

CHAPTER 30

Thwack, thud, thwack!

I slammed the sledgehammer into the bathroom wall and bashed out pieces of drywall. The dust mask covering my face wasn't helping as well as I'd hoped with keeping mold spores from swiftly and vehemently sailing down my airway, but destroying the bathroom at least gave me an opportunity to take out my aggressions.

Technically, they were concerns. It had been a week since Ti and Walker had freed and injected all the Stormforge dragons and the queen had taken Zav home to heal him, and I hadn't heard a peep. Not a single dragon had come to give me an update. I knew it was unlikely I'd hear from the queen herself, but it would have been nice if Zondia had come. Even better would be if *Zav* came.

Dragon healing was powerful. How could he not be better by now?

What if not all was as it seemed? What if the queen had lied to me about withdrawing her objection and she was keeping Zav for punishment and rehabilitation or whatever one did to wayward children?

Thwack, thud, thwack!

"Uhm, Val?" came Dimitri's voice from the door. He also wore a mask and was covered in wood dust and paint chips. "Could you demo a little more quietly? I don't think when the landlord said we could fix the place up that he meant full-scale renovation. I think he imagined paint and trimming the bushes."

"It *needs* full-scale renovation." I picked up a piece of drywall from the floor and showed him the back. Not only had it been warped by water damage, but the inside was fuzzy with black and green splotches of mold. My nose—and my lungs—hadn't been lying to me.

"Yeah, but we can't afford any more materials than I already got." His gaze drifted to the side. "What happened to the bathtub?"

I pointed to a list I'd made on a pad of paper resting on a ledge. *Remove fixtures* and *Retile floor* were at the bottom. "It's in the back yard. Next to the toilet and the sink."

"I knew we were taking out the toilet and sink to redo the plumbing back there, but... how did you lift out a clawfoot bathtub? It was cast iron under the porcelain, wasn't it?"

"Probably, but I'm a beast, Dimitri. I kill bad guys for a living." I flexed an arm and didn't mention that I'd recruited Freysha and her magic to help me. That sucker had been more than two hundred pounds.

"You didn't damage it, did you?" He launched a concerned look down the hall toward the open balcony door I'd been tossing debris out.

"Nope. I gently heaved it into the yard."

"Heaved! Those are worth a fortune, Val." Dimitri sprinted off down the hall as if a dragon were after him. "The plumbing in the *wall* is bad, not the tub!"

I decided to let him discover on his own that it was undamaged and resting on its clawed feet until we finished and could put it back in. Thanks to some very sturdy magical vines, it had been lowered gently to the ground.

I went back to thwacking out bits of drywall, wishing I had some bad guys to kill right now, but Willard said the city had been oddly quiet. Nobody was murdering anyone this week. That was good in theory but left me little to do except tackle the renovation project.

"You were messing with me?" Dimitri returned to the doorway.

"It's fun."

"Do you know what you're doing? Mold remediation is a profession, you know. I think you're supposed to have industrial fans drying everything and air purifiers running around the clock."

"I opened the windows."

"Almost the same."

"Zav said he would help. I thought I'd have him breathe fire—that'll dry everything."

"That'll incinerate the entire second and third floors."

"So long as the mold goes with it."

"I hope you're joking, because my name is on the lease too."

"We could blame the vampire in the basement."

"The vampire who made a concoction that saved the lives of dozens of dragons?"

"I suppose that would be a poor way to repay him." I wished I knew for certain that those lives had been saved. Why wouldn't some relative of Zav's come give me an update?

Thwack, thud, thwack!

The doorbell rang. I knew without using my senses that it wasn't a dragon. On previous occasions, Zav had proven to me that dragons didn't press buttons and politely wait to be let in.

"It is your employer," Freysha called up from below.

"Send her up, please."

A minute later, Willard appeared in the drywall-littered hallway, wrinkling her nose. She was in her civvies and carried one of the envelopes that my payments came in. "What the hell are you doing, Thorvald?"

"Remodeling."

"You didn't *buy* this dilapidated mess, did you?" Willard gawked at the to-do list on the ledge, the pen balancing precariously over the side of the pad.

"No, but I'm thinking about it." I tugged my mask off and wiped sweat from my face.

"With what money? Even if this thing isn't up to code, I'm sure the lot alone is worth more than a half mil."

"The house comes with a vampire-in-the-basement discount. And Nin's grandfather paid me well for the dragon mission."

"Where do you go to convert Gnomish phlanks into US dollars? I'm positive they're not listed on the foreign exchange."

"Is that their currency? How do you know these things?"

"I read books."

"Gnome books?"

"All the books we can get from our moles and informants. After Freysha translates them, someone in the office has to read them and put the information in the database."

"Your job is scintillating."

"Tell me about it."

"Ti paid me in gold. I've since taken it to a dealer, confirmed that it was real, and gotten a very big check. Also a police inquiry, an inquiry from my bank, and a bunch of forms to fill out for the IRS. Apparently, it's suspicious to abruptly acquire large sums of money."

"You think? Well, here." Willard handed me the envelope. "It doesn't sound like you need it now, but I did promise to pay you to free those dragons, and I've heard word that your mission was successful. I've also heard that you and your sword are known to be death to the Silverclaw Clan." She raised her eyebrows.

"Does that mean you heard that relatives of Dob and Shaygor will be coming after me?" It wasn't my fault that dragons from that clan kept attacking me.

"You better watch your back. Or start sleeping with a dragon who'll watch it for you."

"He's more into watching my chest."

"Boob guy, huh? When's the wedding?"

"I don't even know if he's alive." I set the envelope in the bedroom. "How did you learn about everything? Did you hear if Zav is all right?"

"An informant who'd gotten it all from some dwarf traveler."

I wondered if that was Belohk and if I would ever run into the dwarf again. Whether intentionally or not, he'd been responsible for getting me involved in all this. Since I was still alive and now had a substantial financial windfall, I supposed I didn't blame him.

Maybe I would ask Ti how to find him. We'd all returned to Earth together, and the last I'd heard, Ti was helping Nin fill orders for magical weapons while teaching her new crafting tricks. When I'd suggested that they take a vacation somewhere peaceful and relaxing, they'd both looked at me like I was nuts and gone back to hammering on things in the tiny workroom in the back of the food truck.

"And," Willard continued, "I've been hearing from a lot of refugees that the Stormforge Clan is reasserting its majority rule over their Ruling Council and Dragon Justice Court. The refugees are hopeful that their home worlds will return to less stressful times as Stormforge rulers, who are known to be less meddling and more lenient than the Silverclaw dragons that had been taking over, return to prominent positions throughout the Cosmic Realms."

"Does that mean there'll be fewer criminals from other worlds to hunt down on Earth?" Was I going to be out of a job? Ti's payment meant I probably *could* retire early, which my therapist would doubtless cheer, but I would be bored out of my mind within a month. What would I do once I'd fixed up the house?

"I think it means there'll be fewer innocent refugees. I imagine the criminals will still come here to avoid that punishment and rehabilitation. I may even have a new job for you next week. It's been relatively quiet, but someone recently had their throat torn out and their winnings stolen outside of the Tulalip Resort Casino."

"Oh good."

Willard arched her brows again.

"Good that there will continue to be work, not that someone was mugged and half-eaten."

"Does it bother you that the job you love only exists when people are being horribly maimed and killed?"

"It should, shouldn't it? I'll discuss it with Mary."

"Do that. Maybe you should start scheduling an extra therapy session a week."

"I need help that badly, huh?"

"I can't believe you need to ask." Willard stepped back, as if to leave now that she'd delivered my payment, but she paused and squinted at me.

Probably because I was grinning with delight. The dragon I'd been waiting all week for had just flown into my range.

"He's here," I explained, then twirled.

It had been more than thirty years since I'd twirled, but I didn't care. I hugged the sledgehammer as Zav flew closer.

Since I'd moved into this house, he'd been landing in the street instead of on the roof, but maybe he spotted the open balcony door and thought he could come in that way. He landed above us with a thunderous thump—it sounded like a tree falling on the roof.

Willard swore and gripped the doorframe. "What was that?"

"A dragon landing."

"Up *there*?" She stabbed a finger toward the ceiling. "That roof is all angles and points."

"He's as agile as a squirrel."

A great crash came from above, followed by the clatter of something falling. A *lot* of somethings. I opened my mouth in an enlightened "ah" as bricks tumbled past one of the windows.

Willard leaned back into the bathroom, grabbed my to-do list, and wrote *new chimney* at the bottom. "I hope that gnome paid you a *lot*."

The thumps of Zav walking across the roof in his human form came next. As he leaped down to the balcony and strode down the hallway toward us, I couldn't keep a big goofy grin off my face. He was alive. And he looked healthy and fit—and sexy—in his black robe with his powerful aura crackling around him. He was wearing those awful hiking sandals again, but that didn't detract from his allure. Not one iota.

I ran down the hall to meet him halfway. Somehow, I ended up leaping on him, wrapping my legs and arms around him, and kissing him numerous times through my grin. He returned my embrace more calmly—not surprising since *he* hadn't been afraid he was dead—but seemed pleased by my adoration.

"I didn't know you could do that, Thorvald," Willard said in her driest Southern drawl.

"Kiss someone?" I looked back at her without releasing Zav.

"Show affection."

"It's rare. I'm not good at it."

"I'm shocked."

"My mate is a great warrior and vexer of my enemies." Zav patted my back. "If she were effusive all the time, she would not be satisfactory for a dragon. We are stoic and aloof."

"Did he just say he likes you the way you are?" Willard asked.

"Yes. You know how tactful and diplomatic dragons are." I kissed Zav again on the cheek, then decided it was unseemly to have my legs wrapped around him with onlookers present, so I released him. But I gripped his hand and stayed close.

"Oh yes. I observed his tact while he was ordering me to read a two-thousand-page book and assign you as his criminal-capturing assistant."

Zav stepped up to peer at the mess in the bathroom. "Your domicile is in disrepair."

"Especially the chimney," Willard muttered.

Zav ignored her. "Per your earlier request, I have come to fix it for you."

"This should prove interesting," Willard muttered.

I wondered if Zav truly could speed up the process or if he would end up burning down the house and building a dragon cave on the lot. Should I feel hopeful or wary? Or warily hopeful?

I picked up a piece of the moldy drywall, pointed to the pipes, explained that we had replacement materials in the living room downstairs and out in the yard under tarps… and told him I'd feed him after he finished.

His eyes gleamed. "Yes. We will go on a date, and you will feed me barbecue ribs."

"All you can eat *if* you get rid of all the mold and rebuild the pipes and walls."

"A simple matter." Zav pointed to the stairs and extended his hand imperiously to me. "It will be easier if you are not in the way."

"Does that mean me too?" Willard asked. "Because I'm dying to see handyman-dragon in action."

"You also." Zav gave her more of a fly-shooing motion than an imperious gesture.

Willard followed me down the stairs, a smirk flirting with her lips. "I hope you have renters' insurance, Val. And that the landlord has homeowner's insurance."

"We have renters' insurance. I'm not sure what the landlord has. He mentioned some difficulties due to the house being haunted and the vampire in the basement."

"And the dragon in the attic?"

"That's not the attic. It's the second floor."

"It could be the attic by the time he's done up there." Her smirk widened.

"I'm delighted that my home-improvement project is tickling you so much."

I walked her to the front door. I had no idea what Zav had planned or how he and his magic would tackle it, but it might be safer if we left the house entirely.

"Have you seen Dr. Walker since we've been back?" I asked as we walked down the porch steps.

The remains of the chimney lay in a broken heap of bricks next to the rhododendrons.

"I dropped off his payment before yours. To his penthouse loft in South Lake Union." Willard's eye roll wasn't as emphatic as one of Amber's, but it conveyed her feelings adequately. "He'll probably use it for poker games with his wealthy neighbors."

"Is that your main problem with him? That he has money?"

"That he *ostentatiously* has money. And flaunts it. He thinks the sun comes up just to hear him crow."

"Maybe he's trying to impress you." I sensed magic flaring on the second story but decided not to look. Zav's home repair methods were sure to be unorthodox and alarming.

Willard squinted at me. "What are you angling at?"

"Just that he was a good fighter and useful on the mission."

"Maybe he was on good behavior because he was afraid of you and your dragon-slaying sword."

"Please, Willard. You're way scarier than I am."

She snorted and started to respond, but her gaze drifted upward. A stream of dark gray powder was flowing out the window. Ashes? They floated off toward the lake, disappearing from my view before I could determine if Zav was sending them that far for disposal. Magic being used in the house continued to pluck at my senses.

"I bet those were your interior walls," Willard said. "You may end up with a loft too."

"That's okay. Zav doesn't seem to care much about privacy."

"Your roommates may not want to see you going at it like screen doors on a windy day."

"Zoltan spends windy days sleeping in his coffin, Dimitri is always at the shop, and Freysha would be too busy with her studies to notice Zav was in the house."

"If that's true, they'll all be shocked when you invite them to the wedding."

"It's too early to think about weddings. We're only about to go on our first real date. Unless you know something I don't."

"Just that he's up there fixing your house for you. Or trying. What it'll look like when he finishes remains to be seen."

"I was wondering if he might turn the house into a cave. Dragons like caves."

"You better figure out what your living arrangements are going to be before you commit to marriage."

"Hence the dating." I noticed Willard had steered the conversation away from Walker. "I'm not sure how a marriage to someone who isn't a citizen of Earth and spends half his time on another planet would work, but if we ever did get hitched, I would have to invite Walker to the wedding. He was responsible for saving Zav's uncle and the rest of his family."

We pretended not to notice as the bricks floated up to the roof, crumbled and broken ones molding back together as they disappeared over the edge.

"As long as you don't expect me to bring him as my date," Willard said. "I assume *I'm* invited to the wedding too."

"Of course. Would you at least dance with him?"

Willard threw up her hands. "Did Walker *ask* you to try to play matchmaker?"

"No. He just seemed interested in your good opinion."

"Then tell him to stop driving around in a hoity-toity toaster on wheels."

"I don't think he's giving up the butt-massaging seats."

"I'm confused as to how you think this guy is a match for me."

"He's super exotic when he gets furry. Some kind of prehistoric lion with a tail this thick." I demonstrated in the air with my hands. "I think he's part kangaroo."

"Is that supposed to turn me on?" Willard arched her eyebrows.

"I assume other parts are also thick."

Willard didn't look amused.

I lowered my hands. "Look, I know you like reading all those science books. You might find it intriguing to study him. Or just ask him about how he—his animal-shifter side—still exists."

She grunted dubiously.

Your home has been repaired, Zav's voice boomed in my mind. *Enter and see the magnificent abode that my magic has crafted for you.*

"Your dragon just spoke telepathically to me," Willard said.

"To me too. Let's hope the neighbors didn't get the invitation. I wasn't planning on hosting an open house." I climbed the steps to the porch, equal parts curiosity and dread mingling in my gut.

"Send me pictures." Willard lifted a hand and headed to her car.

"You're not going to come see?"

"I saw the look he was giving you up there. If he did even a halfway decent job, I predict you'll be horizontal within ten minutes."

"That's supposed to happen *after* the date."

"I haven't noticed that dragons are well schooled on human cultural protocols."

"True."

"And you can tell Walker I will deign to dance with him at your wedding, but his hands better not roam."

"How is he supposed to mold your heart into gooey lovestruck putty if he can't use his hands?"

"Maybe he can sing me a ballad."

"Is that an invitation to pass that suggestion along?"

"*No.*" She gave me a dark look before driving off.

Well, I'd opened the door. Walker would have to figure out how to get through it on his own.

After a deep, bracing breath, I walked into the house.

All of the materials that had been stacked in the living room were gone, and it was cleaner and tidier than it had been since we moved in. It also smelled fresher. Actually, it didn't smell like anything at all. Neither mold nor old people.

I sniffed my way up the stairs, but the mold scent was gone up there too. Amazingly, the walls *weren't* gone. But everything looked new. Old walls that had been full of ancient wallpaper and flaky lead paint had been replaced and trimmed with wainscoting and moldings that were not only attractive but period appropriate. The bathroom fixtures, including the clawfoot tub, were reinstalled, and they even appeared to be *correctly* installed. The whole second floor of the house looked like something out of a magazine.

"Zav, this is amazing."

He stood in the doorway to my bedroom, his arms folded over his chest and his chin up. "Naturally."

"How did you even know what to do?" I kept peering into rooms as I approached him. They had *all* been renovated.

"I am a dragon, powerful and sublime."

"No, seriously. I was sure you were going to build me a cave."

"I studied human dwellings while I was recuperating."

"You studied human dwellings from your world?"

"Indeed." Zav drew from some extra-dimensional pocket a rolled-up magazine. He showed me the cover. *This Old House.* "I am also now versed in lawn-and-garden care, should you need a dragon-shaped topiary in the yard. Perhaps that would sufficiently warn the sense-dead humans in the area that a mighty dragon is in residence." He rested a hand on his chest.

"That magazine has an article on how to shape bushes like dragons?"

"It has an article on pruning spring foliage. I can extrapolate."

"You're a gifted dragon."

"Yes."

I grinned and hugged him. "Thank you for fixing my home."

"Yes."

I thought about explaining the term *you're welcome* to him, but he kissed me, and that distracted me.

With our lips busy, he switched to telepathy. *You are open to the dragon-shaped topiary?*

If my roommates don't object, it's okay with me. It wasn't until later that I realized I should have asked how *large* a dragon-shaped topiary he had in mind.

But Zav was very good at distracting me with kisses. And other things.

Willard was wrong. It took five minutes, not ten, for us to get horizontal.

EPILOGUE

As an owner in Dimitri's as yet unnamed coffee shop, you would think I would merit a reserved parking spot, but there wasn't a parking lot, so that was a fantasy that would never come to fruition. I found a spot three blocks away and lifted a hand when my front-seat passenger started to get out.

"Hold on, Mom. I want to give you something."

I'd thought about mailing the journal from the elf sanctuary to her, but the idea of it being lost or damaged by some automatic-package-sorting machine had prompted me to ask if she would be willing to come to Seattle for another visit. If she'd said no, I would have gone down there, but her yes had been prompt. She and Rocket were staying at Thad's house. Last I'd heard, Amber had been sharing detailed accounts of how I tortured her in her sword-fighting lessons.

"I told you I'm not wearing shoes in an establishment owned by my own daughter." She wriggled one of her bare feet.

"That's not what I'm giving you, but good luck with the bottle caps and broken glass on the sidewalks between here and there."

"My soles are tough. They can handle it."

"Remind me to get you a nice bed of lava rocks for your next birthday." I pulled the journal out from the side of my seat where I'd been hiding it. On a whim, I'd wrapped it up like a gift. Freysha hadn't read all of it to me, but the gist I'd gotten was that it was positive overall and that Mom would appreciate reading the things Eireth had written about their time together. "This is for your last three birthdays that I missed."

"Thoughtful." As she lifted a hand to accept it, one of my other two passengers stuck his golden nose between us and sniffed the package noisily.

"It doesn't have dog treats inside," I said. "Though you can buy some with the check, I suppose."

This immature overactive oaf is smacking me with his tail, Sindari, my final passenger, announced. *I am considering removing it.*

Don't do that, I replied silently. *He's a service dog. He needs it.*

What service could this tail possibly perform? Sindari's glowering expression was visible in the rear-view mirror. Barely. Rocket's wiggling hips and flapping tail got in the way.

Balance? What's your tail for?

Not thwacking seat mates.

Even with the seats down, there wasn't much room in the back for a tiger and a golden retriever, but it had been a short drive from the house to the coffee shop. And Rocket had spent most of it with his head thrust out the window, meaning he needed less space inside.

"You wrote me a check?" Mom arched an eyebrow as she pulled the package away from Rocket's nose to open it. "That's an odd birthday present."

"I got a nice payday recently. I thought it might help out with your exorbitant property taxes until you can get a new roommate—or a guy to live in a van in your driveway."

"Those people are easier to find than you'd think."

"Are you saying Dimitri isn't a unique and special individual? He'll be wounded."

Mom didn't answer. She'd unwrapped the journal and opened it. Judging by the tender way she ran her fingers over the first page of writing, she recognized the penmanship right away.

"Where did you find it?" she whispered.

"The elven-turned-goblin sanctuary. I could take you there sometime if you want. There's not much left where they lived, but the goblins haven't disturbed the trees back there." We'd have to fight our way past that elven guard creature, but I didn't mention that. After dealing with dragons, a light sparring session with a non-magical predator sounded delightful.

"Thank you. I'll read this later." Meaning she didn't want to get weepy-eyed at the memories it would evoke in front of her daughter? Understandable. She flipped back to the front and looked at the check for the first time. "You put an extra zero in this."

"No, I didn't."

"Val." She frowned sternly at me. "What did you do to get paid this much? Assassinate a king or president?"

"No. That doesn't pay that well. I killed a dragon for a gnome."

She stared at me, like she was trying to figure out if I was joking.

"This is the point where Amber would tell me my life is so weird," I offered, in case she was at a loss for words.

"Is she wrong?"

"No."

Mom fingered the check. "This is nice, Val, but I'm actually thinking of renting out the house in Oregon and moving... somewhere closer."

"Closer to me?"

"Closer to Amber."

"Glad to know where I rank."

"I could visit you too. I'm just realizing that, as much as I like my privacy, I would also like to get to know my granddaughter better. And you."

"Are you thinking of buying a place?" Maybe I should have written a bigger check. "In Seattle?"

"No, just renting for now. And it's way too crowded for me in the city, but maybe out in Fall City or Duvall. Close to the mountains and trails but also close enough to come visit you guys."

"The woods around Duvall are full of goblins." I grimaced, remembering my adventure—misadventure—out at the water-treatment plant.

"Is that a selling point or not?"

"They'll steal all your stuff to build things for their people."

"So, you recommend Fall City."

"And not to leave anything valuable outside in your yard."

"I do have a guard dog."

Rocket turned around to woof at someone walking through the alley. Somehow, his butt ended up toward us with the tail smacking Mom and me on the cheeks.

"A guard dog is a Rottweiler or a Doberman. Something that looks good with leather and spikes on its collar." The tail thwacked me in the eye. "Argh."

You should have let me chew that tail off. Sindari sounded smug.

"Rocket would want to play with the goblins," I added.

"That is true." Mom carefully closed the journal, then folded the check and zipped it into a pocket.

Good. I'd been afraid she would be too proud to accept it.

"I'm ready to see your new business venture," she added.

"It's a little unorthodox, and we're still working out the kinks."

"Amber said it's where all the weirdos in the city go."

"She hasn't been there."

"Apparently, there are rumors on social media sites."

"Well, it hasn't hurt business yet." If anything, there were more trolls, goblins, kobolds, shifters, and various other magical beings there every time I stopped in. "The weirdos need a place to hang out."

"It's interesting that they used to hate you and now come to your coffee shop." She grabbed Rocket's leash and slid out of the Jeep.

"Most of them don't know I'm an owner. But it *has* been almost three weeks since a random magical being tried to assassinate me. I'm not sure if that means that my reputation has gotten better or that rumors have gotten out that I'm sleeping with a dragon."

Rocket jumped out through the window before Mom could open the door for him.

Oaf, Sindari repeated, then opened the other door to let himself out. I'd never figured out how he did that without thumbs, but he stepped regally and maturely out of the Jeep without thwacking anyone with his tail.

Since he used his stealth magic to hide himself from others, our little group didn't get too many stares from people as we walked to the coffee shop. Though Mom stopped at one point to gape at Rocket.

"What happened to his tail?"

Instead of swishing through the air as he walked, it appeared to be attached to one of his hind legs.

I improved it, Sindari informed me.

Rocket looked back at his bound tail and sniffed it.

Mom frowned and knelt to examine it. "Someone tied it to his leg."

How did you manage that? I asked Sindari as Mom gave him a puzzled look.

Me? Sindari held up a paw and spread it wide to show off his lack of thumbs.

"There's some twine here," Mom murmured, then pulled a multi-purpose tool out of a belt pouch. "It's braided from... Is this Rocket's own fur?"

I thought it was an excellent solution, Sindari said. *Why is she going to cut it free?*

Mom likes his tail. It has personality.

The personality of an overzealous oaf.

"Sorry, Mom. I'll dismiss Sindari for the ride back."

Sindari sniffed. *Maybe you should dismiss the drooling canine.*

He's her loyal service pet. He goes everywhere she goes. I wasn't sure that was entirely true, since Rocket was a search-and-rescue dog, not a therapy dog, but I rarely saw her without him, and he did have a snazzy vest.

Sindari sniffed again. *He sounds needy.*

Not everybody can be a Del'nothian tiger.

Alas.

Rocket was extremely excited when his tail was freed. He bounded from one side of the alley to the other until Mom called him over to leash him. Even leashed, he had an extra spring in his step and kept trying to engage Sindari in play. Sindari strode down the alley with his head high and ignored him.

When we walked into the coffee shop, it was as busy as I expected, with no hint of a table free. Somehow, the goblins always managed to hold one down, despite the fact that most of the other clients could have picked them up with one hand and tossed them outside. Given that they always ordered at least twelve mugs of coffee, Dimitri probably helped protect them.

A strange robotic contraption on wheels whirred past our feet, forcing us to pause. It registered a faint magical signature and looked to be made from recycled soda cans and nuts and bolts and bits scavenged from a junkyard. As it zipped toward the aisles of reinforced display cases, sucking up a napkin along the way, Rocket tried to chase after it, but Mom called him back with a word.

Gondo and the troll kid Reb appeared, trailing after the robot, Gondo with a wrench between his teeth as he took notes on a pad of paper, and the boy with a ruler and pliers.

"It's a mystery *why* this place would be getting mentions on social media," Mom murmured, watching the entourage.

Sindari strode away from us and toward the back, where Dimitri was painting on a large banner spread out across a glass display case.

"I'm going to get a coffee," Mom said, not batting an eye at the blue- and green-skinned patrons. Maybe she'd gotten used to magical beings during her visits to Greemaw's valley back in Oregon. "I'll let you know if the quality is good."

"We source it from a local roaster. Willard already vetted it. She said it's excellent. The goblins also say it's superb, but they may be biased since Nin decided we should cater to them by making a special goblin blend."

"Should I try it?"

"It depends on how healthy your heart is. Last I heard, Dimitri hadn't picked up a defibrillator for the first-aid kit yet."

She appeared more intrigued than alarmed. I wouldn't be. Judging by the smell, it was similar to jet fuel.

Dimitri turned out to be painting a sign, though he stopped to rub my regal tiger's ears when Sindari sat expectantly next to him.

"I decided on a name for the shop," Dimitri told me. "I ordered a permanent sign, but it's going to take a few weeks, so I'm making a temporary one."

"Aren't you supposed to consult your fellow business owners before doing something important like picking a name?"

"I consulted Zoltan and Nin. We decided we would surprise you."

I eyed what I could see of the banner—most of it hung off the end of the display case. "Is that a dragon?"

"A *sable* dragon. Hence the name." He lifted the rest of the banner so I could see the words he'd already written. *The Sable Dragon.*

"Sable? Doesn't that just mean black?"

"More or less. But it's more artsy and literary."

"It's one letter away from stable. Zav isn't into saddles or domestication of any kind."

Dimitri gave me an exasperated look. "Nobody is going to think it says stable. Zav can read, right? Do you think he'll like it? Obviously, we were thinking of him. Like honoring him. He made our junker house awesome. Nin doesn't care about that, but she's willing to go along with it because she said dragons are super trendy, and it'll bring people in."

"What did Zoltan say?"

"That if naming the shop after him keeps Zav from breathing down his neck in the basement, he'll sign off."

"Zav has only spent one night in that basement, while Zoltan was experimenting on him."

"I heard there was a lot of neck breathing." Dimitri shook the banner. "Do you like it? The real sign will be a lot cooler. The dragon will be black with neon light."

"He'll be black? Not sable? Won't that be an inaccurate representation?"

"Is it hard work being an assassin *and* a comedian?"

"No, I'm a natural."

Dimitri's gaze shifted toward the front door where a towering woman with short frizzy blonde hair walked in carrying a handful of brochures. She looked around, spotted Dimitri, and started to walk toward him, but then she also noticed me and halted. It was Inga, the half-troll enchanter I'd met up at the fence manufacturer in Woodinville. I hadn't expected to see her again. After frowning at me, she continued toward Dimitri.

"You're the owner, right?" she asked him.

"We're both owners." Dimitri waved at me.

"The Ruin Bringer is an investor in a coffee shop for the magical beings she kills?" Inga asked skeptically.

"No, the ones I kill have to go to Starbucks. The rest are welcome here." I smiled, but she didn't give any indication of appreciating my wit.

Dimitri didn't either. Tough room.

The floor-cleaning contraption whirred past, Gondo still trailing it and taking notes. Reb had a milkshake in hand now and seemed to be there for the show rather than assistance. Dimitri and I might need to have a talk about defining his employment duties a little more.

"Is that Rupert's boy?" Inga asked as they passed.

"Yes. You know him?" I raised my eyebrows.

"I knew Rupert. Met the kid a couple of times." She shrugged. "I'm not that welcome in the troll community, but nobody bugged me if I went for a drink at Rupert's pub. And I talked to him a few times. He gave me some work." Inga handed Dimitri a brochure. "That's what I'm here about. I don't get paid that well at my regular job, and I'm trying to pick up some gigs on the side. If you need any extra security for this place, let me know."

"I'm capable of installing magical security myself," Dimitri said, "but thanks."

"If that's your work—" Inga waved at some yard art in one of the cases, "—it's not horrible, but it's amateurish and unrefined. Did you teach yourself?"

Dimitri's broad pockmarked face always looked a little dyspeptic, but now he added a surly hunch to his shoulders. "Yeah."

"I could teach you. For ten dollars an hour. That's a steal. I was trained by a shaman craftswoman who was apprenticed by a master back on *Agug-gok*."

Dimitri looked at me.

"The troll home world," I explained.

"That's not what the look was for," he whispered. "I was wondering if you thought it was a good idea. Have you seen her work? Is it good?" His eyes turned plaintive. "Better than mine?"

"Why don't you guys have a tinkering session—" I wiggled my fingers, "—and figure it out?"

The cleaning device came through again, this time with Reb riding it and giggling. Rocket came after it, snuffling curiously.

"When you hired the boy," Dimitri muttered to me, "you should have specified he has to use a broom and dustpan for cleaning."

"You're the majority owner and the person who's here full-time. I assumed you would give him guidance."

"You're the one paying him."

"The boy works here?" Inga asked. "You pay him?"

"Just an hour or two a day." I wondered if trolls had laws about child labor and she was about to belt me.

"Good. Troll children need chores. And discipline." She strode after the boy and issued a stern stream of words to him in trollish.

He sprang off the contraption and ran into the back. At first, I thought she'd terrified him into fleeing, but he came back with a mop and bucket and started scrubbing vigorously at splotches of milkshake he'd lost during his ride. From there, he proceeded to mop the rest of the floor.

"Troll children also need parents," Inga said.

"I figured, but I don't think his mom is around, and some dark elves got Rupert."

Inga's voice softened, and for the first time, she looked at me without disapproval. "I heard you got the dark elves."

"With the help of some dragons, yes. Too late to help Rupert though."

Inga eyed the boy, who was still working vigorously, then turned a calculating expression on Dimitri. "You will hire me to install security and instruct you, and I will take care of the boy until we can find true troll parents willing to raise him."

"Uhm," Dimitri said.

"He agrees," I said.

"Val," Dimitri protested. "I haven't even seen her work yet."

"It is excellent. This is a good deal for you." Inga thumped her fist on the table, then walked off to introduce herself to her new foster child.

"Why are all the women in my life so bossy, Val?"

"They want what's best for you."

"What's best for me is another bossy woman? A grumpy half-troll teacher?"

"I'm surprised you have to ask. Just think of what your life was like before you met me and Nin and my mom." Poor Dimitri. He did have a lot of strong-willed—I refused to call us bossy—women in his life. "You lived in a van and could barely make ends meet. Now, you're a successful coffee-shop owner."

"I didn't want a coffee shop."

Gondo rode toward us on the floor cleaner with Rocket woofing and wagging his tail vigorously as he gave chase.

"Are you sure?" I raised my eyebrows. "It's kind of an entertaining workplace."

"I guess."

"You're a hard man to please."

Dimitri slumped forward, gripping his knees in dejection, but he did manage a lopsided grin. "Having enough money to pay rent and buy beer *is* kind of nice."

"So I've heard."

"You should know. You're rich now, aren't you?"

"We'll see how long that lasts. I promised Zav all-you-can-eat ribs from our favorite barbecue restaurant for fixing up the house, but he assumed I meant all-you-can-eat ribs every *day*. In case you were wondering, a dragon can easily consume more than two hundred dollars' worth of ribs in a sitting."

"Maybe we could get a commercial smoker for the back yard."

"Are those affordable?"

"I saw a cool one in a commercial kitchen catalog for thirty-five thousand dollars."

"Nobody warned me how expensive dating a dragon would be."

"I hope he's good in bed."

I knew Dimitri didn't want the details, but I couldn't keep from giving him a wicked grin.

He managed his lopsided half-smile again—until Rocket, Gondo, and the floor cleaner came back through. He didn't straighten and step back quickly enough to avoid being whacked in the balls by a golden retriever tail.

"Ouch." Belatedly, Dimitri covered himself protectively.

I have a solution for that tail. Sindari, who'd been watching the activity without comment, padded after Rocket.

THE END

CONNECT WITH THE AUTHOR

Have a comment? Question? Just want to say hi? Find me online at:
http://www.lindsayburoker.com
http://www.facebook.com/LindsayBuroker
http://twitter.com/GoblinWriter
Thanks for reading!